ALIVE AND KICKING

BY

KATHRYN R. BIEL

BOSTON BUZZARDS #4

Alive and Kicking

Cover design by Sue Traynor and Kathryn R. Biel

DEDICATION

To Ms. Susan Vertucci:
I'm sure you don't remember the time you told me in front of the entire class that I "was no good at math" and that I'd "never amount to anything" because I was "no good at math," but I sure do.
Here are some numbers for you:
22 books published
Over 1.5 million words written
Approximately 400,000 books sold and downloaded worldwide since 2013

Even someone who's "not good at math" can see that those add up to something.

AUTHOR'S NOTE

Dear Readers:

This book explores grief. If you're not in the place currently, this book will be waiting for you in the future.

 *Kathryn*

Content Warnings: This is a fade to black romance that contains off-the-page consensual encounters. There is discussion of sexual relationships and language around that. Cursing and profanity are present.

Trigger Warnings: sibling death, terminal illness, parental abandonment, reading disability

CHAPTER 1: RACHEL

I'm going to die a virgin, so you have to do this for me.

I stare at my sister's—my dead sister, that is— words and fume. She's bullying me from the grave, and there's not a damn thing I can do about it.

Our whole lives, she always had to have the last word. She wasn't going to let something silly like death change that.

"Just because Jason Flemming only lasted two minutes doesn't mean it didn't happen. You didn't magically grow your hymen back!" I yell at my bedroom ceiling as if she can hear me. Maybe she can. Who knows? At least she's not arguing back, for once.

I wish she would.

If I had any tears left in my body, I'd be crying. Again. Frankly, I'm surprised that I was never hospitalized for dehydration during the past six months. Not that I would have gone. We spent enough time in hospitals. I'm never going back to one. Ever.

I pick up the piece of lined paper, the kind we used to use to do our homework on and read her words again. Gram didn't give me Richie's epistle until yesterday, even though she's been gone for six months now. I should be angry at Gram, but I don't have enough energy left for that either. Let's face it, I don't have the energy for anything besides basic bodily functions. She was only trying to protect me, just like she did for Richie and me our whole lives.

Plus, I was in no state to process what my sister had to say to me before this. Hell, I'm still not sure I'm ready, but nonetheless, here we are.

Richie left me a bucket list. Or is it a to-do list? Somehow, even though she was the younger sister, she felt it was her mission in life to boss me around. Once, when I called her out on it, she said that because things were so unpredictable when we were little, she was overcompensating by trying to control everything.

Talk about lives being out of control. Richie obviously had no control over the glioblastoma that entered her cranium and ravaged our lives so completely and quickly. I guess I can give her a pass for this one. She had the audacity to entitle her list "Live Like You're Dying" as if to drive home that I'm still alive and she's not.

I don't need any reminders.

My sister and I could not be any more different if we tried. Aside from the whole living and deceased thing, of course. She had frenetic energy, fueled by caffeine and ADHD. I'm much more mellow and passive, too timid to speak up most of the time; anxiety will do that to you. She was vivacious and lively, while I prefer a night home with a good book. We shared the same pasty white skin, and that's about all we had in common. Where she was a tall, lanky blonde, I'm short with dull brown hair and nondescript brown eyes to match. We used to wonder why we didn't look more alike until we realized we resembled our fathers. Both of them. Mom never told us that we didn't have the same dad, but sharing maternal things was never her strong point or priority either.

Paternity never mattered to us, though. We were a team. A unit. She was my ride or die until, well, she did. And now I'm here all alone, and if I didn't have to help Gram and Gramps with their business to keep a roof over their heads and food on the table, I'd never get out of bed.

And now Richie not only wants me to get up and function every day, but she's given me a to-do list?

This is bullshit.

"Bullshit!" I yell to the ceiling. I squeeze my eyes shut, pressing the heels of my hands into my orbits, hoping—yet again—that when I open them, this will all have been a bad dream.

Spoiler alert, it's not.

Then the three words, which are so harmful yet I've been unable to silence, dance through my brain for the millionth time.

It's not fair.

Richie was going places. She had just finished PA school. She is—was going to help people. She was going to make a difference. She was funny and vivacious and passionate about everything. The exact opposite of me.

God, I hate the past tense.

I'm going nowhere, quite literally. I still live with Gram and Gramps. To be fair, Richie lived here too, up until her death. But she'd planned to move out as soon as she got a job. Instead, she got headaches that weren't just headaches. Eventually, she got a hospital bed in the den.

Me? I'm content to stay where I am. I work at their business, which is on the other side of the property from the house. Gramps has mentioned the idea of me taking it over eventually, which I probably will, but only because I don't know how to tell him no.

It's never been my dream to run a septic pump and grinding operation. I mean, does anyone write that on their first day of kindergarten All About Me board?

I want to work in a business that only exists to take care of what happens after you flush the toilet. I want to answer emails all day and listen to people being hysterical because their houses and yards are filled with human refuse. I want to explain over and over and over that there's no such thing as flushable wipes, and for God's sake, do not flush tampons. I want to work with my crusty old grandfather and my cantankerous uncle and a bunch of men whose butt cracks hang out of their tighty-whities and faded dungarees, and where everyone smells faintly of sewage. Living the dream!

I couldn't tell you my dream for a million dollars.

Whenever I thought about the future, it was never about the career I would have. It was about Richie and me getting our first apartment and decorating it however we wanted, knowing that it would be a disaster because our styles were polar opposites. It was traveling the world together. It was laughing over our favorite movies. It was adopting cats together. It was being the maid of honor in her wedding and the best auntie ever to her kids.

I never really thought about myself outside the context of her.

Another intrusive thought runs through my mind.

God took the wrong sister.

Why her and not me? She would have done a lot of good in this world. She would have healed people. She would have saved lives. She would have made a difference. I help people get shit out of their yard. I mean, it's probably God's work too, but not in the same way.

The words on the page of my sister's "you're alive and I'm not" bucket list are unfocused and hazy. I touch my face, confirming my glasses are on. Maybe they're not strong enough anymore. Maybe the lenses are dirty. Maybe my brain just cannot process looking at Richie's handwriting and seeing her dreams written out in blue ballpoint pen.

The wide cavern of grief rips through my chest again as I realize I'll never see a new piece of her handwriting again. I put the paper down and haul myself out of bed. It's time to go to work. These septic pumps aren't going to sell themselves.

CHAPTER 2: RACHEL

S orry I'm late. Traffic was bad," I huff, dropping my bag on the floor next to my desk. Gramps looks over from where he's studying blueprints hung on the wall. Years ago, when his back started reminding him of his age, his physical therapist, Kim, suggested this modification of hanging materials on the wall so he didn't have to bend over anymore.

"Rachel, we live on the other side of the lot." He turns back to the drawing he's studying, making some marks as to where lines and pumps will go on a new construction job site. An apartment complex, I think.

"Yeah, but I had to pet Butch and then Hazel and then Gus." I'm not lying. The cats were lounging in the yard and demanded tummy and ear scratches. It's almost as bad as a traffic jam.

"Don't get too comfortable. There's a backup over on Baldpate Road. Dale said you should come. Whole side yard flooded, and they're supposed to have a party there this weekend."

My grandfather started Cramer-Romero Associates Pumps with his father-in-law more than fifty years ago. Gramps is the Cramer, and Gram is the Romero. Boxford, where they grew up, was an ideal place for this business because it didn't—and still doesn't—have a public sewer system. How that still exists in the twenty-first century is beyond me. The plan had always been for my mom and my uncle to split the business fifty-fifty. My mom was supposed to handle the pump and grinder install side, while Uncle Robert would do the septic pump repair side. Since Mom took off for the first time when Richie was three and I was five, the business plan has changed slightly. During her intermittent visits, usually between boyfriends and husbands, she would work here, when she bothered to show up. Uncle Robert is out in the field, and now I pick up the slack in the office, doing what should have been my mom's job. Officially, I'm the bookkeeper, but I also do parts ordering, scheduling, and basically anything else no one wants to do. I started here when I was fourteen, so I've worked here more than half my life. Like most small family businesses, weathering economic ups and downs is tricky. The pandemic shutdown nearly did us in.

There was one thing that saved us.

Believe it or not, it's me.

I started making videos for ClikClak. People are fascinated by septic systems, especially when they fail. Sure, it's a niche audience, but we have enough followers to get paid for views. I mean, it's not like I'm super viral, like that hot guy who cooks in his underwear. I'm not one for gratuitous thirst traps, but perhaps I watch for a few seconds before scrolling on. I'm grieving, not dead.

Back to me and my video success. They've also expanded our client area, which is both a good and bad thing. We're going to have to open a secondary office to handle the client requests coming in south of Boston. The guys are getting sick of driving down to the south shore, especially for multi-day jobs. It'll be more cost-effective for the business to have a secondary location than to pay for gas and tolls, wear and tear on the vehicles, lodging, and per diems.

"Lemme get my gear, and I'll head over." My gear officially consists of knee-high rubber muck boots and a tripod. Most days, I'm too lazy to use it, so I just do handheld shots. The tripod, I mean. I'm never *ever* too lazy to use my rubber boots. That's a priority. I don't even bring a microphone, because I'll record voice-overs later on.

I hop in Gramps's Toyota Tundra and head over to Baldpate Road. If the ground is soft, I don't trust my Civic not to sink in. The site is fifteen minutes from the home office. Enough time to jam out to some old-school 2000s pop and forget my life for a brief moment. I consider driving a full-body experience, complete with lead vocals, backup singing, and as much choreography as I can manage without driving off the road.

I'm reserved everywhere but in the driver's seat. There, I'm a star.

However, I am reminded of my reality as I round the corner. Before the truck is even stopped, I can smell it. No matter how many years I've been doing this, I don't think I'll ever get used to it. And it's ten times worse in the late-July heat. The yard is a disaster, probably 12–14 square feet covered in an inch or so of standing water that's created a mud sludge.

But we all know it's not just mud.

I keep meaning to buy Vicks VapoRub and put it under my nose like the coroner in *The Silence of the Lambs*, but I never seem to remember. Sometimes I wish for the good ole days of COVID when you'd lose your sense of smell.

I swear, it invades my nose and lives in my nose hairs for days afterward. I really need to come up with a life plan that doesn't involve poo.

I unplug my phone from the charger and hop out.

This is going to be a good one. I mean, bad for the homeowners and their party this weekend, but probably good for views. The worse the damage, the more people watch. And as we all know, the more people who watch, the more money we make. I've offered on more than one occasion to put it back into the business, but Gram insists that I save the money for myself.

"You never know what'll come up," is her standard reply.

She used to say it to Richie, too. We used her rainy-day fund—not that there was much in it—to pay burial expenses. I mean, dying was one way to get out of paying her student loans back. Extreme, yes, but that was my sister. Her list is proof of that.

The yard is even worse up close, the water squelching under my muck boots. For the record, if it's backing up this much in the yard, there's no way it hasn't backed up in the house. These people's weekend party plans are toast.

Their homeowners' insurance premium is going to go through the roof.

I start recording, taking in the yard. Dale's already got the excavator and has started digging. Uncle Robert walks over, leans on his shovel, and says, "Apparently, they've been here thirty years and have never cleaned out the septic tank."

FYI, it's recommended to clean out your tanks every three to five years.

I wrinkle my nose. "Yuck. It's been sitting in there longer than I've been alive."

"Sure is a long time to be stagnant," he says.

Something about that statement stays with me, like a strand of celery stuck in between my back molars. Annoying and niggling and not going anywhere without significant digging.

Maybe I should ask Dale if I can borrow the excavator for my mind.

I'm on-site for hours, collecting way more footage than I need for a three-minute clip. My work won't be wasted. I'll be able to make a lot of videos from what I recorded today, if I can focus long enough tonight. Next-week me will certainly appreciate that her job is already done.

But even as I spend the rest of the evening at the desktop in the office editing, I can't stop thinking about stagnation. It's not just for sewage! It's me. Ever since I was a little girl, all I've ever wanted was stability and predictability.

Probably because I never had it at home.

It's not hard to psychoanalyze. Freshman Psych 101 kind of stuff really. No matter how hard I've worked to repress the memories, they're still there. The first night Mom dropped us off at Gram and Gramps's house, I thought it was just a sleepover. But I remember the worried looks my grandparents gave each other and the artificially sweet tone to their voices as they kept saying, "Everything will be okay."

As a five-year-old, I had no reason to suspect otherwise. Until that one night turned into weeks and then months. I remember crying myself to sleep but trying to keep it quiet so I didn't wake Richie and so Gram didn't get upset.

She was upset a lot.

At first, I thought it was because of us, something we'd done. Gram never yelled at us, but I could still tell she wasn't happy. When Mom returned, it was a different story.

There was a lot of yelling that night. It was so dark and so late, but Mom said we had to go home.

I was excited. I'd missed my house and the dog who lived next door. He was a great fluffy golden retriever named Hamilton. I think I missed Hamilton most of all. But where she took us was a small apartment where Richie and I had to share a bed. It wasn't home. Being with Mom never felt like home again.

There was a man there. He smelled weird. Immediately, I didn't like him. The feeling was mutual.

This was the start of a long cycle of the same scenario over and over again until Gram and Gramps put their foot down and said we weren't moving out anymore.

Once we went to live with Gram and Gramps for good, things were more stable for sure, but Mom was still in and out. That was the thing—we'd never know when she was going to blow into or out of town. We didn't know whom she'd be dating—or married to—and how long she'd stay.

The only thing predictable about her was her unpredictability.

Richie and I swore we'd never be like that. We'd never let the dude flavor of the month rule our lives. We were gonna put sisters before misters. We were gonna live for us.

Except Richie stopped living in the physical sense, and I never lived in the metaphorical sense. I refuse to take risks and chances. I want to know what's coming next. And if you can't guarantee me a happy ending, I don't want any part of it.

But even as much as I planned, I couldn't predict Richie getting sick, let alone dying. I couldn't predict that my best friend would be gone forever and I'd be stuck here, doing the same thing day in and day out for the rest of my life.

Suddenly, the predictability feels less and less stable and more and more smothering. My ears start to ring as the periphery of my vision gets dark. The vise tightens on my chest as air refuses to enter my lungs. Oh good, maybe I'm dying too, and then I won't have to figure out where I've gone so wrong in my twenty-nine years here on this earth. I frantically look around, trying to find something—anything—to ground me.

In case I forgot to mention, Richie was my emotional support person for my panic attacks. I used to joke that I didn't need a service animal as long as I had her. Joke's on me.

But seriously, if I don't do something, I'm going to puke or pass out or maybe die because I'm pretty sure you have to keep breathing to live. I grab the edge of the desk, hoping the pressure on my hands interrupts this impending and imminent spiral. It doesn't. I reach for my purse, thinking that an Altoid might help. I've apparently lost all motor control as my hand jerks, sending my crossbody careening to the ground.

Since I hadn't bothered zippering the bag all the way, the contents spill out, skittering across the floor. Shit. I drop to my hands and knees, attempting to retrieve my belongings. My hands grasp at the items, but I seem to lack the motor coordination to efficiently clean up my mess. Last thing I need is for the guys to come in and see tampons all over the linoleum. As I shove my personal items back into my purse, my gaze fixes on the folded piece of looseleaf.

With trembling hands, I unfold it, taking in my sister's messy script.

Dear Rachel,

If you're reading this, I'm dead, and you're probably crying. It's time to knock that shit off and put on real pants. Don't even try to lie to me and tell me you're wearing hard pants. I'll haunt your ass.

If I didn't have this stupid brain tumor, these are the things I'd want to accomplish in my life. I know they seem pretty frivolous, and that's a luxury I certainly don't have, so why not ask you to do them? I know you're rolling your eyes at me, but humor me this last time, won't you? Plus, even though these are the things I want to do, I think they'd be good for you. You worry too much, and I won't be there to talk you down. Maybe if you step outside your comfort zone, even a tiny bit, things won't be so hard after I'm gone. You need to live a little, and this list will help you do that. You only live once. Oh, and I know we promised that we wouldn't be like Mom, and you aren't, so don't feel guilty about number 9. Everyone should do that once. It's too late for me. No one will want to screw a bald chick with a brain tumor. I'm going to die a virgin, so you have to do this for me.

Live Like You're Dying
1. Go somewhere on a plane by yourself
2. Jump out of a plane. Just kidding. But at least go parasailing once.
3. Go to a casino
4. Shoot a gun
5. See a moose in the wild
6. Perform on stage in a sexy sequined costume
7. Deliver a baby
8. Meet TJ Doyle from the Boston Buzzards
9. Have a one-night stand (I know, we promised we wouldn't be like her, but this is intentional, so it's okay)
10. Forgive Mom

By the time I get to number ten, I can barely see through my tears. At least I'm no longer hyperventilating. I guess Richie still is my emotional support person. Even so, this list is ridiculous, and there's no way I'm doing any of it. It's her bucket list. Not mine.

I can't believe what she thinks I should be doing. It's totally unachievable, even if I wanted to do these things.

Which I do not.

I mean, it's realistic that Richie, as a physician's assistant, would have the opportunity to deliver a baby. How would I ever go about doing that? And perform on stage in a sexy outfit? Me, the one with the panic attacks? I think not. Completely ridiculous.

I will concede that seeing a moose would be acceptable, as long as it doesn't attack me. If I had to pick a wild animal to observe in nature, it'd be an orca. I'm not one to commune with nature, but if I did, moose wouldn't be at the top of the list.

But don't even get me started on the one-night-stand thing. We promised—*promised*—each other that we'd never put a man before ourselves. That men were scum, and we were better off without them. We were never going to put pleasure above responsibilities. I don't care if she gave me permission to get frisky with a stranger, I'm not doing it. While I could always see Richie eventually settling down with a man who treated her like gold, not unlike how Gramps treats Gram, I never saw that for myself. I have no desire to get entangled and swap bodily fluids with a stranger. That holds no appeal for me. If I was ever going to do that, the guy would have to meet the highest standards. Like, ridiculously perfect. I'm pretty sure that man doesn't exist outside of romance books.

We're not even going to discuss number ten. Completely ridiculous.

So even if I wanted to, I couldn't do this list.

As those thoughts pop in my head, shame washes over me. I've got to at least try. I look at the list again. Anxiety not only takes out the one-night-stand thing and performing on a stage, but flying and shooting a gun, too. About the only thing that seems even quasi-achievable is the Boston Buzzards thing.

They're a soccer team—I'm pretty sure. Richie was a huge sports nut. Probably because she was good at all of them. I, on the other hand, prefer to stay inside with a good book. Maybe I can go to a game or something. If I'm in the same building, it's practically the same thing. That should count.

I take a deep breath. Okay, I can do one last thing for my sister, so she didn't have to die a virgin in vain.

CHAPTER 3: TJ

*9**8 ... 99 ... 100.*

I finish my push-ups, give a knowing smile to the camera, and end the recording. Only 10.7 thousand views, my ass. If the ClikClak algorithm wants to play, I'm here for it. No one can resist a shirtless, sweaty TJ Doyle.

No one's ever going to accuse me of being the smartest out there, but I know what my assets are and how to use them to my advantage. It's not like people are tuning into my account for my witty repartee.

I finish editing and upload the video. I've got to get to practice. I can't be late ... again. Coach Janssen doesn't look kindly on it. Neither do my teammates.

Truth be told, they barely put up with me. I'm not sure why, but I've never really clicked with any of them. I don't mind them, but I get the feeling they don't like me. Sometimes I think it's because I've got the largest social media presence on the team. That's become pretty lucrative. The front office is paying more and more attention to it, keeping players around who draw in the crowds. *Paying* those players better, too.

If I have to strip down to my boxer briefs while I work out, so be it. Cash is king, and I'm wearing the crown right now.

Not to mention, ever since they brought Xavier Henry on in the spring, I keep hearing talk about moving him to midfield. My position. He'd rather play defense, but the truth is, he's faster than I am. If the powers that be decide to make that move, I'm not sure if I'd be dropped back to defender, moved to the bench, or pushed right out the door. At thirty-two, I'm lucky to have played professional soccer for as long as I have. I can't count on it lasting forever.

Add in my frequent tardiness, and really, the only thing keeping me starting is my social media presence. At least for right now.

"Nice of you to join us," Maliq Miller mutters as I stride in, only five minutes late this time.

"I didn't miss anything, did I?" We're starting with warm-ups and then drills and then running plays. I'm already warm from my video workout. Plus, practicing in the August heat warms the muscles pretty damn quick. Sure, we have an air-conditioned facility, but since this whole complex was practically built on a swamp, you can't escape the humidity at this time of year. Sweat pours out of me just sitting still, and there's not a hint of breeze in the air to wick the moisture away.

I may be late to practice, but it doesn't mean I shirk my responsibilities. I work just as hard as everyone else on the Buzzards. I even stay after, continuing my plyometric workout in the weight room.

Okay, I'm doing that to get more videos, but I'm still putting reps in. The results can be seen in my quads and glutes.

I finally call it quits and head to the shower. As I'm walking out, ready to go home for the day, I bump into

Brandon Nix. He's always had quite the attitude, and I half expect him to take a swing at me for running into him. Wouldn't be the first time. He's a total hothead and loose cannon. Instead, I'm surprised when he says, "Hey, Doyle, wanna do a publicity event? It's for charity, but there'll be tons of photo ops."

For a minute, I'm confused. Brandon Nix doesn't do charity. He doesn't do photo ops. He doesn't even have a ClikClak profile, as far as I know. He gets in fights and runs his mouth. I wonder if he has to do some sort of community service or something. I'm pretty sure he's on probation after that last red card and the altercation with the female ref.

Plus, the entire team usually makes fun of my social media presence, Brandon included. They don't understand what a commodity it is.

I'm curious, though. This is totally out of character for him. I need more information. I decide to take the bait.

"Yeah, sure," I answer warily.

"Okay, here's the deal. It's on September first, before our game against the Wave. It's called Soccer for Sibs. We're doing a clinic for siblings of kids with chronic and terminal illnesses."

"Like a Make-a-Wish kind of thing?"

"Sort of, but this is for the healthy siblings of the sick kids. You know, the ones that always get left behind because their brother or sister is the one who gets all the attention. That's who's going to be there. It's gonna be you, me, Landon, and Cally." Then he adds quickly, "Maybe some other people too." He nods awkwardly, mumbles, "thanks," and walks away abruptly.

Okay, that was weird. No one's ever accused Brandon Nix of being slick or polished, though.

But when I think about what I've just gotten myself into, I roll my eyes. My ClikClak and IG are carefully constructed, aesthetically pleasing glimpses of my life.

At least the life I want people to see.

Whiny, needy kids don't really fit into that.

Whatever.

It'll be good for my image. It'll look like I care about someone other than myself. It's not that I *don't* care. It's more that I don't have anyone to care about. I mean, my parents and my brothers and nieces and all that, yeah. Obviously.

I suppose I care about the Boston Buzzards, too. After all, I'm the "local boy makes good" story everyone loves to talk about. Growing up just 35 miles from where I now live out my dream is something the press likes to eat up. I think I'm the only Boston Buzzard who can claim Massachusetts as my home. Hell, I was actually born at Mass General, so I can even say I'm from Boston. There's more than one sign in Sudbury that calls me a "Hometown Hero."

Just because I have six-pack abs and can kick a ball doesn't make me a hero. I haven't *done* anything that truly deserves adoration. I'm lucky because I am physically adept. It's not like I saved the whales or fixed global warming or brokered peace in the Middle East. I haven't even dated a Kardashian.

Most of the time, I'm at a loss for why people like me.

My brother Joey is a stand-up comedian who had his own Netflix special, and my brother Nicky is a Harvard Law graduate who works in the Massachusetts State Senate. I make videos in my underwear. Out of the Doyle brothers, I'm the least interesting.

Soccer is all I have.

I'm not qualified to do anything else, though, so I don't know what to do, other than pretend everything is perfect. During the season, I don't usually go out, so after practice, it's home to a delivered meal kit and filming content. For some reason, next to my workout videos, my cooking videos do the best. I don't necessarily let the world know that my food is all portioned out before I start filming myself cooking.

Chicks dig a man who can cook.

Not that it's helping me. I haven't seriously dated anyone in years. Turns out, despite the face and the body, I've got no rizz when it comes to the ladies. I turn into an idiot who blurts out whatever pops into my feeble brain. Unbelievably, that's not a big turn-on for potential dates.

Also, if I didn't have the recipe and step-by-step directions in front of me, I wouldn't be able to make jack shit. Half the time, I can barely follow the recipe without screwing it up. Another detail I omit while I'm in front of the camera. I make sure to get pictures of my plate so I can post that too. The meals may look okay, but they certainly don't always taste that way, and I have no idea why.

Hell, if it weren't for ClikClak and Insta, I'd probably just eat right out of the pot so I didn't have to do dishes. Truth be told, when Ma drops my laundry off tomorrow, and the kitchen is a mess, she'll probably clean it for me.

Yes, I know. I'm 32 years old, and my mommy still does my laundry. I've never asked her to do that. She just does. She's retired, so it gives her something to do, I guess. Makes her feel needed. We have an unspoken agreement. In return for her picking up after me, I get to have her meddling in my personal life, including near-constant harassment about finding a wife, settling down, and being less of a loner.

It's not perfect, but so far, it works. For her, at least.

I drop my clothes on the floor and fall onto my bed. I should edit videos, but instead I end up doomscrolling until well after midnight. Animal videos. Septic tank fails. Magic tricks. Repeat until 2 a.m. Just like every night.

But when I put down the phone and close my eyes, I can't think of anything else I want to do. Soccer has consumed such a large part of my life that there's been little room for anything else. I can't tell you the last time I read a book. Not even when I was in school. When you're a D1 athlete, they let a lot slide.

I started ClikClak as a hobby during the pandemic, but it's slowly taken over everything that's not already claimed by the Buzzards. Now it feels like work too, but I also can't imagine stepping away. What if I did? How long would it take people to forget about me? How long would it take them to realize I'm nothing special?

Eventually, I doze off, my phone dropping from my hand. I awaken a little while later, my fingers still curled and my thumb making the swiping motion, even though my phone has fallen to the floor. Jesus, this isn't healthy.

In the middle of the night, alone with my thoughts, I will myself not to pick up my cell and start scrolling again.

That lasts for about three minutes.

I think this might be some sort of problem, but what do I know? Hell, at least it's not drugs or alcohol or women. It could always be much worse.

Couldn't it?

CHAPTER 4: RACHEL

The Baldpate Road video is still amassing views. It's also amassing some serious dollars. Sweet. Not that I have anything to spend it on because I have no life.

When I first started making some extra income on ClikClak, I told Richie I'd use the money to help pay her medical bills. I envisioned us being in debt for years, living on ramen and franks and beans. I also envisioned myself being very thin, because I hate beans, so that would mean I'd have to skip every other meal. It's not an ideal plan, but it certainly beats where I am now—debt-free and sisterless.

Because Richie was on her own insurance and over the age of 26, she wasn't a dependent for Gram and Gramps any longer. She didn't own property or have an estate, so both her student loan and medical debts were canceled once we provided her death certificate.

So now I have all this money rolling in and nothing to do with it.

I could plan a trip. I glance at Richie's list, which is never far from my person. I consider laminating it so I don't ruin it, but I want to be able to touch the pen strokes.

Go somewhere on a plane

I've never been on a plane before. It seems like such a big task. Way too much for the first thing to cross off. I freeze, the paper still in my hand. I can't cross things off the list. There's no way I can mark up something Richie did with her own hands. I am now paralyzed by the weight of this problem.

"Rachel, what's wrong? You look like you saw a ghost. Is Richie here?" Uncle Robert laughs as he brushes by me, heading to his desk. I can't blame him, as I'm standing squarely in the middle of the office.

"Richie left me a to-do list, but I can't cross anything off it." I hold the paper out, shaking in my trembling hands.

He ambles over and takes the precious parchment, his lips moving as he reads. "Man, she got you good. She knew you'd never do any of these things without her, and she's guilt-tripping you from the great beyond. God, I miss that kid."

Sometimes I wonder if the roles had been reversed, if anyone would miss me the way we all miss Richie. "Yeah, well, if only I could fly there on a plane, at least I'd get to cross one off, but I can't even do that because I don't want to ruin the letter," I say, hoping he can't see what's really on my mind—the thought of being utterly forgettable.

Uncle Robert shakes his head, handing me back the paper. "For a smart girl, you can be pretty dumb. Make a photocopy." He gestures to the antiquated, hulking machine that takes up the south corner of the office.

Well, that was obvious.

To be safe, I make six copies. Then I carefully fold up Richie's original letter, putting it in my purse for safekeeping. I know where I'll store it at home. All my problems are solved. Except, of course, the big ones.

Gramps walks in. "Bobby, did you hear from Marchand?" Gramps is the only one allowed to call Uncle Robert Bobby. Richie tried … once. It did not go well. I didn't know he could yell that loud.

"Yeah, he says we're good to go on the South Shore expansion." Uncle Robert looks at his email. "Just waiting on the lease for the office space to be finalized. We got the place in the town of Sharon."

Gramps laughs. "You know she's never going to let us forget that." My grandmother's name is Sharon.

I hadn't realized how close to fruition the plan was. "Will you call this location Cramer-Romero Associates Pumps Number 2?"

Uncle Robert laughs. "Or how about Sharon's Cramer-Romero Associates Pumps?"

"Can I design the logo for that? Something in nice shades of brown?" I manage with barely a smile.

Before the jokes get too out of hand, Gramps stops us. You'd think he'd have a better sense of humor, doing what he does, but he really hates toilet jokes.

He's in the wrong business.

"Rachel, I want you to work out of that office. We need someone who knows the ins and outs of how we do things."

My mouth goes dry. My heart starts to race. I don't like new things. I don't like change. I've had enough of that to last a lifetime.

"But Gramps, you need me here," I protest lamely.

"I'll need you more there. You get how I think. I won't have to babysit you. You're mature for your age."

Uncle Robert mutters under his breath, "Because Rachel is an old fart in a young body."

I give him a dirty look. He's not wrong, but that was a little uncalled for. I'm a delicate flower.

Who films shit for a living.

"Wait, where is this new place located? Sharon?" My hand moves the mouse at lightning speed, using Google Maps to calculate the distance. "Holy Pete, do you know what that commute is like? If you think I'm late now, can you even imagine when I have that drive?"

It's an hour without traffic. Around Boston, there's never not traffic.

Gramps looks at Uncle Robert. Then he looks down at his desk. Then he looks out the window. Basically, anywhere but me.

"Gramps?" I stand up and cross to his desk. He'll have no choice but to look at me.

"We think it's time you move out."

He might just as well have kicked me in the stomach. It feels—almost—like hearing Richie's diagnosis for the first time. My body certainly has the same reaction, the bile rising in my throat and threatening to make an appearance. The periphery of my vision begins to darken.

"What do you mean?" Maybe I heard him wrong. I know I didn't, but one can hope.

"Gram and I think it's about time you stepped out on your own."

"I don't want to be on my own."

"Rachel, you're almost thirty. I get why you're a homebody. I understand it. But it's not normal. You have to go out into the world at some point."

"I go out into the world!" My voice rises three octaves. "I went to West Boxford two days ago."

"Only because there was sewage all over the place," Uncle Robert mutters. He is not helping. Seriously, whose team is he on anyway?

"Yeah, well, it's hard working here full time and then doing all the social media. And you both know this business has exploded because of my channel. We're only expanding because of me, and now you're sending me away? You're kicking me out?" My voice breaks on the last word.

"Gram and I aren't kicking you out. We're giving you an opportunity to spread your wings."

"Yeah, by pushing me off the perch!"

"Rachel," Gramps says, his patience wearing thin. "You don't go anywhere. You don't do anything. We're worried about you."

"I go places! I'm planning things." I'm totally not, but my rational brain is shutting down in favor of my go-to, panic brain. My gaze darts around the room, looking for a lifeline—something, *anything*—that will save me and anchor me to this place. I spy the stack of copies of Richie's letter. "I'm going to a professional soccer game." I plop down in my seat and start wiggling my mouse again. "I was just going online to buy myself a ticket."

Gramps folds his arms over his chest. "When?"

"Right now. It's what I was doing before you so rudely interrupted me by kicking me out. It's one of the things on Richie's list." My fingers shake as I do a Google search for the team. "Ah, right here. There's a game on September first." It's almost a month away, so maybe I can use that to delay the inevitability of my moving out.

"Sounds perfect. The Buzzards play right near the new office. It'll be something to do while you get settled down there."

My mouth falls open in disbelief. Before I can respond, Gramps walks back into his office and shuts the door. The discussion—not that there was one—is over.

I'll appeal to a higher power.

"I've got to run back to the house for a minute."

Uncle Robert doesn't look up from his computer. "Coffee kicking in?"

Usually saying I've got to run back to the house is code for needing to use the bathroom. Though we literally make a living on other people's excrement, I don't feel the need to have my own habits analyzed or scrutinized by whoever may be passing through. Plus, I work with a bunch of old dudes, so the bathroom is pretty nasty here.

No, this time, I'm actually appealing to a higher power.

"Gram. GRAM!" I yell as I barge through the kitchen door. She comes bustling in from the living room. She works part-time at the office, but this time of day, she takes a mid-afternoon break. She claims it's to let her lunch digest, but I'm pretty sure she's taking a catnap while her soap operas are on in the background. That woman has been hooked on *General Hospital* for as long as I can remember.

"What is it? Are you okay? Are you bleeding?" That's Gram's code to ask me if I'm physically hurt or if I'm having another panic attack.

"I'm not okay. Gramps said he's sending me down to the south office, and that I have to move there."

Her face melts into a sympathetic expression as she opens her arms to offer a hug. Sometimes I want the contact, but when I'm really heightened, I can't stand the touch. This isn't a panic attack with no rational cause. It's my life, spinning out of control, by no volition of my own.

Again.

I take a step forward and sink into her arms. These are the arms that were there my entire childhood. These are the arms that held me when I cried over a mother who wasn't there. When I had my first panic attack. When I got my first period and thought I was dying. When we found out Richie was literally dying. These arms are where I find comfort and peace, and know everything is going to be okay, even when it's not.

"It's going to work out, Rachel. I told Al I'd talk to you. I can only imagine how he dropped the news on you. That man never did have any tact."

It takes me a minute to process what she's saying. The second I do, I drop my arms and step back as if she's on fire.

"You knew?" I can't keep the betrayal out of my voice. "You knew he was planning on kicking me out, and you didn't do anything to stop him?"

Gram holds my gaze. "Rachel, it's for the best. If we don't pull the Band-Aid off right now, you'll never move on. You'll never get better. You'll never *live*."

I recoil as if she'd slapped me. *Get better?* It's not like childhood trauma can be discarded and stored away like winter boots.

"I'm fine right where I am!" I yell, spittle spraying from my mouth, my arms flailing about.

"But you're not, and you can't see that. Trust me, in a few months, you're going to be happy about this change. It's going to bring wonderful new things into your life. I feel it in my bones."

I'm too stunned by this betrayal to even cry. I take steps backward, small at first, gradually growing larger, until I'm across the room from my grandmother. "I'm happy here."

"Rachel, be real. You're only a breath above catatonic. I've already lost one granddaughter because of a disease in her brain. I'm not going to lose another one."

Her words feel like a physical strike. "I'm sorry my mental health is too much for you to bear. I'll start searching for an apartment today." I whirl around and begin to stomp out. At the last minute, I throw one last parting shot over my shoulder. "I only hope that the Sharon I'm moving to accepts me for me, since you never will."

That was childish. I'll probably regret talking to my grandmother like that at some point in the future, but for right now, I can't be sorry. I'm too angry. Too hurt. They want me out? I'm out.

CHAPTER 5: TJ

Thanks for agreeing to do the Soccer for Sibs thing." Brandon Nix practically grunts as he bench-presses a cool buck ninety-five. Considering he only weighs about one seventy-five, it's impressive.

"Yeah, no problem. What exactly do I have to do anyway?" I add another plate onto the bar, not to be outdone by him. At this rate, I'm going to give myself a hernia, but I don't want him to think less of me for not being able to lift as much as he can.

"We're doing a clinic. Basic skills and drills. Last time I looked, you and Landon are stationed together to work on passing. We thought it'd be easier to have two for that."

"I just have to kick the ball for a while and pose for pictures?"

"No, you have to teach these kids how to kick the ball. And there will be tons of photo ops and autograph signings. You know, the stuff you live for." He's replaced the bar onto the rack and stands up, ready to go.

I reach down into my sock and pull out the Sharpie I carry at all times. "I'm ready."

Brandon laughs. "You're a piece of work."

I don't know exactly what he means by that, but it doesn't sound positive. "Just trying to give the fans what they want."

The Sharpie thing started as a joke with Joey and Nicky one day when we were out grabbing some beers, and some chick approached me for my autograph. When I didn't have anything to sign it with, she pulled out her lipstick and wanted me to sign her chest. I signed a napkin instead because the whole thing made me feel a little sleazy. No one will ask you to sign their breasts with a permanent marker. Now I come prepared, so I'm not put in that position again.

Everyone else thinks it's because I'm so conceited.

My awkward reaction to the whole situation naturally made it into one of Joey's stand-up routines. My candid, unscripted moments have been fodder for my family's entertainment for years. Joey owes me some royalties from his routines because he talks about me so frequently.

Lucky for me, he doesn't mention me by name or that I'm a professional athlete. In his routines, I'm just the stupid little brother. I know my role in the family. Stereotypes exist for a reason, and I certainly fit the pretty boy, dumb jock one.

In high school, I was constantly in danger of being suspended from play because my grades were too low. I learned pretty early on that eventually my grade would get bumped up high enough for me to stay active. See? Maybe I wasn't such a dunce. It wasn't like I tried to fail my classes. I studied, or at least made valid attempts to. But following two years behind Nicky, who was valedictorian and going to Harvard, the mass assumption made by almost every teacher was that I was more than capable, but lazy.

It didn't take long before I realized that soccer was going to be my only way out. I'd never make the grades. I certainly wasn't going to make it with charm or charisma either. I worked to be the best player I could, did enough to get by in school, and miraculously got recruited to play at Maryland.

I was a second-round draft pick with the Buzzards, to the delight of my mom and dad, who have yet to miss a home game, no matter which level of the organization I was playing for. I swear, when my mom watches me play, she still sees the seven-year-old version of me out there, complete with a bowl cut and missing front teeth. It's nice having someone in my corner, rooting for me.

Brandon turns to walk away. I don't know what it is or why, but I want to continue talking about this project and the organization.

"Can you send me information about this event and the charity? I can share it on my socials."

As he pivots to face me, I expect Brandon to make fun of me for this, as members of my team often do. Instead, he nods. "Sure. That's why I asked you. You have the biggest reach." He starts to walk away but then says over his shoulder, "Well, that and because I ran into you outside Leora's office when she said she needed a name fast."

I let out a terse chuckle, trying to mask my offense. "So basically, I was in the wrong place at the wrong time."

Brandon shrugs and walks away.

A moment later, my phone starts buzzing with alerts. Text messages from Brandon, all containing the promotional materials and information that I'd requested. I can probably do something with this. Leora Deventhorpe in the front office is in charge of our publicity, and she's used my official team roster photo on the graphic.

It's not my favorite picture. To be fair, we all have a mug-shot-esque quality in our team pictures. It's especially bad when they remove the background and we're just floating heads. You'd think a professional soccer team could do better.

Once I get home and through the shower, it's the same routine as every night. Prep a meal kit while pretending that I can cook, post some videos that have no point, no message, and no meaning. I'm running out of content ideas. I edit some videos of me working out and throw those up there. Then, it's time to doomscroll until I fall asleep.

It is fascinating, the things people post about their personal lives. It's so easy to fall down the rabbit hole, watching other people struggle. I also get sucked into animal videos, cake-decorating videos—I find those especially soothing—and videos about homeowners undergoing difficulties with their homes. I particularly enjoy the ones about beehives that require removal and septic tank failures. I know it's gross, but it's like watching a train wreck. I can't stop.

My personal favorite, though, is watching people do magic tricks. Probably because when we were little kids, Nicky had a magic set. He wouldn't ever let me play with it. I was always the audience, and I could never figure out how he was doing those tricks. Before I discovered soccer, I wanted to be a magician. Granted, I was five. When Nicky outgrew the set, I inherited it. No matter how many times I read the book, my tricks never worked. I could never figure out how to do magic. The whole thing remains a mystery to me.

Morning brings another identical day. Practice, training, workout, back home. Lather, rinse, repeat.

My job is enviable and something only a few ever achieve. No matter how cool it is, I feel the clock ticking. Any minute now, the guillotine could lower and—SNAP—my career is done.

And then what?

Out of sheer boredom, I make a video post about the Soccer for Sibs event.

I don't talk about my family here much, but let me introduce you to my two best friends and worst enemies. My brothers, Joey and Nicky.

I cut to a picture of the three of us as grubby little boys who had just experienced the bliss of playing in the dirt pile in the backyard when my parents were putting an addition onto the house.

I'm lucky that these two knuckleheads have been there every step of the way with me during my life. But some kids aren't so lucky. Some kids have to watch their siblings get sick and go to the hospital. Some kids, instead of supporting their brothers and sisters at soccer games and spelling bees, are supporting them through chemo and rehab. The Boston Buzzards, in conjunction with JustSibs, want to celebrate those kids. The ones often left on the sidelines when the focus needs to be on their brothers and sisters. Come and learn how to play soccer with me and a few of my Buzzards teammates, then stay for the game as we look to crush the Wave on September first. You've been the best cheerleader, and now it's time for you to be a starting player! Link is in my bio for details! Let's keep kicking!

I sit on my black leather sofa and stare at my phone. I've uploaded hundreds—maybe even thousands—of posts. This one feels different. Good different. I almost want to smile. Maybe because it's not all about me? There's a purpose to it, substance behind it. It's not simply showing off my body or my athletic prowess.

I spend over an hour exploring every link on the JustSibs website, reading the stories, and seeing what the CopingSpace organization does.

I guess I never thought about the fact that kids get sick. We were all healthy and happy. We were lucky, it would seem. I, until this moment, did not realize how growing up like that would impact the healthy siblings. My chest feels tight, thinking about what it would have been like if Joey or Nicky had been sick.

Sometimes I want to kill them, but that's totally different than them having some fatal disease with no known cure.

I shoot a text to Brandon.

>*Me: Thanks for including me in the event. Seems like a really good cause. I just posted on ClikClak about it, so hopefully we get some interest.*

It's a few minutes before I get a response.

>*Brandon: Are you drunk or high? Should we get you drug tested tomorrow?*

What is he talking about?

>*Me: No, why?*

>*Brandon: Because you're excited about doing a charity event. No one gets excited about that. Even me, who came up with the idea in the first place.*

>*Me: Don't you think it's a good cause?*

>*Brandon: Of course, but they're still awkward AF. And it's not like I'm really good with people, let alone kids.*

>*Me: You can't punch anyone.*

>*Brandon: I'll try to remember that.*

I slide my screen back to ClikClak. The video already has a hundred thousand views. I nod in satisfaction. With this sort of traction early on, this video will probably do pretty well.

And I didn't even have to take my shirt off.

It's almost as if I had something important to say, and people listened.

Weird.

CHAPTER 6: RACHEL

My plan to buy a ticket to a Boston Buzzards game was not enough proof of my growth to prevent my grandparents from kicking me out. They think they're helping me. All it's doing is hurting me. I didn't think I could be sadder than when I lost Richie. This is a new low, even for me. Every time I try to convince myself that this might not be horrible, my gram's words ricochet around my brain

You'll always have a home with us.

It's not true anymore.

There's no such thing as always. At least not for me.

I have to move. I have no choice. But also, the real estate market in Sharon, Massachusetts, where my new office is going to be, is ridiculously expensive, so I'm forced to live a few towns away in Mansfield in order to save about $1000 each month. My commute will take at least twelve to fifteen minutes, and that doesn't include any extra time to stop and pet cats along the way.

The apartment complex where I find a rental that won't break the bank was built in the early '70s. No matter what kind of renovations they do on the inside, there's no disguising it. It has a sad pool that I'll probably never go in. The apartment interior is a wash of tan and white. From the oak kitchen cabinets to the beige carpets to the white vertical blinds that cover the sliding glass door to the tiny balcony, the whole thing has about as much personality as a piece of dry toast.

Perfect for me.

I mean, it's not. It's not at all what I would pick if I were moving into my dream place. This whole thing is more of a nightmare than a dream, sort of like the story of my life. It's available and cheap, and it'll do. What other choice do I have?

The past two weeks have been a whirlwind, sapping my already sparse energy. I currently vacillate between seething and sobbing. Both are draining. Who knew how tiring it would be to find a place to live, pack up all my stuff, buy furniture, and make sure I have internet? Adulting totally sucks. I've driven up and down I-95 more times in the past fourteen days than I probably have in the last fourteen years.

All the work of getting moved in doesn't even include my job responsibilities in setting up the new office. My first day there will be September fifth. To soften the blow, Gramps made me South Regional Director. It's a fancy way of saying I'm in charge in the new office.

It's a sizeable promotion, complete with a sizeable pay raise, and I'd be honored if I didn't have to leave my home. If I wasn't so alone.

My new place smells weird, like desperation masked with cheap primer. At least it smells better than my day job, though that's not saying much. The bar's pretty low for that one.

Through some creative negotiation—okay, I cried in the rental office—I was able to move into my apartment the last week of the month rather than on the first. The delivery truck from Bob's Discount Furniture is a frequent visitor; my only visitor. The Target is less than five miles away, and I make that trip at least once, if not twice per day.

That's all it took to move me out on my own.

Packing up my room at home was harder than I expected it to be. It'd been easy when I was little, as often as I had to do it. Mom dropped us off with Gram and Gramps almost yearly and then stumbled back into town to claim us about six months later. When we were with her, we'd move once or twice, depending on the state of her relationships. About two months after the last relationship would end, she'd drop us back at Gram and Gramps's. I used to be good at packing up all my life's belongings on a moment's notice.

This time was different. I'd hoped I'd be so fueled by rage that it wouldn't bother me. Now, though, when I'm going to sleep in some strange place, I have to face the fact that Richie won't be with me. She'll never set foot in this apartment. There will be no trace of her in here.

Whenever we'd spend the first night back with Mom, we'd snuggle in our shared bed, and we'd plan what things we'd have in our house when we grew up. In the days before Pinterest, we'd snag old *Better Homes & Gardens* and *Martha Stewart Living* magazines from Gram and cut out pictures of how our safe haven would be decorated.

Our house. Together. I'm not supposed to be by myself.

The absolute ache I feel in my chest deepens. Some days, I'm afraid to look in the mirror, afraid that there will be a literal hole right through me, where my heart used to be before my sister's death ripped it out.

I'm on my own, in Target for the billionth time this week, trying to make decisions without any input from her.

It's a constant reminder she's not here to pick out furniture or tell me what color shower curtain I should get. For the record, she'd have picked the peach ruffly one, but I go for something called "Bohemian Stripe" that has turquoise and orange and gold and black designs. It's not my style either, but I figure the bright colors will break up the monotony of the apartment. Maybe I can fool myself into cheering up if I mix enough bright colors and bold patterns together.

And even though I'm tempted to get the one she would have picked, I can't decorate my apartment for her. I have to start living for me. Isn't that the point of all this? Isn't that why Gram and Gramps kicked me out?

So here I am, in this new place that feels like a stiff pair of shoes a size too big, with nothing to do except sit with my own emotions, none of them good. I pick up my phone and open up ClikClak. The video of Baldpate Road is still getting views. I re-edit some of the footage and post another video. Next week, when the new office opens, I'll have lots of great material. Until then, I'm trying to be creative with recycling footage from previous job sites.

I finish uploading and go out to the feed, relaxing back on my brand-new Bob-o-pedic couch. I glance up at my brand-new bookshelf, two shelves filled with my all-time favorites. I should read a book. It's been months since I found solace in the words on a page.

Instead, my gaze drifts back to my phone because it's easier than getting up and trying to figure out what I'm in the mood to read. I swipe a few times, barely processing what's flashing before my eyes. An ad for concealer. Three videos in a row of people dancing to the same '80s pop song. An ad for a weight loss supplement. A guy talking. I swipe up and then immediately pull the video back down to watch as my brain, lagging behind the speed of my fingers, processes the username.

TJ Doyle.

I've read his name so many times that it's emblazoned in my memory. Holy shit, it's the guy who usually cooks practically naked! How did I not connect his name with those videos before? Probably because I expected him to be doing something sports-y or with a ball. Right now, he's fully dressed—I almost didn't recognize him disguised in a shirt—sitting on a black couch, talking about his brothers.

But then it shifts into talking about having a sibling with cancer and this charity event he's doing.

—with me and a few of my Buzzards teammates, then stay for the game as we look to crush the Wave on September first.

September first. That's the game I said I was going to go to, way back when. Okay, it was only three weeks ago, but it seems like a different lifetime. I click on the link in his bio, and it directs me to the website.

"Meet Boston Buzzards superstars Brandon Nix, Landon Stubbs, TJ Doyle, and goalie Callaghan Entay!"

My heart starts to race. My hands grow clammy. I might actually be able to do something on Richie's list. Like, for real. I can meet this guy, whom she undoubtedly had a crush on because he bears a striking resemblance to Chris Evans, and then I can cross it off. I don't think I ever noticed his face before. Damn if my sister didn't have a type.

After I fill out my name and email, the first question on the list is, "Do you have or have you had a sibling with a life-threatening, life-altering, or terminal medical condition?"

A big ole yupper on that one.

I keep getting prompted to fill out more.

Glioblastoma. Check.

Only sibling. Check.

I pay the fee of $250, which includes a commemorative T-shirt, a professional photo, and two tickets to the game.

I don't have anyone to take, obviously, but if there's an open seat next to me, at least I won't have to make small talk about a sport I know absolutely nothing about. I can probably bring a book to read.

What am I doing? This is stupid. I don't even like sports. I go back to the website, only to see a huge red banner dashing across the page. "EVENT SOLD OUT."

Did I get the last tickets? What if there's someone else out there who really wanted them? My buyer's remorse is immediate and strong, especially at that price point.

My phone dings with a confirmation email. I open it up, looking for contact information so I can try to get out of this. NO REFUNDS.

Dammit.

I open the itinerary and read. Registration begins at 11:30 with the event starting at noon. Then my mouth goes dry, and my heart sinks as I read what I should bring on Saturday. Cleats are preferred. Shin guards. Water will be provided.

Oh no.

I was so excited that I'd get to meet TJ Doyle that I didn't process what the event was. It's not just standing around, shaking hands, and taking pictures like at a comic con. It's a soccer clinic. Like where they teach you how to play soccer. Maybe I should have paid attention to the fact that the whole stupid thing is called Soccer for Sibs.

Me, playing soccer.

That's got to be the most ridiculous thing I've ever heard. I couldn't catch a ball if my life depended on it. I've never been to a sporting event in my life. I've never even watched one on TV. Once I got past middle school PE, I don't think I've touched a ball.

And I paid two hundred and fifty bucks for this.

"You're expensive even when you're dead," I yell to the ceiling. Gramps always said Richie had champagne taste on a beer budget. When we were little, we had no idea what he meant by that. Now, I'd say it tracks.

Again, Richie doesn't answer me. Bitch.

In my apartment by myself, I have between now and Saturday morning to obsessively spiral about what a stupid thing I've done, and there's no one here to stop me.

Usually, that's said with an evil laugh, but for me, it's a scary voice inside my heart talking. I want to call Gram, but I'm trying to stay strong. Maybe it's childish, but I'm mad at her for kicking me out. Rationally, it makes sense not to have me commute all this way, especially considering my punctuality issues.

I don't feel like being rational.

It's the hurt that overwhelms me, tasting like bile in my mouth. My mom didn't want us. My sister had no choice but to leave. My grandparents said I had to go.

It's hard when no one wants you long enough to stay.

It doesn't take a rocket scientist or world-renowned psychologist to figure out that I'd rather be alone than face rejection ever again. I'll take survival mechanisms for 100, Alex. I'll work and come back to my '70s apartment. Maybe I'll take up a hobby like knitting.

I should get some cats.

Yikes, that's a dark place to go to. I mean, I love cats, and my grandparents always had at least two at a time my entire life. Somehow now, that seems like a cry for help. I need to be strong. I need to be productive. I need to show them all that I am just fine on my own, and that I don't need anyone to love me. I need to be a self-contained unit that doesn't need anyone or anything.

I will also avoid the animal shelter for now.

If only to give myself something else to focus on, I walk to my new bedroom and try to figure out what I'm going to wear for this soccer thing. There is nothing even remotely athletic in my closet. Or in my suitcase, which has yet to be unpacked because I haven't assembled my dresser yet.

I sit down on my floor, overwhelmed by the state of my apartment. The state of my life. Everything is all brand new, and I hate all of it. I make a vow to never leave my apartment or speak to anyone again in protest of all the change.

I can almost hear Richie tsk'ing at me from the great beyond. She'd say, "Rach, you're *this* close to meeting TJ Doyle. To making physical contact. To sniffing him. Don't let me down now."

Okay, fine. I can do this one thing from the list. One thing, and one thing only. If Richie has a problem with that, she can come back and haunt me herself.

But now, in all seriousness, what do I wear to this thing?

CHAPTER 7: TJ

I'm actually on time. Someone write this down. I walk into the field house, which is our typical practice facility, and take some video footage. Brandon Nix is already there, talking with Callaghan Entay. Brandon's wearing his glasses. He usually reserves those for the mornings after late nights, so I expect him to be surly and hungover.

When I approach, I'm surprised to find him in a good mood. There are a bunch of staff members from JustSibs running around in their turquoise T-shirts, setting up stations and marking zones off with cones and sticks and orange tape.

Landon Stubbs joins us, and we start joking around with the ball, bouncing it off our legs to one another, like you'd do with a Hacky Sack. None of us is the type to stand still, and we're not friends enough to really talk about anything important. Brandon, however, is talking a mile a minute about nothing and everything.

"Dude, are you on something?" I ask. I didn't peg him as one to risk his career with drugs, but he's definitely more high-strung and jittery than normal.

"No, just excited about this event."

He's acting weird. I look over and I see Hannah, Entay's girlfriend, recording us. She does the social media accounts for the Patriots, so I'm surprised to see her at a Buzzards event. Callaghan has drifted off, talking to someone near the goal. Since I don't have to worry about him taking my head off for talking to his woman, I call out, "Hey, send me what you get." I add a quick "Please and thanks!" at the end so I don't sound like a complete and total jerk.

I'm the opposite of smooth.

One of the handlers from Soccer for Sibs comes over and explains our assignments. Leora Deventhorpe had already sent us the itinerary with this on it, so it's not a surprise.

The official person says, "Remember, today is about the siblings. Do what you can to make them feel special. We expect lots of social media posts, so make sure to smile big. Take your time with them. Thank you for donating your time and names to this event today."

I take that as my cue to whip out my phone and do some recording. I get footage of the field house, some of the stations, and, of course, me navigating it all. I'll get the guys in this, too. I walk back to where they're still standing and hear Brandon say, "I'd show them how to really kick a ball."

Hannah laughs. "Oh, to have your confidence. We should have you put your money where your mouth is."

This is the Brandon we're all used to. He seems a little calmer. Now that it doesn't look like he's tweaking out, I turn my phone lens toward him. "What's Brandon talking smack about now? I want to record this for posterity."

Brandon swats at the phone. "You want to go viral at my expense."

They all make fun of my social media. I don't think any of them realize how lucrative it can be. They think it's a stupid hobby for a stupid guy. I laugh with Brandon so he can't laugh at me. "Same difference. What's the bet?"

Brandon glances at Hannah, like it's some secret. Some club I'm not smart enough to belong to. Just when I'm about to walk away, Brandon says, "That I can kick a ball further than the kicker for the Patriots. Bring him over. We should do this. Get Chris Todd, and let's have a kickoff contest. I've got time before the game."

The dude's balls are the size of boulders, I swear. I bet he's never had an insecure moment in his life.

Callaghan Entay, always mindful of his duty as team captain, squashes this before it can go anywhere. "Sounds like it'd be worth watching, but not on a match day. Save your leg for the game, especially in this heat."

He's not wrong. Like most of August was, today's a soupy, humid, upper-80s day. The weather doesn't seem to realize it's supposed to be fall, and it can start cooling down now. I can practically feel the dehydration cramps starting now. We're all going to be mainlining the electrolyte gels by game time.

Brandon crosses his arms over his chest and pouts like a petulant toddler. "Cally Entay is always spoiling the fun." I'm of course getting all of this on video. Callaghan *hates* being called that, and Brandon is a grade A button pusher.

I *think* Brandon's trying to be funny. I also don't think Callaghan appreciates it, though his parents should have thought twice about his name. I have to say, over the past few months, Brandon's seemed a little more relaxed.

Definitely less aggressive and irritable.

Almost likable.

Usually, this kind of chill only happens when a guy is getting it regularly. Brandon's never brought anyone around. Hell, there's not even any rumors of him dating a supermodel or anything currently. The only thing I've seen on social media is mentions of him and Andi Nichols, the referee. Like that would ever happen. The way she tossed his ass out of the last game she officiated for us—yeah, no. It's clear she hates Brandon.

She's here, working this event too. I look around quickly. She's on the other side of the field house and hasn't even as much as glanced in Brandon's direction. Yeah, I don't think there's anything to that one.

There's got to be some other explanation for Brandon's good mood.

There's no more time for analysis, as it's time to report to our stations. There's a line of kids and parents in the doorway. Everyone's wearing the same turquoise T-shirts emblazoned with the logo for the JustSibs organization. Landon and I head to the midfield zone to teach some agility skills, including dribbling and passing. Brandon's teaching how to do penalty kicks at one end of the field, while Callaghan is, of course, in goal, teaching goalkeeping. Andi Nichols, the referee, is at the other end, with frequent whistle sounds coming from that direction.

That's not at all annoying.

There are six to eight kids in each group, with their parents standing back, phones obscuring almost every single adult face. It only takes a minute or two to tell which adult belongs to which child, so I try to make sure angles work for the best pictures and videos. The groups are mostly made up of boys between the ages of eight and twelve. There are only a few girls in each cohort.

I wonder if we had partnered with the New England Crush, our USSL women's affiliate, if we'd have had a more balanced turnout? Maybe I should mention that for next year.

A buzzer sounds, signaling the end of this rotation. There's a little girl in this group, probably about five or six, who reminds me of my niece Cami. Her mom is standing right next to her, instead of stepping back like the rest of the parents.

"I'll keep an eye on her," I say, jogging up. "You can go stand over there. She's in good hands with me." I squat down in front of the little girl. "What's your name?"

"Alivia," she says, her eyes bright behind her glasses. "Watch what I can do." She proceeds to drop to her stomach, put her hands down, and roll her legs up over her head until her toes touch the ground, effectively bending her in half.

"Jesus," I say, jumping back. I look at her mom, who just stands there. She looks on the young side to be this girl's mom, which might explain why she stands there staring instead of telling this child not to snap her spine. "Does she do this often?" My back hurts just looking at her.

Alivia drops her legs back down and stands before I know it. I watch her mom for a reaction. Any kind of reaction. There is none. "Does she always do that? Doesn't it hurt?" I could seriously do Pilates and yoga every day for the rest of my life and never have a fraction of that flexibility.

The mom doesn't respond, instead staring at me with big brown eyes that are the exact same color as her hair. It's as if she's trying to look right into my soul. I glance down to make sure I'm not inadvertently exposing anything.

Nope, still covered.

But I swear, this woman is looking at me as if she can see me naked. Not in a lustful kind of way. More the soul-baring, knows-all-my-deep-dark-secrets kind of way. Also, she's pretty, in a woman-out-of-her-element kind of way. Though I probably shouldn't be thinking about hitting on someone's mom at a charity event.

A foot flies in the air. It's the little girl doing a cartwheel. I could picture her on the soccer field, twirling and flipping and doing anything but kicking the ball. I wonder why her mother made her come to this. An event with Simone Biles would be much more appropriate.

The corners of my lips rest in an uneasy smile. I look around, trying to see if I'm being pranked or something. The rest of the event is proceeding as it has been. Why isn't this mother doing anything to stop her kid and make her pay attention?

"Alivia!" a voice calls. I glance over. It's coming from where the parents are standing. Seriously, if Alivia's mom isn't going to do anything, the least she can do is go stand with the rest of the adults. I see who's calling Alivia. It's an older version of Alivia. A mom-sized version. If that's her mom, who's this lady standing next to her? What the hell is going on here?

"Are you with her?" I point at Alivia. The woman shakes her head. "Then who are you with?"

She's maybe a few years younger than I am. Totally unprepared for soccer. Bike shorts, canvas sneakers, no cleats, no shin guards. She's gripping her phone like it's a lifeline.

"Do you play soccer?" I yell over the din.

She shakes her head.

"Ready to learn?"

Another headshake.

"Then why are you here?" I tilt my head, waiting for the answer. This seems like a big thing to do, especially if you're not into soccer.

"Can I just take a quick picture with you for my sister?" Her voice shakes.

It's starting to make sense. All the kids here have sick siblings. I bet this woman is no exception. Jesus, I'm a dumbass for not realizing that sooner. "Is she the soccer fan?"

She swallows hard and nods. "She always wanted to meet you." The pain in her voice is evident. It practically punches me in the gut. I'd do anything to make it go away.

"Let's play some soccer, and then we can get a quick picture. I'll make it fun. Deal?"

She nods the slightest of nods. It's obvious she has no idea what's going on.

"Okay, we're going to run up the line and then Alivia here is going to kick us the ball."

I start off in a trot with this woman next to me. Once we're about ten yards away, I stop and set up to receive the kick. The woman places her hands on her knees, panting. "So," she gasps, "Is there a rule about subbing in oxygen tanks? Asking for … me."

I grin. "You haven't even touched the ball yet."

"Yeah, that's because I don't want to embarrass the ball."

I have to laugh. "Too late. The ball's going to need therapy." I signal to Alivia, who kicks the ball down our way. It ricochets off the woman's legs—bet she wishes she had shin guards on now—and skitters across the turf. One of the little boys in the group runs after it.

I'm busy watching the ball, so I don't see the whirling dervish tumbling toward us. Alivia does some sort of flip, landing just inches in front of the woman. She backpedals to get out of the way but trips on a cone. She lands with a hard thud on her back.

"Oh my God, are you okay?"

She splays her arms and legs out wide. "This is a play I like to call defensive starfish."

I reach down and grab her hands to pull her back up. "It's highly effective, especially when you're trying to block grass stains. I'll have to try it in my next game."

I can't help but grin.

For a split second, the corners of her mouth threaten to quirk up at the edges, but then a loud airhorn startles her. The panicked look is back on her face.

"Okay, I'll put you out of your misery. You can have your picture." I give the signal, one of the workers steps up, and the woman hands her phone off. I hold the ball under my arm and stand next to the woman. I half expect her to put her arms around me, like women often do when they request a selfie. Seeing as how her sister's the fan, maybe she's not touching me out of respect for her.

We get the picture, and I turn to face her. "What's your name?" I ask so I can sign the headshot we have to give out.

"Rachel," she says quietly.

It's seriously so hard to hear her over the noise in here. "Can you spell that?" People get really pissed when you spell their names wrong. Trust me on this one.

"It's R-I-C-H-E-L-L-E."

I repeat it back as I write it and then frown. That can't be right. That's not how you spell Rachel. Dammit. I can't even spell a simple name without screwing it up. "I'm sorry, I messed up." I look around for the person with all our pictures, but she's now moved over to Landon. I try to catch her attention. "Hang on, let me get another picture. Spell it again for me?"

I can't believe I was such an idiot. I often have trouble spelling names right. I should probably have people write down their names for me before I sign, so I can get it right. I might not be smart enough to sound things out and not reverse letters, but I can at least copy it without messing it up.

Rachel takes the picture, her eyes shimmering wet with tears. "This is perfect. Thank you." And then she walks away, heading right to the door.

"Look what I can do!" Alivia does a flip, almost kicking me in the chin. I put my hands up and take a step back. When I look up again, I can't find Rachel anywhere.

She's gone.

All because I'm too stupid to write her name.

CHAPTER 8: RACHEL

I clutch the picture and hold my breath, willing the tears to stay in my eyes before they explode onto my face and take over my whole body. Something I've learned about myself this past year: I'm an ugly crier.

There are no crystalline drops of liquid lightly tracing down my cheeks while my eyes grow more vivid in color. Oh no, there's grotesque contortions of all my facial muscles, it seems, while the increased saline from my eyes triggers an avalanche of snot through my nose. Then add in the shoulder shaking and the wailing sound that automatically comes from my mouth.

It is not a pretty picture at all.

Crying in public should be avoided at all costs, and that is my number one priority as I race off the field and into a deserted corridor only lit by emergency lights. It's likely I'm not supposed to be here, but my need for solitude outweighs any rule-following right at this moment.

I slide down the wall, sinking my head to my knees and focusing on my breathing. In for four, hold for five, out for seven. In for four, hold for five, out for seven. I do this over and over until the urge to sob and wail passes.

I can hear the buzzer and whistles and the din of people talking, but it feels far away. Or maybe I'm just far away. Far away from a world in which I can function without grief overtaking me.

I didn't think this would be this hard.

I look at the glossy photo in my hand and the words scrawled across it.

Richelle, Keep Kicking! TJ Doyle #8

Eight was Richie's favorite number. Being born on the eighth day of the eighth month will do that. The year she was turning eight, she declared that it would be the best year ever because it was her lucky year.

That's the year that Mom dropped us off at Gram and Gramps for the last time before she disappeared for three years. That was probably the best thing that could have happened to us, so maybe Richie was right.

I wonder if Richie liked this player because of his number. I take a closer look at his headshot. He looked way better in person. Or at least I thought he did. I pull out my cell phone to look at the picture we took.

God, I look awful.

It comes as a little bit of a shock, how bad I look. I don't know what I thought I looked like, but this isn't it. I've never been the type to spend hours looking at myself in the mirror. Hell, I don't even appear on camera for any of my ClikClak videos. I stare at my tired eyes, complete with puffy bags and shaggy hair that hasn't even had a trim in a year, my bob now grown out. I put my contacts in today, so I don't even have my glasses to distract from the disaster I am. I barely recognize myself.

TJ Doyle, on the other hand, is way hotter in this picture than he is in his headshot. I thought professional pictures were supposed to make you look your best. He definitely looks better in the candid shot.

And I made a complete and total ass out of myself in front of him. *Defensive starfish?* Where the hell did that come from?

I don't think I've ever met someone so photogenic before. Short light brown hair and a matching close-cut beard. Dark blue eyes that would be so easy to get lost in. A sleek nose and prominent cheekbones. I wonder what he'd look like without the beard?

Or without his clothes. I bet he has abs of steel to match the buns of steel I spied when he first walked in. I should have sniffed him when I had the chance. I bet he smells like leather and sandalwood and man and all those other things that romance books use to describe their hunky heroes. This man has main character energy.

That intrusive thought makes me sit up straight. What the hell was that? I am not sitting here, lusting over the man my sister lusted over. That would be wrong on so many levels, like cheating on her with her boyfriend.

This is so messed up.

What am I even doing here? I should go. I can cross one thing off the list. That should be enough. I can go back to my apartment and ...

And what? What's waiting for me back there?

Absolutely nothing.

Sitting here on this dirty floor, I realize I'm at a crossroads. My life as I knew it is gone. I don't have the option of going back to how things were. I can be stuck forever, or I can take a step forward. I can return to my apartment and never leave again, or I can stay out in the world.

It'd be easier to hide forever. I pull out Richie's list and look at it. *You only live once.* Is what I'm doing even living?

My place is so new that I don't even have memories in it yet. I'll never have any of Richie there anyway. Maybe it's better if I stay out. I did buy two heinously expensive tickets to the game, so I should probably stick around and at least see what a professional soccer game is like. I could ogle TJ Doyle for a while, and no one would be the wiser. I'm not sure how long a soccer game lasts, but it's probably a few hours in which I can think impure thoughts and picture him as a romance novel hero. I wish it were an item on Richie's list so I could cross it off, too.

I can do this. I can make the choice to rejoin the world of the living.

I mean, I didn't already die of embarrassment yet today, so that's a start.

Besides, worst-case scenario, I can always ogle TJ Doyle's buns of steel from the safety of my seat. A girl's gotta have goals.

CHAPTER 9: RACHEL

The problem with deciding to "rejoin the world of the living" is that the world of the living doesn't come with an instruction manual that says, *Congratulations, you've decided not to become a reclusive cat lady before your thirtieth birthday! Here's how: Step one: try to stand up. Step two: buy spandex shorts that you'll never wear again. Step three: stop dwelling on TJ Doyle's buns and what a total ass you made out of yourself.*

I wish I had a step-by-step set of directions. Lacking that, I do what any socially awkward, grief-stricken woman would do. I reward myself for my bravery. Coffee and books. Maybe a little sweet treat, too. If I can't handle people, I can at least handle carbs and paperbacks.

Instead of heading home, like I'm so tempted to do, I point my car in the direction Google tells me, toward an indie bookstore with the suspiciously optimistic name *An Unlikely Story.* It seems only fitting. Me, attempting to play soccer, is a very unlikely story.

I expect the business to be a tiny shop stuffed in a depressing strip mall, smashed in between a Chinese restaurant and a vape shop. Instead, I find a sprawling three-story building with a large front porch and gorgeous hardwood floors, and books for days. Is this heaven? No, it's an indie bookstore.

Complete with a coffee shop.

It's easy to pass the time in a haven like this. It's so homey it feels like … home. For a little while, buried between row after row of stories, I feel like my old self; the one who would escape for hours—even days—in the pages of a novel. I pick up book after book, looking at the cover, reading the back, and then putting them down. Nothing is jumping out at me right away. To say I've been in a reading slump is an understatement. It's hard to read about happily ever afters when your world is falling apart. Conversely, it's hard to read about sad things when you're practically drowning in your own grief.

I was the one always reading when we were growing up. Richie was too busy studying and playing sports to curl up with a good book. I spent much of my teens and early twenties curled up with a cozy romance rather than dating. I didn't have a social life to get in my way, but I didn't mind. The happy endings in my romance books never let me down the way real people did.

Richie was a late convert to romance books, but when she did, like everything else, it was go big or go home. In the last few weeks of her life, Richie couldn't see the print well enough, so she had me read them to her. Her preference: the smuttier the better. I'm almost positive it was because of how embarrassed I got reading them. I believe it gave her great amusement to watch my face turn various shades of crimson while using words like folds and organ and slick and moist.

There were other words she delighted in hearing, but I can't repeat them in polite conversation.

I offered to get her audiobooks, but she said my voice was more comforting. I call bull. Even as she was dying, she was still being a pain in the ass little sister.

My taste in books, like everything else with Richie, differed. I prefer the deep emotional connection of a couple falling in love. The push and pull of forbidden attraction. The rivals-to-lovers or opposites-attract. The witty banter that makes me kick my feet in delight. You know, the type of things writers dream up and put in their books that never quite happen in real life.

With the exception of my grandparents, I can't think of a love story, filled with romance and longing, true soul mates and all that jazz, that exists outside the confines of the pages of a book. We romanticize books and movies because it doesn't happen in real life. There is no prince on a white horse, ready to swoop in and solve all the problems. In reality, guys send dick pics in hopes of getting laid and then ghost you as soon as they do. Moms don't want to be moms and follow random guys all over the place rather than staying with their kids. Sisters die.

Shit happens.

And I can say that with authority, considering my job.

So maybe a smushy romance is not what I need right now. I need something that is totally fictional so my brain doesn't start thinking about happy endings for myself that will never come to fruition. I settle on an indie book called *Super Serial* that's described as a dark comedy thriller about a pastry-obsessed bounty hunter in a corporate-dystopian world. Sounds perfect.

I buy the book and head to the cafe, where a grilled cheese on white seems like it will hit the spot. You can't go wrong with carbs and dairy. An iced coffee completes the meal. I'm surprised when I look up to find my cup down to the ice and the clock indicating it's time to drive back to the stadium.

In spite of myself, this was a pleasant afternoon. Richie would be proud of me for stepping outside my comfort zone. I consider calling Gram to let her know where I'm going, but then I remember I'm still mad at her. It's okay. I don't need to share this day with anyone else. I'm doing it for me.

Well, I'm doing it for my sister, but that's a detail I don't need to focus on.

The stadium is massive, especially compared to the facility next door where the event had been. Even though the calendar has just flipped to September, the heat and humidity are more like August. I'm sweating like a stuck pig. I feel my throat tighten a little, and my blood begins to pound in my ears at the thought of being shoved in like a sardine with thousands of people. How many does this place hold anyway?

Over 65,000. I should not have looked that up. I'm definitely going to have a panic attack. But when I get inside, there are fewer people than I would have thought. Helpful ushers point me in the direction of my seats. The bottom two tiers are packed, but the uppermost seating is empty. I bet those are sold out for football games.

My panic starts to ebb as I take in the sight.

I'm in section 108, row 3. If I liked sports, these would be fantastic seats, located right behind the Buzzards' bench. I look around and see that most of this section and the one next to us are filled with people wearing the Soccer for Sibs T-shirts. I left mine in my car.

I settle in and pull out my book. Sweat pours off me. It takes me a little while to be able to tune out the crowd and focus on what I'm reading. Several times, I'm startled out of my own world when the crowd erupts into massive applause and the PA system blares, "GOOOOAAAAAL!" The scoreboard at one end of the field reports that the Buzzards are winning.

The people sitting next to me are super into the game. It's an older couple, probably in their sixties, with two men whom I'd guess to be their sons, if the familial resemblance is any indication. I can't imagine what it'd be like to be a grown adult and spend time with my parents. In theory, it could happen, but I haven't talked to my mom since the funeral. Every few minutes, the family next to me is on their feet, yelling and screaming in thick Boston accents. There's been a lot of cheering from them, so they must be happy with whatever's happening on the field.

The mom looks over at me, book in hand, and smiles. "Soccer not your cup of tea?"

My face flushes, and I hastily close my book, my finger still caught between the pages. "Not really."

"Why are you here then?" one of the sons asks. "And why did you pay so much for these seats if you weren't even going to watch the game?"

I open my mouth to tell them about the whole charity event when something on the field draws their attention. Several whistles sound as the crowd boos. I look to see a player being helped to his feet by a teammate. I'm pretty sure he was one of the ones at the event today. I don't know his name. The referee places the ball in front of him, holding his hand up in the air. The player backs up, takes a few steps forward, and launches the ball with his foot. It sails down almost half the field and right over the outstretched arms of the goalie.

The entire stadium erupts in a cacophony as the now familiar "GOOOOAAAAAL!" echoes through the stadium. The player pumps his arms as he runs to a teammate, jumping on him. The crowd begins tossing their hats onto the field, chanting "Hat trick! Hat trick!"

"What's going on?" I ask the woman. It's not that I really care, but the stadium is abuzz with excitement. It'd be nice to be on the inside for once, instead of on the outside looking in. She's still on her feet, her hair matted to her head from sweat now that it's been freed of the baseball cap she'd been wearing.

"Brandon Nix scored a hat trick."

"What's that?" I ask as the officials are picking up all the hats from the field.

"It's when a player scores three goals in one game."

I nod, unsure of what else to say. I'm sure that's a good thing. I slide my book into my bag and watch what's going on for a minute. The opposing team—Miami, I guess—has the ball at the center of the field and is kicking it. The players are running, chasing the ball as it darts here and there. My gaze locks in on number eight in the middle of the pack running forward, then changing direction.

Holy leg muscles, Batman.

Reflexively, I fan myself. Now I know why sports romance is a thing. You'd think soccer romance books would be way more popular.

A player from the Wave has the ball. One of the Buzzards tries to get it away from him, and the two of them tumble out of bounds. The Miami player slams right into the female referee on the sidelines, both of them falling to the ground with a heavy thud.

Ouch, that had to hurt.

I never realized how physical soccer is. No wonder Richie liked it. She was the rough and tumble of the two of us. It doesn't hurt that a lot of these players are serious eye candy, either. Maybe I should become a soccer fan. The player who took out the referee jumps to his feet and reaches for the woman. He pulls her to her feet in an act of sportsmanship. I guess for all the physicality, soccer is still a very refined sport.

Wait? What was that? Did that guy just grab her ass in front of thousands of people? I shake my head. I cannot have seen what I think I just saw. But I did, because she's waving her hand and yelling "Red, dammit, red!"

Then out of nowhere, one of the Buzzards' guys comes charging, fists ablaze, and begins to pummel the ass-grabbing Wave player. I'm sure this is against the rules, but that is satisfying to watch.

The family next to me is on their feet, yelling and screaming. The entire stadium erupts into chaos. There are whistles and air horns to add to the shouting. It's hard to even tell what is going on now, because there's just a massive huddle of people on the field. Eventually, the officials break it up, and the puncher walks off the field, head down, while the head referee holds up a red card. He doesn't even look at it.

The group of referees is conferring, and it looks like they're about to throw fists themselves. Finally, there are a few more whistles, and another red card is issued. This one is to the punchee, who is bleeding. Good. He has to leave the game as well. Also good. I don't know much about soccer, but I know this guy should not be allowed to play anymore, especially if he's going to manhandle women like that.

"See, isn't this more interesting than some dumb ole book?" one of the guys sitting next to me says. It's the sort of thing that's supposed to be funny but isn't.

I shrug. "To each his own."

The other guy says, "Don't let Joey give you a hard time. He's just jealous because he's still working on reading books without pictures."

"Boys, stop it," the mother admonishes.

I don't know how to respond, so I don't. I pretend to be engrossed in the goings-on on the field. The rest of the game takes about ten minutes, in which absolutely nothing interesting happens. Apparently, we've fulfilled the excitement quota for pro soccer. I'm itching to get back to my book. The final whistle sounds, and I stand up to leave. The family sitting next to me is not moving. I look around. Trying to rush out now would probably be futile, since everyone is pressing toward a few narrow doorways.

Reason and sensibility do not stop me from wanting to get out immediately. I'm standing, shifting my weight from one foot to the other, willing the bodies in front of me to move. Even though it's night, the temperature and humidity haven't decreased yet. I'm sure in a month or two, I'll be longing for this kind of warmth, but for now, I'm hot and sweaty and fairly confident I have significant BO.

It's time for me to go home.

Good thing I don't have to go anywhere for the next four days. It's going to take me that long to recuperate from one day out. I've had my dose of being with people for the rest of the year.

The mom of the group finally stands and leans in to make conversation. "Do you have plans after the game?"

The response inside my head is, "Do I look like the kind of person to have plans?" but I know Gram would kill me for being sassy. Instead I say, "A cold shower, air conditioning, and my book."

The woman laughs. "That sounds heavenly." Her head tilts as she looks me over. "You know, we have a family tradition of going out for ice cream after every game. Started when the boys were little, and we've never seemed to move on. You look like you could use some ice cream. Why don't you join us?"

While I'm never one to pass up ice cream, my immediate inclination is to say no. She must sense my hesitation, and she quickly adds with a laugh, "I'm sorry. I know that came out of nowhere. We don't even know each other. I'm Maureen, and this is my husband, Tom, and my sons Joey and Nicky. Tyler will join us there."

I'm about to politely decline when she says, "My doctor says I need to lay off the ice cream because of my cholesterol, but I say you only live once. Isn't that right, dear? Now what do you say?"

You only live once.

It's like Richie is giving me a message. I can practically hear her saying, "This is a chance to do something. To connect. Also, you really like ice cream. Don't pass this up!"

Maybe my dead sister did communicate with me. Maybe I'm hallucinating from the heat. Maybe I'm just in the mood for ice cream. Doesn't matter because I find myself nodding in agreement. "I'm Rachel," I add. "I'd love to join you."

I guess I'm doing this.

CHAPTER 10: TJ

The end of the game was absolutely nuts. There's speculation about whether Brandon Nix will be fired or if he'll just have a massive financial penalty. Any other time, if you'd asked me about Brandon, I'd have said he was a loose cannon and a major asshole.

His actions today, beating Seamus O'Marra to the ground, were totally reasonable. We all saw what O'Marra did to Andi Nichols. He probably deserved worse.

I'm sure it's all over social media. My fingers twitch, jonesing to check ClikClak. I spent the break between Soccer for Sibs and the game posting my videos from the event. As much as I'm tempted to open the app, my family is waiting for me. Win or lose, unless there are extenuating circumstances, we go out for ice cream after games. They make the effort to come to the games, driving almost an hour each way. The least I can do is debrief with them for a few minutes after.

It keeps Ma happy, and that's all that really matters.

I check my phone for the confirmation text. Because most ice cream places close before the end of the game,

Ma or Dad calls ahead and asks them to stay open. We pay the staff handsomely, of course. Most are accommodating, and they love the social media exposure I give them. With approximately seventeen home games, we've found a list of nearby places that we rotate through. Improving the local economy one ice cream sundae at a time.

Tonight's location is Three Pugs Creamery, located about four miles from the stadium. I don't even need to look at the menu to know that I'll be ordering The Enzo, which is a hot fudge sundae built on chocolate chip cookies. My mouth salivates in anticipation.

Once showered, I head for my car and drive to the ice cream shop. I see Dad's Jeep Compass parked next to Joey's Dodge Charger. Nick rode down with one of them. There are two other cars in the parking lot. They must have two workers staying for us tonight.

Probably fans who want details about the fight at the game.

If I'm lucky, Ma will have ordered my sundae already. When I get home, I'll heat up leftovers for dinner. I'd prefer to get my protein in before I fill up on fats and sugars, but some traditions are worth messing up my macros.

It wouldn't feel like a game day was complete without this.

As I walk in, I'm immediately confused. There isn't a lot of table space inside to begin with, but there are more people here than should be. No one will ever accuse me of being a math wizard, but even I know there are five people here when there should be four. I look closer.

It's the woman from Soccer for Sibs!

"What are you doing here? Are you stalking me?" The words come flying out of my mouth before I can stop them. Okay, probably not the nicest thing to say, but what else am I supposed to think? I've never needed security before, but I might have to look into it. How'd she connect with my family? How'd she even know they are my family?

"Tyler, don't be rude! I invited Rachel." My mom stands up and whacks me on the back of the head.

Rachel's mouth hangs open, her eyes equally wide. If I didn't know any better, I'd think she was truly surprised to see me. Instead, I think she's a fantastic actress. I grab her elbow and pull her up to standing. "That's it. Time to go."

"Wha—" she manages to splutter before Joey jumps in.

"Ty, let go of her." He pries my fingers off her arm and shoves me back. I'm not expecting that—partially because I'm two inches taller than Joey, but also because we're grown-ass adults, not little kids who fight over their favorite toy. It gets even worse when Nicky joins, and the two of them drag me across the shop, pushing me into a chair.

It's a teeny shop, so it's not that far.

And for the record, I'm way more muscular than either one of them, so if I'd been prepared, I could have kicked both their asses.

Nicky still views me as a threat, so he sits on me. That's right. Mr. Harvard himself sits on me.

"Ma!" I shout. "Tell Nicky to get off of me." I thrash to get out from underneath him. I almost manage to buck him off, but then Joey comes and sits on top of Nicky, and there's no way I can thrust 400 lbs. off of me. I should have worked harder on leg day.

"Oh, the baby's crying to Mommy again. We're gonna sit here like this until you can remember what it's like to be a human being," Joey says.

I feel like I'm six.

I cannot believe my brothers are sitting on me for punishment, and my parents are allowing it to happen.

No matter how humiliated I might be, I still have to protect my family. "Ma, you don't understand. I think she's stalking me."

"Oh honey, no. Rachel's not like that. She wasn't at the game for you."

I peek out around the sides of my brothers to see Rachel's gaze drop to the floor. I point in triumph. "See! Look at her. She's lying to you. She was at the game because of me."

Her gaze slowly returns to mine. Her cheeks are bright red. Her big brown eyes remind me of the hot fudge on the sundae I'm not currently eating. "I ... I was kind of there because of him."

With that admission, my two brothers, whom I'm about to disown, stand up. My quads, already sore from the game, are screaming. I'm going to need to visit the massage therapist first thing in the morning. Gingerly, I get to my feet. "And her name isn't actually Rachel. It's—" I can't remember what she had me write. And there I was, feeling bad because I can't spell, when it was all a lie. "She made up some cock-and-bull story about a sick sister, and it was her sister who likes soccer, not her. All while she's at an event for siblings of sick kids. And then she just so happens to end up—wait, how is she even here? How did this all come about?"

"Rachel was sitting next to us at the game," my mom supplies, looking from me to Rachel and back again. I can see her wheels are turning.

"Yeah, and how did that happen?" I ask.

Every eye in the place turns to Rachel. Or whatever her name is.

"Tho ... Those were the seats they gave me with the tickets for the event," she stammers. "I didn't pick them. I didn't even know who I was sitting next to."

Nicky volunteers, "She didn't even watch the game. She was reading a book."

A book? People still read books? "Who comes to a professional soccer game and reads a book?" I shout. I don't know if I'm more shocked or offended.

She shrugs. "Someone who doesn't care about soccer. But also someone who paid $250 for that stupid event and tickets just to fulfill my sister's dying wish." With that, she walks out the door.

That shuts me up fast.

She did say her sister was the fan.

Was.

Past tense. Shit. I truly am an idiot.

Which my brothers promptly remind me of the minute the door closes with Rachel on the other side. Even my mom chides me. "Tyler Jeremiah, I did not raise you to be rude like that. You should go apologize to that poor young lady."

I nod. I should.

"Jesus, Tyler, go!" my dad barks. He's a man of few words, so when he speaks, I tend to listen. I hightail it out to the parking lot, reaching her Honda Civic just as the engine roars to life. Well, as much as the engine of a Honda Civic can roar. I'm waving frantically. It must look foolish enough to get her attention because she rolls down the window.

"Let the record show that you approached me, lest you accuse me of stalking and forcing this interaction," she says with her mouth pulled into a tight line.

"You a lawyer?" I ask. I hold my hands up as if in surrender.

"I don't feel like talking about my shitty job. Can you just say what you have to say so I can go home? It's been a long day."

Right. Now what was I going to say? Oh, yeah. That. "Um." I look at my feet and kick some of the gravel in the parking lot. "I ... uh ... I mean, your sister. The one who wants to meet me ..." If I phrase it that way, she can correct me, and I don't have to ask directly.

"Wanted."

Her solitary word hits me like a punch to the gut. For as much as I want to kill my brothers most of the time—like right now—I cannot imagine a world without them in it. "I'm sorry." I don't know what else to say.

Her gaze drops, and sadness wafts off her. It envelops her. I don't know how I didn't see it before. "And I'm guessing my mom basically forced herself into your space and then demanded you go out for ice cream in such a way that you felt you had no choice. She's a very pushy woman. Don't let her small stature fool you. I'm scared shitless of her."

A tiny smile cracks through, but it doesn't reach her eyes.

I'm on a roll. Might as well continue. "And you thought this would be what your sister would want you to do, to hang out with me."

The smile's gone, and she shakes her head in a vehement denial. "I had no idea who I was sitting next to. Your mom said they were meeting up with Tyler."

"That's my name."

"Yeah, but I only know you as TJ. That's what Richie put on her list, and that's what your ClikClak handle says. I didn't do a deep dive."

Interesting, if she's telling the truth. "She left you a list?"

Rachel shrugs. "Pretty much. There's not much on it I can actually accomplish, except for meeting you. And now I have and can cross it off. Good enough." Her window begins to roll up.

Good enough? That can't be her response. Her sister had to have reasons for putting these things on the list. Like me. Why was I on her list? "Is there anything I can do to help fulfill this experience?" The words leave my mouth before I can stop them. Why am I so invested?

Her nose crinkles as if someone farted. I hope it wasn't me. "No, and what's it to you anyway?"

"I don't know. It's just ... interesting." It's like watching a ClikClak in real life. I can spend hours watching other people live their lives. It fascinates me.

Plus, you learn all sorts of cool shit. Except how to do magic tricks. I still can't figure those out.

"Well, glad I could entertain you. Now, if you don't mind stepping back so I don't run you over, I'll be off."

Again, I hold up my hands and step back. I watch her taillights until I can't see them anymore in the dark September night. I wish she would come back because there's something I want to know.

What could her sister have possibly found so interesting in me that meeting me became her dying wish?

CHAPTER 11: RACHEL

It could have gone worse. It could have gone a lot better, too. No matter how many times I replay my interactions with TJ Doyle in my brain, the large consensus is that it could have been worse.

That's a win in my book.

I mean, accusing me of being a stalker was a low point, but I rebounded from there. Thanks, Richie, for bailing me out. It goes without saying that I wouldn't have been in that situation in the first place if it weren't for Richie, but that seems like a small detail to harp on, with her being dead and all.

It's also important to mention that I have never had any kind of interaction with someone that attractive in my life. I thought being that good-looking was the result of a skillful combination of makeup application, Photoshop, and AI. But there he was, TJ Doyle, walking around like some kind of Greek god or Marvel hero. It's probably a good thing that I was super awkward because of the whole dead sister thing. Otherwise, I would have acted like an idiot because of who I am, and that's a harder pill to swallow. At least I can blame Richie for this.

If I were in the business of having celebrity crushes, TJ Doyle would 100 percent be it for me. Good thing I'm not that delusional.

Still, I awake the next morning with a sense of accomplishment and a slightly renewed vigor. It'd be more renewed if I had a cup of coffee, because it is the first thing in the morning, and I'm not quite awake yet. Maybe I should do something wild and crazy, like going to a local cafe rather than brewing my java at home? I did decide to start a new chapter in the book of my life, after all. That can include going out for coffee.

It's slightly overcast, but my phone tells me that the twenty percent chance of rain doesn't kick in for another hour or so. Plenty of time to get caffeinated and get back to my place before the weather turns crappy.

After another consultation with the almighty Google, I determine there's a small coffee shop less than a mile from here. I could walk there. It's highly unlikely the exercise could be bad for me.

New town, new me. That's going to be my fake-it-'til-I-make-it motto.

Isn't that what Gram and Gramps want?

Why couldn't they see that I was content in my life? In the bedroom where I'd finally felt safe? In the job that I knew inside and out and could do with my eyes closed? I've had enough transitions to last a lifetime, and I'm not even thirty yet. Why couldn't they see that staying still was what I needed instead of all this change?

But things change, even if we don't want them to.

I have no choice but to try to roll with it. Richie would think it's best. She wouldn't have left me that list otherwise. Something pushes on the inside of my chest. It's a little different than the tight clench I feel when I am missing Richie. No, this is my heart moving in the opposite direction—briefly swelling with pride that I was able to cross something off.

I did something for my sister. I did something for me.

It feels good.

I doubt there's anything else I'll be able to cross off, but at least I did something. Yes, this accomplishment definitely deserves a cup of coffee. Probably a tasty pastry too.

Then, I can hibernate in my apartment for a while and recharge.

I find a pair of loose-fitting yoga shorts and throw on a neon pink T-shirt that we had made years ago for breast cancer awareness month. We're lucky that breast cancer hasn't directly affected our family, but that doesn't mean Cramer-Romero won't miss a promotional opportunity. I dig out an old pair of running sneakers from a trash bag of shoes that is still sitting in the corner of my room. The cute canvas ones I wore yesterday had no support, and my feet are talking to me about it.

According to Google Maps, Lawadessa Cafe is only 0.8 miles from my new apartment complex. Even in my perpetual couch potato state, I should be able to manage that. I walk to the end of the access road that leads to my building and turn left onto Oakland Street. There's a massive brick building across the street that looks like it used to be some kind of factory. The year 1903 is etched in limestone at the top of the center tower. I'll have to find out what its story is. I bet there's some history there.

My mind craves a connection to the past in this town that is to be my future.

Even though I've been here for over a week, I haven't explored my new neighborhood on foot yet. Exploration is part of the new leaf territory I decided to turn over. I'm tempted to call Gram and let her know what I'm doing.

It would make her happy.

It would make me unhappy. I still feel betrayed by her. But even calling Gram is a substitute. A distant second. Who I really want to talk about this experience with is Richie. We'd always talked about getting our own place together. We were waiting for her to finish PA school and get a job. Instead, she got cancer.

No, I will not let those thoughts enter my mind right now. I'll be here and be present and be sweaty. Super sweaty. Gross sweaty. The air feels like you could cut it with a knife, thanks to the sky-high humidity. The air conditioning of the cutest coffee shop ever provides immediate relief.

It smells divine in here. If I weren't in public, I'd yell to the ceiling and ask my sister if this is what heaven smells like. Coffee beans, vanilla, and cinnamon drift through the air. Two swings hang on ropes on one side of the shop. They remind me of the swings Gramps made for Richie and me.

I order an iced mocha and a cinnamon roll and then go sit on the swings to wait. I'm gently rocking back and forth, back and forth, remembering the hours spent in the weeping willow tree in the backyard. Richie and I would have contests to see who could go the highest. Though heights have never been my favorite thing—Richie was obviously the daredevil—I could pump a swing like no one's business.

I close my eyes and can practically feel the wind rushing over my face and through my hair as I soar into the sky.

"Rachel? Is that you? What are you doing here?"

The voice startles me out of my reverie, and I jump, which causes me to nearly fall off the swing.

"No, seriously, are you stalking me?" TJ Doyle asks, looking down at me. Between my sitting position on the swing and his tall stature, it's quite intimidating, at least from this vantage point. Also, it's not super comfortable to stare up at him, yet I can't stare straight ahead because that's not socially acceptable to have your gaze on someone's crotch either.

"Rachel! Order ready for Rachel!" the barista yells. Thank God.

I manage to stand, my legs rubbery from the shock of his accusation. Well, actually, from the shock of being called out in public at all. He only takes the tiniest of steps backward to allow me to get up. There's about a millimeter of space between us. I can feel the heat wafting off his body. Jesus.

Also, standing up doesn't do much to improve the height difference. He's got to be over six feet tall, while I clock in around 5'2".

"Nope, I was here first. I think you're stalking me," I somehow manage to say. With that, I put my fingertips on his chest—dear Lord, is he made of granite?—and push him back slightly.

No one—not even this Adonis—stands between me and my food.

I head to the counter and pick up my order. The cinnamon roll is still warm with a thick buttercream frosting oozing down the side. I'm salivating. I immediately take a bite, letting out a small reflexive groan of pleasure when the confectionary masterpiece hits my taste buds.

This may be the best thing I've ever tasted.

It's so good, I shove a little more into my mouth than is polite. On one hand, I want to savor the perfection, while on the other, I want to inhale it whole. If I could mainline it, I would.

"Good?" TJ Doyle asks, a wicked amusement dancing through his blue eyes.

"Mmmm hmmm," I manage, my mouth too full to answer. I set my iced mocha down on a table, point to the cinnamon roll still in my hands, and then give a thumbs-up.

"I'll take that under consideration."

"Tyler! Order ready for Tyler!" It's his turn to pick up his stuff.

I sit down and take a sip of my coffee. My head is clearing from the shock. What is TJ Doyle doing here, in my coffee shop? Okay, I've only lived in the neighborhood for like ten minutes, but it's still mine. I was here first. I hereby brand this seat at this table in this shop *Mine*.

Now that that's settled between me and my inner monologue, I try to distract myself by pulling out Richie's list and reading it over. Maybe there's another item I can cross off just as easily as meeting TJ Doyle. Maybe—

I don't get to finish the thought because the paper is snatched out of my hands.

"What's this?" TJ says as he flips the list over. In one effortless move, he's placed his smoothie down on the table, straddled the chair, and begins to read.

I have no idea how anyone moves that fast and that smoothly. Is it some kind of witchcraft? Is his perfection actually CGI, and I'm now living in some sort of virtual-reality Matrix-type universe?

"Give that back to me," I say, reaching for my sister's list. I snatch it out of his hands and hug it to my chest, feeling the paper wrinkle against my body.

"I saw my name on there." He lifts his cup and takes a long pull on the straw, never breaking eye contact. That makes something deep within my stomach flutter. Probably from eating the cinnamon roll too fast.

Then, he breaks his intense stare by picking up his phone and snapping a selfie with his beverage, the logo on the cup prominently displayed. He sets his drink down and begins furiously typing.

Suddenly, I'm sweating in places I didn't know I sweated. I blink rapidly, apparently losing all control of my facial muscles. "No, you didn't."

"Yes, I did," he says, still typing on his phone. "I may uphold every single stereotype there is for the dumb jock, but I can at least recognize my name in print." Finally, he turns his gaze to mine.

Man, his eyes are blue. Deep pools to get lost in, like in every clichéd romance book. I wince reflexively at his words. "You're not dumb." I don't know why I say this. Maybe he is. I don't know him at all. I just hate to hear someone talk so poorly about themselves.

"Yeah, well, I ain't never gonna be a rose scholar." He winks at me. *Winks*.

"Rhodes," I correct automatically. As soon as the word is out of my mouth, I instantly wish I could grab it from the air and shove it down my throat.

TJ doesn't seem to mind. Instead, his face breaks into a wide grin, perfectly straight white teeth gleaming. "You proved my point. Why is my name on your paper if you're not stalking me?"

This again? I'm tired of it. Something in me snaps. No one is content to let me be in a vegetative state, yet when I try to go out, I'm getting critiqued.

I slam my hand down on the table in protest. "I was here first, buddy. This is my neighborhood coffee shop. I like it here. There are swings, and the cinnamon roll is orgasmic. So if you have a problem with me being here, I suggest you find another place for your smoothies and egg white protein bowls." He's not eating an egg white protein bowl, but I assume that's what someone with his physique would eat. Probably a lot of vegetables too.

He stares at me, all expression gone.

Okay, maybe that rant was a little excessive, especially the orgasm part. I can't believe I said that to him. I feel the heat fill my face, and I know it's now beet red. Great. If I didn't think it would totally destroy Gram and Gramps, I would die right here and right now of embarrassment.

"How can this be your neighborhood coffee shop? This is my neighborhood coffee shop," he says, clearing his throat.

"It's pretty clear that, by some great cosmic coincidence, we live in the same neighborhood. So, we're apt to run into each other. Please stop accusing me of stalking each time it happens. I swear, yesterday was a series of un—" I stutter, almost saying unfortunate. But none of it was unfortunate. No, yesterday was the best day I've had in a very long time. "Unplanned events. Like this, right now."

"You could say it's all a coincidence."

I nod in agreement. I don't think it's the right time to tell him that there's a chance my sister is pulling the puppet strings from the great beyond.

"So why is my name on your paper then?" TJ raises an eyebrow, the devilish glint back in his eyes.

Gah, he won't let this go. I might as well fess up. "It's my sister's list."

He frowns. "Your sister's list?"

Doesn't he remember? "Yeah, her to-do list?" We just had this conversation the night before.

"Oh, right. I didn't think it was an actual list. More like things she might have said to you. Who writes all that stuff down?"

"Someone who knows she's dying and won't make it to her twenty-seventh birthday, but who, despite being the younger sister, is bossy." That's Richie in a nutshell.

His voice softens. "I'm sorry. Can I see it?"

I've never let anyone read it. It's mine, and sharing it with someone else feels too vulnerable and raw. On the other hand, besides a random chance meeting here at Lawadessa Cafe, it's not like I'm going to see him regularly. He's not going to be a part of my life. He means nothing to me. If anything, I think Richie would be delighted that this man, who meant so much to her as to be on her bucket list, is interested in what she wanted to do.

What can it hurt?

CHAPTER 12: TJ

I'm dying to know what's on that list. I don't know why. Maybe it's because I spend so much time scrolling ClikClak that I am used to getting the inside details of complete strangers' personal lives, and it's made me nosy. Who knows?

I have to see that paper.

I want to know what else would be on a list that includes meeting me. I'm still trying to process that someone thought about me, thought I was worthy enough to include on their dying wish list.

Also, that someone actually took the time to write it down. Weird.

Rachel is looking at me with those big, sad eyes. She also has some of the frosting from the cinnamon roll on the corner of her mouth. I can't stop staring at it. Thoughts of how to remove it dance through my brain.

All involve touching her, and some involve my tongue.

She's totally not my type, so I don't know why my brain is going there.

"You can't laugh at it. Richie wrote this for me." Her hand is shaking as she holds the paper out. "I can't believe I'm doing this," she mutters softly.

Tell me about it. When I walked into Lawadessa and saw her sitting there on the swing, I did not have control over my feet. They moved directly to her. Why? I have no idea. I would typically *never* seek out a crazy fan. In fact, most times when I'm out in public, I try to conceal my identity with a baseball hat and sunglasses.

With the skies being gray and the humidity oppressive, I didn't bother with them today. Too hot for a hat, and wearing sunglasses would probably call more attention to me.

I glance down at the list. It's a photocopy of a piece of notebook paper. I can see the faint lines that I know are blue, though they appear light gray. There's a swirly handwriting that starts off neat but is visibly shaky by the bottom of the page.

The first line says, "Dear Rachel, If you're reading this, I'm dead, and you're probably crying. It's time to knock that shit off and put on real pants. Don't even try to lie to me and tell me you're wearing hard pants. I'll haunt your ass."

Before I can read more, the paper disappears from my hands. I look up. "Hey, I was reading that."

Rachel is clutching the paper against her chest. "I changed my mind. I'm not ready to share it yet."

I look at her for a minute before nodding. Again, I can't imagine what it'd be like to lose one of my brothers. I'd probably be a little nutso too. While the curious part of me wants to know what's in the letter, there's a burning need to have something else explained.

"What are hard pants?"

Rachel's face breaks into a momentary smile. "You know, pants that are hard. Jeans. Khakis. Dress pants.

Pants you wear to be professional and a functional human being. The opposite of soft pants. Sweatpants. Yoga pants. Pajama pants. One has a high content of Lycra and spandex, while the other doesn't."

I bend over to look under the table and then sit back up. She's wearing loose-fitting shorts over her thin legs. "Those are soft pants."

"Yes, but it's a Sunday morning, and I was out for a walk. You don't exercise in hard pants."

She has a valid point.

Rachel continues. "And furthermore, I don't need dressy pants for my job, and Richie knew that. I can be a completely functional human being *and* be comfortable. The two are not mutually exclusive." She punctuates her rant with a small fist pound on the table.

I put my hands up. "Easy there, killer. I didn't mean to get you all riled up. I wear soft pants for my job too." I want her to know I'm on her side.

"I'm just sick and tired of everyone thinking they know what's best for me. I can make my own decisions. Am I sad? Yes. Terribly so. My sister was my best friend. Watching her suffer and die was the worst thing I could possibly imagine. I'm allowed to grieve. I'm allowed to process it the way I want to process it. I don't need everyone up my grill all the time about how I'm grieving."

There's obviously a lot more going on here than just the list. It's probably time for me to leave. And maybe move so I don't have any more accidental run-ins. That's too bad, because I really like my apartment.

Awareness dawns on Rachel's face, her eyes huge and her mouth forming an "O." She quickly covers it with her hand. I'm embarrassed for her. "I'm sorry," she adds, practically jumping to her feet. In the process, she almost flips the table. The jolt is enough to send my half-full smoothie toppling over. It hits the table with enough force that the lid disengages, and I'm left with a lapful of almond, avocado, and oat milk.

Awesome.

Rachel lurches forward, grabbing a handful of napkins as they're skittering toward the edge of the table. Immediately, she begins blotting.

She's blotting the smoothie that landed on my lap.

Right there.

Now it's my turn to jump up, using my hands to block hers, otherwise I'll be the mortified one. After a split second, she realizes where she's been rubbing. She lets out a squeak and then proceeds to run toward the door. She didn't even grab her coffee.

I look from the entrance to my soaking black shorts and back, the bell jangling in her wake. Almost immediately, two cafe workers with mops and towels appear and begin cleaning up the mess. I mumble a quick, "Sorry," dropping a few bills on the table, and then I head for the door myself, grabbing Rachel's iced mocha for her.

The cafe is located on the corner, so she could have gone in one of four directions. I do a quick scan and see her bright pink T-shirt. She's crossed Chauncey Street and is heading up North Main toward Oakland.

There's not much traffic on this Sunday morning, so I sprint across all four lanes of Chauncey, not paying any attention to the walk signal. Rachel's walking at a good clip, but I can run a hell of a lot faster than she can move.

"Rachel, wait! Rachel!"

She slows and then stops as I run up beside her. She turns and looks at me like I've got three heads. Or a crotchful of smoothie and a half woody.

Then, the tears start. "What do you want? Can't you just let this end?" Her hands drop to her knees, and she bends over trying to catch her breath.

I hold out her cup. "You forgot your coffee."

Her head pops up, her eyebrows arched. "You chased after me to give me my coffee?" She straightens, hands on her hips, chest still heaving. "And how did you catch me so fast, and why aren't you out of breath?" she asks between gasps of air.

"You were only walking."

"I was ... speed ... walking," she huffs out.

"For one, my legs are a lot longer than yours. And for two, I'm a professional soccer player. I run for a living. If I can't catch up with you walking, I probably shouldn't have a job."

"Fair point." She takes the drink and takes a long sip. "I'm sorry about"—her gaze drops down to my groin and then quickly back up—"that. I don't know what got into me."

"It's fine. I haven't been felt up in public in a while, so it's no biggie."

Rachel's eyes pinch shut. "Richie would die if I told her this story." Her eyes open. "I should really get going, and no offense, so should you. You're a mess."

"Okay. You heading this way?" I point down North Main. "Me too."

We start walking, not saying anything for a minute. I'm not sure what to say next. This whole experience is out of character for me. Hell, it beats staying inside, aimlessly scrolling on my phone, but I have no idea why I keep pestering this poor girl who is obviously mortified beyond all belief. I can't help myself.

"I'm up on Oakland," Rachel says. "Not too far."

"I live on Oakland. We must be neighbors," I reply, relief rushing through my veins to finally have a connection to this place. I live in an apartment complex that is a converted chocolate factory. There have to be at least 100 units in my building. I don't think I've spoken to a single neighbor since I've moved in.

Wish I knew what was prompting this bout of reclusiveness. The last few years, it's been getting worse and worse. I don't like being around people anymore. It's like, unless it's my family, I have no idea how to be real anymore. Even with my teammates, I'm putting on a show of who I think they want me to be. I'm always thinking about the aesthetics of everything. I worry constantly that I won't get the right angle or the perfect shot, or that people will be able to tell it's all fake.

And if I'm not perfect, they'll laugh at me.

Except Rachel is real and vulnerable in a way she can't hide. She doesn't even bother. Since she's not hiding, I don't feel the need to either. She's probably one of those people on ClikClak who airs all her dirty laundry and train wreck of a life, and gets millions of views because of it.

Hell, I bet I've seen her videos.

I realize that the entire time I've been with Rachel, I haven't been thinking about what I'm going to post. Other than the shot of my smoothie, which I'm wearing more than I was able to drink. It's somewhat refreshing not to have to worry about what the internet will think of me right now. It's almost as if I can take a deep breath for the first time in years. If I were the deep-thinking type, which we've established I'm not, I'd analyze this and try to figure out what it means.

We continue walking side by side in silence. I glance down at her. She's got to be close to a foot shorter than my 6'1" frame. No wonder we're moving so slowly. It's fine. I don't have to be at the facility until this afternoon. All that awaits at home is scrolling ClikClak and trying to think about what content I should be creating for this week.

After what feels like three hours, but is only about fifteen minutes, we reach my building. I'm about to announce that we've reached my place, but I stop myself. While I'm 99 percent sure Rachel is not a stalker, I don't know that I want her knowing exactly where I live. Being in close proximity to fame can make people unpredictable and a little unhinged.

I don't know if Rachel needs any more help with that. She seems to have enough on her plate right now.

"How much further are you? I can walk you home," I offer. It seems like the gentlemanly thing to do. My mom would be pleased. Actually, I think she would be pleased about this whole encounter, aside from the junk rubbing. She's always on me to go out and be more social, like with real people, not just online friends.

Hell, if it means socializing, Ma would probably be okay with the junk rubbing too.

And she already tried to adopt Rachel. I'm not sure Rachel was aware of that last night when Ma invited her out for ice cream. My mom makes it her mission to make sure everyone is taken care of. It's why she still does everything for me that she does. I'd be shocked if my mom didn't try to get Rachel's number, if only so she can continue checking in on her.

"I'm just up here, on the right." She points to a sign that says "Twin Oaks Apartments." It looks like it has been there since the '70s. I have to will myself not to scrunch my nose at the dated building.

"I can get there myself," she says, looking toward the sky. "I think I felt a raindrop. You don't want to get soaked."

Maybe she doesn't want me to know the details of where she lives either. Can't be too smart in this day and age. If everything she says is true—which it seems to be so far—she doesn't know me from Adam. I could be one of those guys who's looking for the next conquest. I could be looking to take advantage of her.

I'm not, but she doesn't know that.

I start to reassure her when, without warning, there's a thunderclap so loud the windows on the building rattle. The heavens open into a deluge. Rachel screams. I grab her hand and yell, "Run!" like the raindrops are acid, and we're about to melt. Like I've never played 90 minutes of soccer in conditions worse than this.

The front door to my building is only a few feet away, but the rain is so intense that we're soaked by the time we get there.

"We can't just go into a random building." Rachel's hair is plastered to her head, and that oversized t-shirt is starting to cling in all the right places.

"It's not a random building. I live here," I tell her.

"You live here?" she repeats, seemingly confused by this development.

I nod. "Down this way. Let's get dried off."

Her feet stop moving, and her eyes narrow. "I don't think so. I may not be the most experienced out there, but I know a line when I hear one. What's next, do you want to get cleaned off, and then I'm naked in your apartment? Do you think I'm one of those girls who loses her head at the sight of a hot guy? Do you think just because you have abs and buns of steel and because I accidentally already rubbed your penis, I'm just going to take off my clothes and let you use me until you're sick of me and toss me aside like yesterday's Chipotle wrapper?"

That seems oddly specific and like it may not have anything to actually do with me, other than the abs and buns of steel. And the penis touching. That much is true.

I try to reassure her. "I can 100 percent believe that you are not the type to go to a stranger's apartment and take your clothes off. Yeah, I can believe that. Also, I wasn't feeding you a line. I wasn't planning on making a move. I was planning on offering you a towel. You've met my parents. You know I come from people who like to help other people."

"Oh."

Oh is right. As in oh boy, what have I gotten myself into?

CHAPTER 13: RACHEL

If I were using my rational brain, I'd say I don't think I have to worry about TJ Doyle making a move on me. Ever. Anyone with eyes knows something like that would never, *ever*, happen.

However, if someone were writing a list of what *not* to do in the presence of a guy, I think I'd have checked every one off.

Don't accidentally make friends with his mom. Check.

Don't freak out over every single thing he says. Check.

Don't accidentally touch where his bathing suit covers when you spill his drink on him. Check.

Don't assume he's trying to get in your pants when he clearly has no interest. Check. Check. Check.

Finally, I throw my hands up, losing the battle to my inner monologue. "Look, I appreciate that you're being nice. I just haven't dealt with many people since my sister died, and I think I've forgotten how to do it. Not that I was that good at it before, but I'm definitely worse now. Yeah, a lot worse. In case you couldn't tell. Also, in case I haven't made it incredibly obvious, I have some trust issues I'm working through right now, too."

Water drips off his hair and runs down his temple. He raises an eyebrow. "You? Have issues? Say it isn't so."

I force a small smile. This is why I don't like to talk to people. Because when I do, they have no context for me or my life, and I just end up looking like a freak. When I was in grade school, my classmates didn't understand why sometimes I would have new clothes, and then I'd be in the same outfit for days. It was too hard to explain that I had lots of clothes at my grandparents' house, but sometimes my mom made us leave our belongings behind when she stormed out of a relationship. It became easier not to talk to people than to explain why I couldn't have friends over or why I had to make sure Richie had her lunch every day.

Maybe I can explain. "Okay, do you want the short version or the long version?"

"I don't want any version right now. I want to go put some dry clothes on and warm up before I get too tight. I've got practice in a little bit, and I don't want to be more sore than I need to be."

Yup. I have definitely overstayed my welcome. "Good point. I'll just go." I hitch my thumb over my shoulder in the direction of the door. This will be for the best. It's easier to keep to myself than get into why I am the way I am. I look out at the parking lot. The rain has escalated, and it's now coming down sideways, pelting the pavement. It's going to sting, I just know it.

Then I look closer and see tiny white pellets bouncing off the ground. Hail can damage cars. I can only imagine what it'll do to me. I'm going to be bruised and battered. At least my outsides will finally match my insides.

"Don't be stupid. Just come and get dried off, and give this a chance to pass. I promise, I won't make a move."

Of course, he won't make a move. I can't even believe I said that. There is no way in hell someone who looks like him would go for someone like me. Not that I want him to. I don't. I'm still not interested in dating because it's nothing but heartbreak.

But it's not like he's asking me out. Or even flirting with me. Perhaps he's simply being nice. I spent an hour or so with his parents and brothers yesterday after the game. They do seem like the type of people who like to help. It wouldn't be a stretch to think he was raised to be kind as well.

Okay, maybe I should take him at his word. Just a little. Just for right now. "I mean, it's probably not the best idea to go out in the hail."

"If that's what you describe as 'not the best idea,' I sort of want to be there for what one of your worst ideas is. And when I say be there, I mean sitting on the sideline, eating popcorn, and watching that shit show. I'm this way." He tips his head down the hall.

We head to the elevator, where he pushes the number five.

If you looked up awkward in the dictionary, it would have a picture of this moment. The two of us, standing side by side. Me, looking like a drowned rat with my brown hair parted down the middle, falling out of the sloppy bun at the nape of my neck, and plastered to my head. I'd actually put some mascara on this morning, and it's undoubtedly tracking down my cheeks, so that I now resemble a deranged raccoon. TJ Doyle, on the other hand, is one of those mythical creatures who actually gets hotter when he's soaking wet, like Mr. Darcy walking out of the lake. His black T-shirt is now hugging every single muscle on his torso and arms.

I totally understand why he made it to Richie's bucket list. He should be on every woman's bucket list. And free pass list. He should be on all the lists.

I should break the silence. I should make small talk. I should do something—*anything*—to make this elevator trip less uncomfortable. We're only going up five floors, but it might as well be fifty. Are there minions pulling this elevator by hand? Maybe a hamster on a wheel?

I try to think of something to say and draw a complete and total blank. Why am I so bad at this?

Oh, right. I don't talk to many people, unless it has to do with sewage. Even I know that's a topic to steer clear of in casual conversation. I virtually never speak to a member of the opposite sex if he isn't related to me or if he doesn't work with me. Dear Lord, it's as if I've lost all ability to function in a social context.

Normally, I'd say it doesn't bother me, but I'm blowing this for Richie. I fulfilled her wish, technically, but I have to make more out of this experience. For some reason unbeknownst to me, he keeps landing in my path, and fate keeps pushing us together. It has to be because I need to do more for Richie.

"So, what do you do when you're not playing soccer?"

TJ turns to look at me. Based on the expression on his face, I quickly glance at myself in the mirrored doors to see if I've suddenly sprouted an extra head that I'm not aware of. Nope, just me in all my drowned-rat glory.

Thank God I put on a bra today, otherwise I'd be ready to compete in a frumpy wet T-shirt contest. I'm a mess.

"What's it to you?"

If I didn't know better, I'd say there was a distinct snap in his tone. I don't know if I should redirect the conversation to something else or if standing here in the most painfully awkward silence ever is the preferred option.

I open my mouth, but the doors part, sparing—or prolonging—my misery. I follow him down the hall and to the door that leads to his place. He unlocks it and pushes it open, gesturing for me to go in front of him.

I walk in and immediately halt, too busy taking everything in to move further. This apartment is stunning. High ceilings showing wood slats and beams. Visible ductwork in shiny chrome. White walls and exposed brick. It's a total fusion of the past and present and is uber chic.

If I hadn't had to move so quickly, and if I could afford it, I'd love to live in a place like this. It's got so much more personality than my sad, tan apartment.

"Wow," I say. "This is amazing." I'm looking up, around, turning in a circle.

TJ disappears down the hall, returning a moment later with a thick, fluffy towel in his hand. He hands it to me and disappears again. I'm still holding my iced mocha. I set it on the counter and try to dry off. I wipe my face off, and then my arms and legs. How we got so wet in so little time is beyond me. I throw the towel over my shoulders like a cape and wait.

A moment later, TJ returns. He's in gray sweatpants and is pulling a shirt over his head. I catch a glimpse of a flat, muscular stomach.

Is it hot in here?

Holy shit, I didn't think people looked like that in real life. Sure, I've seen people like that on TV, or even on ClikClak, but I assumed that they were using filters or airbrushing. While I generally have no interest in sports or athletics, I do enjoy the occasional eye-candy video. Just because I'm a homebody doesn't mean I don't have a libido. They give me inspiration for how to picture my favorite book heroes. And the authors are always going on about gray sweatpants. I had no idea why, until now.

It all makes sense.

Then I realize I'm staring, so I abruptly turn away, looking back at the ceiling. "So this used to be a factory? What kind? Like a textile mill or something?"

"Um, I'd guess chocolate."

I turn back around. "Chocolate? Why do you think that?"

"Because it's called The Chocolate Factory. I never looked into it, though. The space is nice, and it's close to work. I didn't want to have to worry about taking care of a house just yet."

Mmm, chocolate.

Of course, at my job, when someone says "chocolate factory," they mean something totally different.

"Well, this place is amazing. Thanks for this," I say, pulling the towel tighter around my shoulders. I look toward the living room area and try to see what's going on outside. The windows are splattered with rain, so it makes it tough to see if it's still coming down. The air conditioning is cranked, and I shiver in response.

"Are you cold?" He walks over to the thermostat and presses some buttons. Instantly, silence befalls the apartment, with the exception of the rain hitting the window. Guess that answers that question. "Let me get you a change of clothes. Hang on."

Before I can protest, he's gone again. I wish I could tell Richie all about this. She'd die all over again. "Richie," I whisper, looking at the ceiling, "you will not believe where I am."

"Did you say something? I put some stuff in the bathroom for you."

"Um, thanks." Ignoring his question, I practically run to the bathroom. He's put out a pair of flannel pajama pants and a gray Boston Buzzards sweatshirt. The pants look brand new. They're way too big for me, so I pull the drawstring and roll the cuffs. The crewneck sweatshirt comes down to mid-thigh. The sleeves have to be rolled up, too.

As if I could look any more ridiculous.

My hair is beyond help, short of ripping the elastic out and using my fingers to comb through it. Then I take a second to confirm that, yes, my mascara has run down my face. Of course it has. Tissues aren't the best at cleaning up makeup, but it's the best I can do. I only glance in the mirror momentarily. It's not going to get any better than this.

I walk out with my clothes folded under my arm.

"Here, let me toss them in the dryer for a few minutes." He holds his hands out, waiting for my clothes. I pass them over but then remember my folded-up list. It's been somewhat protected in the pocket of my shorts. It doesn't appear to be too wet—just a little damp. Good thing there's a stack of copies in my apartment.

Maybe I'll make some more, just in case. Can't be too careful.

TJ disappears down the hall, and then I hear him opening the dryer door. Then comes the sound of him pressing buttons. Beep. Beep. Beep-beep-beep. The dryer door opens and closes. Beep-beep-beep-beep. I'm sure he has a top-of-the-line washer and dryer, but it can't be that complicated. I shuffle down the hall to see what he's doing, delicately holding the hem of the too-long pants up like a Regency heroine.

He pushes one button, and then another. He opens the door. He closes it. He pushes more buttons. He puts his hands on his hips. He scratches his head. It's quite clear he has no idea what he's doing.

"Um, do you need a little help?" I offer.

"I know you're supposed to do something so you don't shrink clothes." He's scratching his head again.

I step up and look at the Samsung dryer. Three quick taps and it hums to life. I set it for a twenty-minute cycle. Turning around to look at him, I say, "It shouldn't be long."

He doesn't break my gaze. "I should probably learn how this thing works."

"Yeah, you should. I have to go down to the basement to do laundry in my building. The machines still take quarters."

"Ma usually comes down once or twice a week for my laundry. Sometimes she does it here, but most times she takes it home and brings it back."

I've met his mother, so I can totally see her doing that. She's like a force of nature, but in a nurturing kind of way. However, the thought of having a mother who would take that kind of care of her grown children is mind-boggling.

"Your mom still does your laundry?"

"Yeah, I travel a lot, and I'm pretty busy. Ma always did it for me growing up, and somehow"—he looks around the room as if searching for the answer—"she just never stopped."

The mere thought of that level of caring and commitment from a parent has me green with envy. "Oh. How old are you?" I ask and then quickly regret it. I don't need to know any personal details.

"Thirty-two. You?"

"Twenty-nine. Richie was only twenty-six when she died. Her birthday was a few weeks ago. Eight-eight. I think that's why she liked you, because you're number eight. You were number eight on her list." I'm rambling.

He looks down at his feet for a moment. Talking about my dead sister usually has this effect on people. It's a good reason for me not to talk to anyone.

"Why don't we go have a seat while we wait for your clothes to dry? Should only be a few more minutes, and then you can go," he says.

Right. He can't wait to get me out of his place.
Can't say I blame him.

CHAPTER 14: TJ

She's got to think I'm the world's biggest moron, not knowing how to operate my own dryer. I want to explain, but she changed the subject, and now I don't know how to get it back to why appliances flummox me. She's met my mom, but maybe she didn't get the full picture. With a woman like Maureen Doyle, it's easier to let her bulldoze over you than stand up to her. She wants to do my laundry? I'm gonna let her. It's easier than fighting with her about it and being on the receiving end of her disappointment. I'm her failure-to-launch child, and I'll never get over letting her and my dad down like that.

When she brings up her sister again, it makes me think about the list. She's still holding it in her hand. I try to take a peek. "Is that what she said on the list? The number eight thing?"

Rachel shakes her head. "No, but I know—knew—my sister better than she knew herself."

I slide onto one of my kitchen counter stools, and Rachel does the same. "So you knew about the list then?

Did you try and do anything with your sister before she died, or was she too sick?"

I wanna ask her why I made the list. Why did her sister think I was that special?

Rachel looks away, her gaze focused out the window, shaking her head slightly. "My grandmother blindsided me with it a few weeks ago. Just after her birthday." She turns back to me, her gaze sharpening. "I can't believe she did this to me. She knows I'm going to have to do things for her, but she also knows I'm going to hate every single one of them."

Like meeting me. Ouch. I can't control the expression on my face, my eyes and mouth immediately drooping. My thoughts are no doubt written all over my face.

"Oh no, I don't mean you!" She attempts to backpedal. "I meant, I'm pretty introverted, and going out and hunting down a professional athlete is not anything I'd ever do. Anything that involves me leaving my bedroom is a stretch for me."

If she were any other woman, I'd probably make a flirtatious comment about never leaving her bedroom. Even I know that is the wrong thing to say right now. Instead, I offer her a small smile. I 100 percent believe that she spends very little time talking to people. It shows.

Yet somehow, it's endearing.

"I think that Richie knew I was going to be even more of a recluse after, and so she put the most absurd things on the list to try and get me to live a little."

I offer a different perspective. "Maybe she didn't want you wasting the gift of your life when hers was going to end so soon."

Rachel stares at me, wide-eyed. I don't know what I could have possibly said that upset her, but unless she blinks soon, I'm afraid her eyeballs are going to fall out of her head. Then her eyes narrow. "Are you sure you never met her? Are you sure she didn't put you up to this?"

I've met a lot of people in my life. While I can't guarantee I never met her sister, I can honestly say I'm not in cahoots with her. Or anyone else, for that matter. I shake my head. "There is no great plot. She's doing this on her own."

Curiosity is gnawing away again. I have to know what's on her list. "What else is on there? Maybe there's something you can do that's not as bad as you think."

Rachel's lips become a thin line for a moment. Then, she folds the top of the paper back and slides it over to me, her hand remaining on the paper. Only the list is exposed.

Some of the items are simple. Some are totally ridiculous. Nothing makes sense together, and none of them has anything to do with each other.

"This is pretty … random." I struggle for something to say, hoping to break this uncomfortable silence.

Rachel appears to be studying the list upside down. I'm sure she's read it so much already that she has it committed to memory. Her hand contracts, pulling the list back. She quickly folds it and places both her hands on top of it. "Yeah, well, she did have a brain tumor, so that could be part of it."

"She died of a brain tumor?" I ask before I can help myself. "That sounds awful."

Rachel nods. "She didn't fit the demographic for the type of cancer she had, so it shocked everyone. She'd just finished PA school. So for her, delivering a baby makes sense. She really wanted to do that. Me, not so much."

I think about the list for a minute. I don't know much about Rachel at all, but none of it vibes with the woman sitting across from me.

Rachel slaps her hands down on the counter, making me jump. "That's it!" she declares. "That's it. I'm sick of being sad. I'm sick of grieving. I'm sick of being afraid all the time. I just want to be. I want to be happy. I don't want to be the girl with the troubled mom and the dead sister and the panic attacks. I want to be me. But I don't know who that is."

Her statement strikes a chord with me. I want to be me, too. Not my brothers' stupid little brother. Not my mother's man-child, whom she still has to parent. Not just a soccer player. Not just eye candy on the internet.

Except I don't know what or who else I am, either.

Our deep thoughts are interrupted by the musical intonations of my dryer. It's full-on playing an entire song that goes on forever. I'm not sure I've ever heard that before. "Is it supposed to sound like that?"

"If it's a Samsung, yes. That's what they all sound like."

How does she know this? Is there a secret dryer-sound cult, and is she a part of it?

"Really?" I ask.

"Yeah. It's actually a song, like a classical one. I think maybe Schubert? I feel like I saw a ClikClak about it one time." She pulls out her phone and begins scrolling.

"Oh, are you on ClikClak? What's your handle?" I pick up my phone and swipe open the app. After a moment, I realize she hasn't said anything. I glance at her. "What's your handle?"

She shakes her head and stands. "My clothes are done." Abruptly, she turns and heads down the hall. I hear the dryer door open and close. Then the same for the bathroom door. A moment later, Rachel returns, dressed in her bright pink T-shirt and shapeless gray shorts.

She looked better in my clothes. I bet she'd look pretty damn good without any clothes on.

"Well, thanks for everything. I should be going now." She jerks her thumb toward the door. "I'll just see myself out."

"Hang on, I'll walk you home." My mom would be proud of me for being so chivalrous. As we head toward the door, I catch the time on my microwave. "Oh shit, I can't. I've got to get to practice." I'm going to have to hurry or else I'm going to be late. Again. "I'm so sorry."

Rachel offers me a small smile. It's one of the few I've seen grace her face this whole time. It does something magical to her. It makes her seem years younger and lighter. *She's pretty.* "No, please. I'm sorry I took so much of your time. Thank you for being kind and not thinking I'm a weirdo."

I laugh. "Well, I never said *that*."

Her smile grows. "Now I know why Richie liked you. I hope she can see this. I hope she knows how great you've been to me."

I don't think I've been particularly great or even anything special. I wonder who Rachel's been spending time with that makes her feel so small. "Well, we're bound to run into each other at the coffee shop, or somewhere else in the neighborhood. If you ever want to teach me how to do laundry, hit me up. I'm usually free."

She raises an eyebrow.

"Right, I mean, except for the whole soccer thing. But other than that, I have some time." Jesus, I sound like the bumbling idiot I am. I'm not even trying to hit on this chick. Something deep within screams to me that she, above all else, needs a friend.

Or maybe I do.

I'm not sure I'm friend material, but I can be nice. My parents raised me to at least be that. I think about number ten on her list about her mom. I wonder what that story is? Not everyone is as lucky as the Doyle brothers.

After I close the door behind Rachel, I scramble to get ready for practice. I haven't eaten enough to fuel me for the upcoming workout, so I grab two protein drinks and swallow them down as I'm driving. This is bound to cause stomach cramps, but desperate times call for desperate measures.

I pull into the field house, grab my bag out of the back seat, and make it in with one minute to spare. No one can give me shit for being late today.

Except I'm the last thing on everyone's mind when I walk in. Brandon Nix is out.

I drop my bag on the locker room bench. "Was he fired for pounding O'Marra? Dude deserved it."

Maliq Miller's at his locker next to mine. "I heard he quit."

Merriweather Hayes calls from across the room, "That's stupid. Why would he quit? He's our top scorer."

I glance over at Landon Stubbs, who's suspiciously quiet. I wouldn't say Brandon Nix has many friends on this team—it's hard to make friends when you're a blowhard—but if he did, Landon would be one of them.

"Stubbs, you're awfully quiet," I call. He knows something. I can tell. "What's the real story?"

And once again, I cannot figure out why I'm so damn nosy about other people's personal lives. I just have to know.

Landon won't meet my gaze. He's looking down at his feet and pretending to be busy rearranging something in his bag. He didn't even look this uncomfortable when he came out and introduced us to his boyfriend, Carlos.

"Come on, Stubbs. I know you know," I goad.

"Shut up, Doyle." Callaghan Entay practically growls. "Leave Landon alone."

"Listen up," a voice booms from the entrance of the locker room. We all turn our attention to Coach Janssen. "As you may be aware, Brandon Nix has left the Boston Buzzards organization. Not that we need to provide you with any information at all"—he glowers right at me—"but we can't have any of you spreading rumors about your former teammate." His gaze remains trained on me.

"I can't believe I have to have this conversation, like you're a bunch of preteen schoolgirls," he mutters, running his hand through his graying hair. One of the assistant coaches hands him an iPad, and he reads off it in a monotone voice: "This is the official statement from the front office. Commenting or posting anything besides the official statement will be subject to disciplinary actions." He takes a deep breath and continues. "The Boston Buzzards have announced that Brandon Nix left the team, terminating his contract, of his own accord with no punitive actions pending, and the organization wishes him well in his future endeavors. The Boston Buzzards stand firm that all employees of the United States Soccer League and the United States Soccer League Referee Association should be treated with respect and dignity, including freedom from harassment and assault, regardless of gender, orientation, or race." With a curt nod of his head, he spins on his heel and is gone.

The team sits in silence for a moment. There's a lot to unpack and process. It's obviously a dig against Seamus O'Marra and his touching of the female referee. That's totally bullshit. You can't grab a woman's ass, and everyone knows that. Especially when she's officiating a game. The referees are totally off-limits—

"Wait a minute!" I yell, the pieces falling together. "Are Nix and Andi Nichols hooking up?"

That would explain why he went after O'Marra the way he did. There have been rumors swirling around on ClikClak ever since that video of her red-carding him went viral.

What I wouldn't give for that sort of traction.

But also, there was that warning about punitive actions, like that can keep the gossip mill down. Not in this day and age with social media.

"Okay, guys, enough of this. I need you ready to go for warm-ups in three," Claude Kenley, our strength and conditioning coach, calls.

Walking out to the practice pitch, I realize that if I can't talk about this on social media, there's no one I can share it with.

Fuck, that's depressing.

That thought rams around my brain throughout the entire practice. Sure, I could call my brothers or even my parents. They have to take my calls. It's family code. But aside from that, I only have four million strangers to talk to.

Shit, I need to figure this out. I should probably go talk to our team shrink, Watson Ross. I can only imagine what he'd have to say about me. Yeah, I probably don't want to hear that.

How did I get this alone?

Immediately, Rachel pops into my mind. She's totally alone, too. She seems super sad about it. I'm not sad. I'm just ... I don't know. Ambivalent, I guess, if ambivalence feels like itching in the bottom of my feet and restlessness in my legs and uneasiness in my stomach.

I feel like ambivalence should feel like less, not more.

Funny, I didn't feel this way when Rachel was here.

Weird.

CHAPTER 15: RACHEL

He doesn't even know how to do laundry!" I shout at the ceiling. Seriously, Richie needs to know what kind of man she spent her limited time lusting over. Once again, Richie has nothing to say for herself. Would it be too much to ask of her to slam a door or knock over a lamp or do some moaning, just so I know she's still with me?

But no, she's silent. Everything is silent. Now I know what they mean when they say silence is deafening. I've always been one for quiet, but this is oppressive. I lie on my bed, staring at the ceiling, but nothing changes.

If Richie were here, I'd tell her about running into TJ Doyle. I'd tell her that out of all the apartment complexes in all the world, he had to live in the one across the street from mine. I'd tell her that he was kind of … sweet. Almost nurturing.

Let me be clear, I don't think he has any idea how to truly nurture someone else. But he's obviously been well cared for in his life, and it seems to be second nature to extend that caregiving to those around him. His family is the kind I used to dream about having when I was growing up. A mom and a dad who showed up to school functions and did things like go out for ice cream afterward.

He's a grown-ass adult, and his family is still doing that.

I wonder if he even knows how lucky he is. Probably not. If I was ever going to talk to him again, which I probably won't, I'd tell him. Sometimes people don't appreciate what's right in front of their faces.

And speaking of faces ... I fan myself. He is, without a doubt, the hottest guy I've ever talked to. Is lust contagious? If so, I've caught it from my sister.

I roll onto my stomach, open up ClikClak, and search his profile. There are several accounts with various versions of his name. Then the real one pops up, with the green star, indicating that it's a verified account.

Damn, he's got over four million followers.

It only takes me about 30 seconds to figure out why. Most of his content is of him working out. Barely clothed. My face flushes, and my body feels as if it's on fire. Holy crap. He's like a walking ... I don't even know what. My brain is short-circuiting too much to even come up with a good analogy.

Logically, being a professional athlete, you know he has to have good physical fitness. I saw him play. I know that takes a certain prowess that someone like me would never ever possess. But dear God, this man rivals something Michelangelo would have carved.

"Okay, I get it now!" I yell to the ceiling.

The only account I have for ClikClak is the one I use for the business. There is no way in hell I'd message him from that one. I would die of embarrassment if he ever found out that I film shit for a living.

Quickly, before I have too much time to overthink what I'm doing, I create a new account. I follow him and a few pages that I already follow, mostly people who make me laugh. I take a picture of myself and upload it, putting it to music, so there's at least one video of me. Then, I send him a DM.

>*Me: Thanks again for letting me dry off yesterday. I appreciate it.*
>
>*Me: And sorry about the crotch thing again.*

I probably will never hear from TJ Doyle again, but I did want to let him know that I saw his kindness and thank him for it. And also that I was apologetic for the inappropriate touching. People who grow up in loving and supportive homes often take that for granted. Not the inappropriate touching—the kindness part. Gram and Gramps did everything they could for Richie and me, but once that seed of doubt and insecurity was planted, nothing could erase it. I never expect unprompted kindness.

My phone buzzes with a notification. I scramble to sit upright. This cannot be happening.

>*TJ: No problem. You get home ok?*

I smile. I can't help myself.

>*Me: Yes. It's just across the road. You make it to practice ok?*
>
>*TJ: One minute to spare. That's notable for me.*
>
>*Me: I tend to run late too. And that was when I just had to walk across the yard to get to work. Now that I have to drive, it's going to be interesting.*

As soon as I type it, I want to hit unsend. To erase. Because I know what's going to come next.

>*TJ: Where do you work?*

Yup, there it is.

It's not that I'm ashamed of what I do. Working for my grandfather has been great. Well, it's been okay. Alright, my job sucks, but I'm helping the family out, and it's a steady paycheck. Until I can find something else I want to do more, it'll suffice. I keep thinking one day, I'll wake up and BAM! Suddenly, I'll know what I want to do with my life.

That morning has yet to arrive.

TJ: You said you moved here for work?

Sigh. I'd better get this over with.

Me: Yes, I work for my grandfather's company. I'm 4th gen. We're opening up a new satellite office in Sharon. My official title is "South Regional Director," but I think that just means I get to handle all the bullshit.

Me: Do you still have practice even though it's Labor Day?

I figure if I change the subject, maybe I can avoid the word sewage. I've already embarrassed myself enough in front of this man. Talking about my job will only send things down the drain, quite literally.

TJ: If it's in season, we're practicing. A slightly smaller workout, so a few free hours today. Whoopie.

Me: What are you going to do with all your spare time? Also, trying to wrap my brain around the fact that a "slightly smaller" workout gives you hours. My body is sore just thinking about it.

TJ: Cookout at my parents.

A cookout. That must be nice. Gramps and Uncle Robert were usually on call on weekends, and there always seemed to be some sewer emergency, so we didn't have many of those growing up.

Me: With hot dogs and hamburgers and potato salad salmonella and everything?

TJ: 100%, which is why I steer clear of anything with mayo.

I'm trying to think of something witty to say that doesn't involve a bodily function when the next text comes in.

TJ: Wanna come with me?

This has me jumping to my feet. What? Why? How? I don't understand what's happening. With shaking hands that drop my phone not once but twice, I send my reply.

Me: Did you mean to send that to me? I'm Rachel Cramer. You know, the girl you thought was stalking you. The girl who spilled your smoothie on you.

TJ: Dammit, I thought I was sending this to the girl who started to get frisky patting my junk in public.

My face burns. I still can't believe I touched him *there*. What the hell was I thinking?

Me: She sounds like a piece of work. She also wants to know what she should bring, because her grandmother raised her never to show up anywhere empty-handed.

That's true. Gram is as old-fashioned as they come. Homemade apple pies, chocolate chip cookies (the Toll House recipe, naturally), and Italian Jeannettes were her specialty. Since I have neither the time nor the ingredients to whip any of those up, I'm going to have to resort to plan B.

TJ: Ma will just be so happy that I didn't scare you off with my antics. Don't worry about it.

Me: I'm going to worry about it, so at least give me time to run and grab something from Stop & Shop. Or better yet, Fresh Market. Their baked goods are better.

TJ: Seriously, you don't need anything.

I don't think this man understands that I can't just show up with nothing. As it is, it's going to be uncomfortable enough that I'm going.

Me: Text me the address and the time, and I'll meet you there.

I have no idea what is happening. Who am I and what am I doing? This was not what I had in mind when I decided to turn over a new leaf. This is all spiraling out of control. Fast. My breathing picks up as my pulse quickens. I'm going to need to listen to a meditation app all the way there to keep me from totally freaking out.

TJ: It's stupid for both of us to drive all the way up there. I'll pick you up in 30.

I sigh. He's not going to let this go. "You picked a stubborn ass," I yell to the ceiling. I don't even wait for her to not answer; I've got to get ready.

For the second time in three days, I'm faced with the dilemma of what to wear when going to see TJ Doyle. My clothing choices have not dramatically improved, but at least I don't have to pretend to be athletic. It's cooler today after the storm yesterday. Not quite fall, but you can tell summer has one foot out the door, not unlike my mom most of my life.

I pull out one of my favorite dresses, black cotton with fluttery sleeves and a tiered bottom. I wear it to the office if I have to look nice, but it's also fine for just running errands. Of course, I throw a pair of bike shorts on underneath because Gram would have a fit if I didn't. Flip-flops because I don't own cute shoes. I grab the denim jacket I've had since 2015 in case it gets a little cold.

Now, on to the hair and face. I never put my contacts in this morning, and I don't feel like doing it now. I'm already putting forth a lot of effort. I don't want to overtax myself. My hair's a little hopeless, about fourteen months overdue for a cut. Before Richie got sick, I wore it in a cute above-the-shoulder bob. Now it hangs limply down past my collarbones. There's probably no helping it now. Claw clip it is.

I throw a little mascara and lip gloss on. It's about all I know how to do. Then, realizing that I'm fixing my face for a man, I wipe it off. I will not do that. I will be me. But really, it actually made me look a little less dowdy, so I put it back on. Shit. What am I doing? I'm about to wipe it off again when my phone dings with a text alert.

TJ: Which building are you?

I'm out of time to war with myself about turning into my mother. The makeup stays on.

Me: Second building on the left. Be right out.

TJ: I'm the one in the Grand Cherokee Trackhawk.

He says that like it means something to me.

Me: I don't know anything about cars.

TJ: It's bright red. You can't miss me.

As I run down the stairs, a little faster than I'm used to moving, I push down the intrusive thought that's wormed its way into my brain.

Like mother, like daughter.

CHAPTER 16: TJ

I'm definitely going to have to make an appointment with Watson Ross to unpack my behavior. This doesn't have anything to do with soccer, but I won't tell the sports psychologist that until after I'm lying on his couch. My first mistake was telling Ma about running into Rachel. I only did it because she was on me—again—about being alone too much. She's well-meaning, as all moms are, but it annoys me. Does she think I don't realize I come home to an empty place and eat all alone every night?

Ma always asks me why I can't find someone. After ten years playing soccer in the USSL, I know people tolerate me for two reasons: because I'm a professional athlete and because I'm conventionally attractive. That's it. My teammates don't really like me; they put up with me. I'm the butt of many jokes, both on and off the field.

Sure, women want to date me, but it's just for the clout—and the money. Joke's on them. I do okay, but it's not like I'm one of the highest-paid players in the league. I don't have an agent, so no deals are coming my way. It's one reason why I've worked so hard on my social media income. I have a few brand deals, but it's not like I'm posing in my underwear or having shoes named after me. When I stop playing, which is bound to happen sooner rather than later, that cash cow will dry up.

Dad invests my money for me. His favorite phrases are "soccer players aren't ballers, so don't live like one" and "maybe you should save it for a rainy day." I hear one or the other the second I talk about making a big purchase, like my car.

When Ma started in again last night, I needed her to stop, so I blurted out that Rachel lives in my neighborhood, and that we'd hung out. It was a knee-jerk reaction. I didn't anticipate it would have any other repercussions.

She got so excited that I didn't have the heart to mention that it was only an act of nature that forced Rachel to spend time with me. Ma went on for at least five minutes about how I should bring her around because she got the impression that Rachel was lonely and sad. Ma wasn't wrong about that.

Rachel probably needs someone to look after her a little, like Ma does for me. I had no idea how to bring that up to her. Or how I'd even talk to Rachel again, for that matter. Truth be told, it's been so long since I've met someone in real life that I have no idea what to do anymore. There's a big difference between sliding into someone's DMs to hook up and actually having a face-to-face conversation. Not that Rachel is that great at it either.

Seems like she's pretty out of practice, too.

I was completely, but not unpleasantly, surprised when she messaged me. Good surprised. I smiled, surprised. There are so many DMs in my inbox that it would have been easy to miss. Except there it was, and I didn't miss it. Naturally, I wasted no time clicking on her profile. She doesn't have much up there, probably because she doesn't use the app a whole lot. I might be better off if I don't tell her I legit think I'm addicted to it.

Not addicted as much as I enjoy the access it gives me to other people's experiences. It's not an addiction. I can stop any time I want to. I just don't have anything better to do with my time.

Just like I didn't have to reply to her immediately. And keep replying. And invite her to my parents' house for the Labor Day cookout. When I texted Ma that Rachel was coming, I could practically hear her shouting with joy all the way down in Mansfield.

I mean, Ma told me to invite her. I didn't come up with that one all on my own. She had zero confidence that I actually would. Hell, I didn't think I actually would.

What I did not stop to think about is the fact that we'd have to spend almost an hour—each way—in the car with nothing but small talk to break it up. Before I pick her up, I try to think of topics that we can talk about. I could make a list, like the one she carries with her. It's clear she's not a sports person, so that's out. She was reading at the soccer game. I'm not a book person, so that's out too.

She said she works for her grandfather at the family business. I'll get her to tell me all about that. That should kill some time on the way up at least.

I have the same feeling that I get before a big match. Hyped up. Excited. A little nervous. I can't run my pregame routine, so I have to hope it goes away.

As I pull up to the second building on the left, I see Rachel step off the curb and quickly approach my SUV. She's wearing a black dress and denim jacket, with big round glasses on, and her hair pulled up in one of those clip things that girls use. A large purse is slung over her shoulder, and she carries a water bottle.

She's cute. Like in a best friend's little sister kind of way. Or the shy neighbor kind of way. Which she is, I guess. The glasses give her a librarian vibe. The kind that could pull off the sexy librarian with some persuasion.

Whoa. Where did that come from?

"Thanks for picking me up," she says as she slides into the seat, quickly pulling her seat belt on.

"Thanks for agreeing to come. I happened to mention to Ma that I ran into you, and she was all up my grill about when we were going to hang out again." I glance over at Rachel just in time to see her shoulders sag a little. Shit. "I mean, that's not why I asked you today. I mean, it is, because Ma wanted you to come, but I—"

"It's fine. I get it," she says quietly.

Great. I've screwed things up already. Typical Tyler.

"Well, I know you've met my parents and my brothers. Nick and his wife Sasha will be there. Joey's wife, Amanda, will also be there, along with their girls Cami and Ella. I feel the need to warn you now. Cami has more energy than a nuclear power plant. I swear, they must feed her pure caffeine and sugar, with a side of speed. She kind of reminds me of that girl who was in your group at the Soccer for Sibs thing. The one who kept flipping and contorting and stuff. I swear, I thought she was going to snap her spine." I'm rambling. I know I am, and there's nothing I can do to stop it.

This is why I like ClikClak. I can do multiple takes and edits and make it seem like I'm not a bumbling idiot. People only see the best, polished version of me. Not the real me.

Rachel laughs, though. "Right? Her feet were more in the air than on the ground. I thought I was going to get a foot to the face more than once." She pauses for a moment and then continues. "She didn't seem that interested in soccer. Seems like a gymnastics event would have been more her speed."

I slap the steering wheel with both hands. "That's what I thought too! But on the other hand, there weren't that many girls there, so I'm glad she came. I was thinking about reaching out and suggesting that if we do it again, we pair up with the New England Crush."

"What's the New England Crush?"

"It's our USSL women's team." I glance over again. She has a blank look on her face. "United States Soccer League. Women's professional soccer." Still nothing.

Rachel shrugs. "I'm not a sportsball person. I'm a book person." She pulls one out of her bag and stares at it for a moment before saying, "Although I'd gotten out of the habit of reading after Richie died. I'm just starting again." Her voice turns wistful. "I'd forgotten how much I loved it."

"You brought a book?" Who brings a book to a cookout?

"Yeah. Like I said, I'm just getting back into it again, and it's hard to form a habit if you don't have access to it."

A pit forms in my stomach, realizing how long a ride this is going to be. This was such a stupid idea to bring her. We have absolutely nothing in common. She has no interest in soccer, and there's no way I can talk about books. Then I remember my plan.

"So, tell me about your family business," I say, a little too abruptly. Smooth. Real smooth. Good thing I'm not trying to impress this woman. I'd have failed miserably already, and we've just reached I-95.

"It's pretty boring. I work in the office. I've done it since I was fourteen. There's not much else to say." The finality in her tone is unmistakable. She does not want to talk about it. I wonder what kind of business it is. Is it something shady? Is her family in the mob? Is it a strip club?

I may never know.

The curious part of me that feels it has a right to every detail of everyone's life wants to ask her more questions. From somewhere in the dark recesses of my brain, the underdeveloped part of me that is ruled by tact and empathy tells me to drop it.

He doesn't come out much, so I listen to him when he makes his rare appearances.

I try something different. "Where did you grow up?"

"Mostly around Boxford. We lived with our grandparents more than anyone else, and that's where they live."

"Like you and your parents and your siblings all lived with your grandparents?" Jeez, that must have been crowded. I can't imagine what the fight for the bathroom was like.

"No, just my sister and me." There's that tone again.

Good thing I'm not a baseball player, because everything I say is a swing and a miss.

As the ride goes on, Rachel becomes less and less responsive until we're sitting in uncomfortable silence. I should put the radio on or something, but I have a feeling that will offend her too. I have no idea why she's upset, but it's clear she is. She's very still, except for her fingers, which are in constant motion, her index fingers running over the nail beds of her thumbs. Every so often, she clenches her whole hand into a fist and then relaxes.

If I didn't know better, I'd say she was nervous or anxious.

I steal another glance. She's got her eyes closed and is taking deep, exaggerated breaths. Her hands are now clenched tightly in fists. There's a sheen of sweat on her forehead.

"Hey, are you okay?" She is definitely not okay.

She doesn't say anything. Shit.

"Rachel, are you okay? Do you need me to stop or something? Are you carsick? Please don't ralph all over my car."

"I'm fine," she practically gasps.

"Listen, I'm not the brightest bulb in the drawer, but even I know you're not fine. Because if this"—I wave my hand in a circle in her general direction—"is fine, then I don't want to see not fine."

"I'm a little anxious. Trying to do some grounding so I don't have a panic attack."

Panic attack? Why is she having a panic attack? What's there to panic about? From the recesses of my brain, I remember a ClikClak I saw about this. For a while, I got a lot of videos about people with anxiety, probably because I thought their experiences were interesting. Now what was it they said to do?

Then I remember. "Alexa, play I Gotta Feeling." Immediately, the rhythmic synthesizer beat begins pulsing through the sound system. "Trust me on this and do what I tell you," I tell her.

Rachel is now staring at me. Her hands are opening up in her lap. "The Black Eyed Peas?"

I nod, partially to her and to the beat. This song is a banger. "Yup. The second repeat of the verse, your job is to sing all the ad-libs. Not the main part, but the extras that they yell in the background. I'm taking lead vocals."

"What are you talking about?"

I don't care that she is having a panic attack. That's not a problem. It will be a problem if she doesn't know this song. I get that she might be sheltered, but not knowing the Black Eyed Peas would be extreme. "Do you know this song or not?"

She nods.

"Okay then. From here on out, you are not to sing any of the main vocals. Just all the extras and background stuff they do. Got it?"

Another nod. I hear a soft "whoo hoo" at the right place. Then the verse comes. I sing the main part, and she chimes in with the random phrases. This time, my glance is met with a small smile. As the song picks up, we are both singing, much louder than is acceptable for the general public, but totally perfect for a car concert.

After almost five minutes of bouncing and dancing and yelling, Rachel ends with a closing "Whoo hoo" and sags back into her seat.

"You good, or do we need to do it again?"

"I'm good. Where did you come up with that?" She sounds a little breathless.

"Saw a ClikClak about using that for anxiety. I thought it might be good because sometimes I get a little too in my head before games. I put it on my playlist."

"ClikClak, huh? Is that your go-to for advice?"

Bobbing my head up and down, I reply, "Of course. Where else am I supposed to find out how to remove a beehive or snake a drain or frost a cake? It's all there."

"That's not what you post, though."

"I post the things that will gain views to make money. I won't be able to play soccer forever, and I'm not good at anything else. The monetization is crazy." As soon as the words are out of my mouth, I wish I could pull them back in. One thing my dad has told me over and over and over again is not to talk about money with anyone. Shit.

"Yeah, I run an account for my grandfather's business. It's a niche world, but it makes a nice little extra income. I've funded many a Target run through my monetization."

My body sags back into the seat. She gets it. I'm about to reply when she hurriedly adds, "I tried putting the money back into the company, but Gramps won't let me. He says the increased work generated from my videos is enough, and that I should consider my video money as a company bonus. If I want more money, I make more content to get more views. Of course, keeping the algorithm happy with a constant stream of videos is work in and of itself."

This girl understands my life. I feel something in my chest lift and expand. "Tell me about it. And then you spend more time on the app, and then you get consumed with what you're going to post. Next thing you know, you've been scrolling for hours and it's after two in the morning."

"Um, well, I've not really had that experience with ClikClak. I pretty much post my videos and turn it off."

Oh. Yeah, totally misread that one. Typical for me. That balloon feeling deflates. I can practically hear it going "Pfffftttt" from inside me.

"I mean," she continues, "I've had that happen with books, though. I've stayed up reading almost all night on more than one occasion. I'll forget I need sleep."

"Never have I ever read a book that made me forget I need sleep." Mostly because I don't read, but she doesn't need to know that.

"You don't know what you're missing. There's no better way to escape from reality than in the pages of a book."

I consider her words. Maybe I should give reading a try.

CHAPTER 17: RACHEL

I'll be damned if the Black Eyed Peas didn't pull me out of my brewing panic attack. I can't believe that worked. I also can't believe TJ Doyle is that into ClikClak.

He can never ever find my work account.

I've already done some mortifying things in front of him, but that would take the cake. I cannot have this man find out what I do for a living. Nearly having a panic attack after having to talk about my family was bad enough.

Rather than spiral back into panic, I force myself to stay in the present. "So, is there somewhere we can stop so I can pick up a dessert or a bottle of wine or something?"

"I told you, you don't need anything. Trust me."

Trust. Easy for him to say and probably do. "I'd like to, but if I called my grandmother right now, she'd be mortified by me walking in empty-handed."

"And if you show up and hand Maureen Doyle food, she'll be offended that you didn't think she'd have enough to go around."

We are at an impasse.

I feel my heart starting to race a little. I've got to let this go. "Okay, fine. But I'm going to tell her I wanted to bring something, and that you wouldn't let me."

"Fine."

"Fine." I cross my arms over my chest in a huff.

The awkward silence returns to the car for a moment.

This is so weird. All because of Richie's stupid list. I pull it out to study it again.

"What are you reading?"

I answer without looking up. "My sister's list. Trying to figure out if there's any way I can do at least one more thing."

"What's on it again?"

I read the list to him, tripping over the one-night-stand part. Real smooth, Rachel. Even if I were propositioning him—which I'm totally not—there's no way he'd go for it. Not someone like him with someone like me.

He doesn't seem to notice. "This list is easy. You just need a travel agent. You book a trip to Alaska that requires you to have a layover in Vegas. There are slot machines in the airport, so you don't even have to leave. Then you head to Alaska, where you'll definitely see moose. You can even go to a firing range while you're up there. That's like four things in one weekend trip."

I'm impressed with his plan. I would never do any of it, but it's a good effort. "I don't think playing slots is the same as going to a casino. Nice try, though."

"Why moose?" he asks.

I know exactly why. "One year, Gram and Gramps took Richie and me up to Old Orchard Beach in Maine for a little vacation. It was one of the few we ever went on. We saw so many cars with the bumper sticker that said, 'I brake for moose.' We thought they'd be all over the place, but we didn't see any. One of many disappointments in our lives."

"I hear they're mean and nasty. You probably don't want to run into one."

I shrug. "Maybe, but when you're nine and eleven, you don't think about those things." I think about the list. "She never got to see one," I say softly.

He's quiet for a minute. "Maybe I'm not the best person to help you plan your list. It never occurred to me that Maine would be a lot easier to get to than Alaska." He shrugs. "No one has ever accused me of being the brains of the operation."

"Don't sell yourself short. I've been so paralyzed by everything that I didn't think of Maine either."

We've exited I-95 and are driving down Route 20, through Weston and then Wayland. When TJ begins making turns off the main road, I know we're getting close. I can do this. I don't need to panic. Of course, if telling yourself not to panic worked, no one would ever have panic attacks again. It's about as helpful as telling someone to calm down.

As if TJ can sense my increasing stress level, he says, "Everything will be fine. You don't have to worry about my family."

I think back to the ice cream shop. "Your brothers sat on you."

His mouth pulls back into a tight line. "I said you didn't have anything to worry about. They'll still pick on me. They always do. Joey's a comedian. He routinely uses me for material in his stand-up act. You might have seen it on Netflix."

I look down at my hands. "I haven't been much in the mood for things like that lately, but I can check it out. Is it good?"

"Yeah, Joey's wicked funny. People love him." I can hear the hero worship in his voice.

"And the other one?" I can't remember his name. "What does he do?"

"Nicky's a lawyer who works for the State Senate. He went to Harvard."

Wow. "So you're all a bunch of underachievers and slackers then."

His mouth is in that tight line again. "I wouldn't compare what I do with them. I just kick a ball around. Three-year-olds can play soccer."

My eyebrows shoot up. He can't be serious. "Listen, I don't know a lot about soccer. That's an understatement. I don't know *anything* about soccer, but I do know what I saw out on the field the other day is not something that a three-year-old could do."

He doesn't say anything as he pulls into the driveway of an oversized gray Cape Cod. There are several other cars parked on the cobblestone driveway already.

TJ hops out and walks around to my side where he proceeds to open the door.

"Are we late?" I ask as I attempt to slide out of the SUV. It's not nearly as warm as it's been the last few days, but my nervous sweating has made the back of my thighs stick to the leather seats. Finally managing to disengage without leaving a layer of skin behind, I get out and brush my dress down.

TJ stands there. "Of course we're late. It's me. I'd probably give Ma a coronary if I ever showed up anywhere on time. You gonna be okay?"

We're standing about six inches apart.

"As okay as I'll ever be," I offer.

"I promise, my family won't bite. You'll be okay. You'll be safe." He pushes a strand of hair behind my ear. "I'll look out for you."

His touch sends shivers down my spine. Despite the fact that he's so tall and built of solid muscle, his fingers are delicate, feeling more like a whisper. "Is this because I had a panic attack on the way down?"

He nods, pulling his hand back. "It was scary, but not as scary as thinking you might boot all over my car."

I can't help but smile. The stupid, ridiculous type of smile that this man makes me do. If I were a cartoon character, I'd have stars in my eyes.

"C'mon, let's go face the firing squad. I promise they'll be nice to you. I can absolutely guarantee they won't be nice to me."

I half expect—or just want—him to take my hand to lead me, but he doesn't. I rush to catch up to his long legs, my flip-flops making thwacking noises on the walkway.

"It's easiest to get to the backyard through the house," he says.

I can hear a cacophony of voices already. I wonder how many people are here. What am I getting myself into? Despite the fact that TJ's assured me they'll be nice, my old friend anxiety is back to make sure I don't have a comfortable moment ever.

As I follow him through the house, I try to take in the details to ground myself. It's an older home—the whitewashed brick fireplace, blonde oak floors, and wood trim give it away. There have been several renovations, including a cool black-and-white geometric tile floor that spans from the entryway into a modern kitchen that is most certainly not original to the house. There are pictures of the three boys everywhere at all different ages and stages. It feels like a home.

The noise from the back of the house is getting louder. It's not just a jovial party. It's yelling. A lot of yelling. I glance at TJ to see if this is normal for his family. They seem to be typical Boston-Irish, if the last name is any indication, and they are not known for being passive wallflowers. The look on his face confirms that this might be more than the usual boisterous crowd.

His pace quickens through the house, and I follow, not wanting to be separated from him. We exit through the sliding glass door onto a screened-in porch that overlooks the yard. Due to the hill the house was built into, we are on the second level, looking down on a kidney-shaped pool and an expanse of flat, green grass. In the middle of the lawn is a patch of grass that's brighter and denser than the rest.

Oh no.

If that weren't enough of a tell-tale giveaway of an overflowing septic tank, the smell reveals it all. I'd know that smell anywhere.

"Jesus, Cami, get out of there! You smell like shit!" Joey is yelling at a little towheaded girl, who's having the time of her life running and sliding through the lush section of grass. She looks fresh out of the pool, but that's about the only thing fresh on her. Her swimsuit is streaked in brown. Peals of squeals and laughter carry on the wind. She pays no attention to her father. Or to the woman with a neat, pale blonde bob that must be her mother. Or to Maureen or Tom.

"What's going on?" TJ yells, his voice joining in the chaos.

My hand holds my phone, fingers twitching with the impulse to start recording. This would be ClikClak gold.

"Get her in the bath!" Nicky yells.

Joey marches over and picks her up. Though he's more than double her size, Joey is no match for the bundle of energy. That and she's slick with goo that makes her impossible to hold. She slides out of his arms. He reaches down to grab her again but misses and lands face first with a squelchy thud. It splashes everywhere.

Another little girl, even smaller, wriggles out of her mother's grasp and makes a beeline for her father and sister.

"ELLA, STOP!" Tom yells. It's too late. She's jumping in the puddles.

Oh dear Lord.

A very "muddy" Joey finally wrangles Cami and Ella and marches across the yard with them under his arm, straight toward the house.

I can't believe I didn't record that. It would go viral almost instantaneously. I mean, I couldn't whip out my phone because I barely know these people, and that would be taking advantage of their generosity. It would have been an invasion of their privacy.

These people have been kind to me. It's time to return the favor. I send an S.O.S. text to Uncle Robert.

"What's the address here?" I ask, typing as quickly as I can.

"270 Old Lancaster Road," TJ answers absentmindedly, watching the chaos. Then it registers. "Why?"

"I'm getting your parents some help. They haven't called a septic service yet, have they?"

"MA!" TJ bellows so loudly that I want to cover my ears. "Did you call a septic service?"

"What are you talking about? Our yard is flooded. It's probably from the creek from the rain yesterday," she yells back.

"It's not flooding. The septic is overflowing," I say. "When was the last time they had it pumped?"

TJ turns and looks at me, his eyes wide in bewilderment.

My gaze drops to my feet. I talk fast so I don't have time to think about what I'm saying. "I've gotta guy. He'll be here in about an hour. In the meantime, don't use the toilets unless you have to. You should probably shut off the water to the house." I raise my gaze. I have to fess up now.

"DO NOT GO IN THE HOUSE!" Maureen yells to Joey.

"I gotta put them in the tub!" Joey yells back. Cami is still thrashing and screaming. Ella is giggling.

These people seem to yell an awful lot. There's so much to see. I put my hand on TJ's arm to get his attention. "They can't shower in here. It'll be too much on the system. The septic's already full. Trust me, it'll get much, much worse if they start running the water in the house."

"What are they supposed to do? They're covered in ..."

"Yeah, I know what they're covered in." Everyone with a working olfactory sense knows what they've been rolling around in. "How close are you with the neighbors? Can they go over there and hose off?"

Because it was my idea, TJ and I get tasked with escorting the girls to the next-door neighbor's house and borrowing their hose. I carry a load of towels, soap, and a change of clothes.

For a five- and three-year-old, getting sprayed down, soaped up, and rinsed off in the driveway next door is super fun. The girls are laughing and squealing with delight, prancing around with so much soap on their hair that it looks like they're wearing wigs. We lather the soap right on top of their bathing suits, but these'll definitely need a good washing. Probably with bleach.

Finally, the girls are clean enough to be returned to their mother, who's waiting with the dry set of clothes. Now it's Joey's turn, but he can soap himself up. TJ and I head back across the front lawn to his parents' house.

As we get to the front door, TJ turns and looks at me, his eyes narrowing. "How do you know so much about this?"

I look at my feet.

"Rachel? Oh, wait—I know! You watch all those ClikClaks too! The ones from Oh Crap!"

He knows my ClikClak handle. He's watched my videos.

Maybe the earth will spontaneously open up and swallow me whole. I wait. There's not even a tremble from underneath my feet that indicates my salvation is coming. What there is, though, is the tell-tale woosh of the air brakes of the vacuum truck pulling up outside the front of the house.

Time to go to work.

I open up my phone and start recording. Uncle Robert slides out, hiking up his dungarees, and gives me a curt nod. "He the homeowner?"

"I'm Tyler. This is my parents' house. You're ..." I see the moment he recognizes the logo on the side of the truck. He looks from me to Uncle Robert and back again. He sees the phone in my hand. "You're the one who does the videos?"

"Yeah, Rach here has put us on the map. We can't keep up with the business," Uncle Robert answers. "We're opening a second location because of her videos. I don't know what morons find watching this entertaining, but who am I to look a gift horse in the mouth?"

TJ's face fills with color.

"Okay, Uncle Robert, let's get going," I say, pulling his elbow and walking him back toward the truck.

Ninety minutes later, the Doyles' septic tank is empty and their yard is torn up by deep tire tracks. Joey and his kids are clean and almost dry.

"Rachel, darling, we can't thank you enough for getting us help." Maureen pulls me into a big hug. This is what I always imagined a mother's hug to feel like. "Promise me you'll come back again."

I glance at TJ. He's never going to want to see me after this.

CHAPTER 18: TJ

W ell, that was amazing," I say on the drive home. I'm still in awe of how Rachel handled that whole mess. Also, I'm amazed that I've been following her ClikClak without knowing it was her. She's one of my favorite accounts.

"It's not really. It's just sewage removal."

"No, you don't understand, I love your videos."

She shifts in the passenger seat of my SUV. "It's literally shit removal. The only glamorous part of the job, if you want to call it that, is the grinder pump installation on new construction, but those videos don't do anything. I don't know what it is about septic tanks."

"There's something fascinating about it. Also, until I saw it on the side of the truck in person, I didn't put it together. Cramer-Romero Associates Pumps. C.R.A.P."

Rachel twists her hands together in her lap. "Yeah, Gramps was quite the clever one with that. Ironically, he hates poop jokes. No one's allowed to make any in his presence."

"No wonder you knew so much about ClikClak. You have a big account."

"Well, the videos practically shoot themselves. I still can't figure out why people want to watch them," she mutters, shaking her head.

I can't explain it myself. Instead, I say, "Yeah, coming up with content ideas sucks. It stresses me out. I'm not bright enough to have a good platform or pitch, so I end up taking my shirt off." I shrug. "Works okay for now."

"I'll say. You have over four million followers."

"Yeah, but it's all I have." My words hang in the air between us.

"That's not all you have," she says. "You have a family. A loud family. A very loud family. Are they always that loud?" She laughs.

"Yeah, pretty much, though there was a little more panic this time. You know, Ma has already said you have to come back again when there's not a crisis."

Rachel is quiet. I steal a glance. She's looking out the window. The sadness is back. I'd seen it lift when we were washing the girls, but now it's like a heavy curtain has dropped over her face.

"I'd like you to come back too."

She turns to look at me, her face getting harder and harder to see in the fading light. "Why?"

"You seem like you need a friend." It's probably the wrong thing to say, but it's the truth. What I don't say to her is that I need a friend.

"And you want to be my friend?" She's turned her body to face me.

I pull into a parking space in her building's lot. Shutting off the car, I angle my body toward hers. "Yeah, sure. It makes sense. We live in the same neighborhood. We're bound to run into one another. It'd make more sense for us to be friends than for me to keep accusing you of stalking me."

Rachel laughs. "Richie would absolutely die if she knew this was happening." She looks up at the ceiling of my SUV and yells, "TJ Doyle and I are now friends. Stick that in your pipe and smoke it." Then, sheepishly, she looks at me. "I still have to talk to her. I know it makes me crazy."

I shake my head and put my hand gently on hers. "No, it doesn't. I'm sure you have a lot to tell her." I try to think of what my mom or dad would say to comfort someone in a situation like this.

"I keep waiting for her to answer me." Rachel's eyes are beginning to glisten.

"Well, *that* makes you crazy," I say deadpan.

It's enough to break the tension. Wiping her eyes, Rachel starts to laugh.

"And you can call me Tyler. It's what my friends and family call me."

"Tyler," she says, trying it out. It sounds good coming from her mouth. "Well, good night, Tyler. Thank you for today. It helped. More than I can say."

"You were a tremendous help, too. You saved my parents' house. We owe you big time."

"It's nothing."

Silence overtakes the SUV. I don't know what else to say. Seems like Rachel doesn't either. Odd to think that three days ago, I didn't know this person at all, but sitting here in the dark, I'm already thinking about what I should say the next time we talk. All because of some list.

"The list!" I exclaim, suddenly remembering why we're together. "We need to do the list."

"Um, there's no 'we' here." I see Rachel's hand move to the door handle.

"Okay, you need to do the list, but I can help. Or at least be a sounding board. An accountability partner." Jesus, I sound desperate.

Her hand stills for a moment. "Why?"

I'd like to know that too. "I need something to do." It's about as close to the truth as I can bear to admit.

She stays facing the door. I have to strain to hear her voice. "I'm not a charity case."

"I'm not treating you like one. I lie there alone every night, watching videos of other people live their lives. I feel like I have the opportunity to not just be a spectator for once. Will you let me not be a spectator?"

I'm practically begging. Truth is, I have no idea why this means so much to me. Something deep within my gut is telling me to pursue this. To make Rachel pursue this.

Rachel stares at me over her shoulder for a long moment. She lets out a sigh. "Fine. I'll think about it." With that, she opens the door and slides out. "Thanks again for the ride."

She closes the door and crosses in front of the vehicle. I watch her walk to the end of the building and then disappear up the stairs.

Before I pull out, I send her a text.

Me: You get in ok?

Rachel: I'm in and locked.

Rachel: Thanks again.

Me: Thanks for coming. I had a good time.

Three dots wave for much longer than I'd like.

Rachel: Me too. Sewage aside, but that's literally the story of my life.

Me: You're a book person. You can just turn the page and start a new chapter.

I don't know where those prophetic words came from, but I'm pleased with myself.

I'm only home for a few minutes when the temptation to start scrolling ClikClak comes back. I can let myself. I was out for a long time today, and I barely touched my phone. In fact, other than texting Rachel, I haven't wanted to use my phone.

This is new.

"Wow, four days in a row on time? What's the occasion?" Maliq Miller always seems to be watching the clock when it comes to me.

"Shut up, Miller. Who are you, the time police?" I slam my locker door shut a little too hard. If Rachel can start a new chapter, so can I. At least that's what I've been telling myself.

"Hey, Crew, make sure you're on time. Otherwise, Miller here will be up your grill every single minute of every single day." I feel the need to warn the new guy, Crew Benequista, who was moved up from our minor league affiliate to fill the vacancy left by Brandon Nix. "Other than that, we're a chill group."

As one of the more senior players, I should make him feel welcome. I've been with the Buzzards since the beginning of my career.

"Alright, guys," Coach Janssen announces. "As you know, we're at home tomorrow and then in Las Vegas next weekend. The travel itinerary is being emailed to you today. We are taking the red-eye back on Sunday night to give you a little time off. While what happens in Vegas stays in Vegas, please remember that we're very much in contention for the championship this year, and every single point will help our standing going into the postseason. We have casinos right here in New England, so don't think that this trip is an occasion to go wild. Do that on your own time after we beat the Renegades."

Coach's speech echoes in my head throughout the rest of practice, but I can't figure out why. We travel for half our games, so it's not like this is new news. Maybe the warning about Vegas. Last time we were out there, Andy Bracer and Pressley Samson missed our flight home because they were MIA. The resultant social media posts solved that mystery, and both were stuck with a hefty conduct fine, and Pressley started marriage counseling.

It's not until I'm on Oakland Street, about to make the left into my parking lot, when the sign for Rachel's complex catches my eye, and everything clicks together. I'm so excited that I don't even bother going inside before I shoot off my round of text messages.

Me: I'm playing in Vegas next week.

Me: You should come.

Me: You have to fly out there.

Me: We can go parasailing on Lake Mead.

I'm about to type another one when I make myself put my phone in my pocket and wait. This could be unwelcome. She could not want to talk about this. I haven't heard from her since Monday, and it's now Friday. I should be staying in the hotel with the rest of the team tonight, as we usually do before home games, but I convinced Coach Janssen that I'd get better sleep in my own bed.

So now, instead of bonding with a teammate, I'm by myself, cooking dinner for myself, and thinking about my brilliant—if I do say so myself—plan.

Me: Hello? Is this thing on?

Finally, my phone dings with a text.

Rachel: I don't think so.

She can't say no. She hasn't even had time to think about it. It's so perfect!

Me: You don't think your phone is on? Then how are you responding?

I smile at my joke. At least I find myself funny. I can have a fan club of one.

Me: Come over so we can talk about it. I'm making dinner.

Rachel: I'm tired. My social battery is low.

Okay. My chest feels a little heavy with ... disappointment. I totally thought she'd be all over this. Plus, all week I've wanted to talk to her, and I couldn't think of a non-lame reason. I was so proud of myself for thinking that this would be a great way for her to get some of her list done. Like I could help her.

Like she'd want my help.

Obviously, that's a big fat no.

CHAPTER 19: RACHEL

I stare at my phone, not really believing what I'm seeing. I read and re-read the string of messages from TJ Doyle. *Tyler.*

I change the name in my contacts. I have to type it three times before I spell it right. Then I change it back to TJ.

I wasn't lying. I am tired from the past two days, working remotely to get the new office up and running. I don't like it one bit. There's not one aspect of my life that seems familiar anymore. It's as if I'm walking around in someone else's shoes. Ones that are several sizes too large.

Also, I'm very deep into a bottle of pinot grigio, but that seems like a detail best kept to myself. I take another long drink.

Yes, this new life in this new apartment with a new workplace and a new superhot, super famous friend feels much too big for me. Any minute, I'm going to wake up, and this will all have been some kind of melatonin-induced fever dream.

But every day, I wake up and I'm still here. Richie is still dead, and I still have to go to work for CRAP #2. That's the abbreviation for the Sharon office. Pretty fitting, if you ask me. What's especially crappy is we haven't been able to get into the building yet, so I'm doing everything remotely.

You'd think I'd like it, but I hate working remotely. It blurs the line between my safe haven and work.

And now today, there's a string of text messages asking me to go to Vegas and watch TJ Doyle play soccer again. It's actually a solid plan—if I intended to carry out any more of Richie's list. Which I don't, because the more I thought about it, the more I realized it wasn't ever achievable.

It's not even the baby thing. That seems improbable but not impossible.

No, the impossible thing on the list is forgiving Mom. There's no way in hell I will be doing that. "I'm not forgiving Mom!" I yell at the ceiling. Since I won't be able to complete the list, it seems foolish to try to do any of the other things on it.

How do I explain that to TJ? He was only being helpful. Nice. Kind. Why?

What could he possibly want from me in return? There's only one way to find out.

Me: Why are you trying to help me with this?

When my phone doesn't ding with an immediate response, I finish the bottle of wine. Then I start pacing. Or as close to pacing as I can do in my current state. There may be some stumbling involved. He thinks I'm rude. He hates me now. I don't want him to hate me. I want to understand why he likes me. That's the problem with texting. You can't infer tone. You certainly can't understand the years of wondering when, or if, my mom was going to show up, and the tremendous shadow that it's cast on my entire life.

She didn't even come to see Richie until the very end.

Me: I don't mean that in a nasty way. I really want to know why this matters to you.

TJ: It would be easier to say in person.

He's not wrong.

I run to the bathroom, brush my teeth, and reapply my deodorant. I've already taken out my contacts, put my glasses on, and changed into sweatpants and an old T-shirt. It'll have to do. My apartment is far too hazy right now to attempt to make myself look better.

Why am I always trying to figure out what to wear for this man? Seriously, he needs to accept me as I am—no dressing to impress. No, sir. I'm not *her.* I smile at my little rhyme. At least I find myself funny.

Then, confirming his apartment number, I stumble across the street to find out why my sister's bucket list means so much to him.

My knuckles barely rap on the door when he yanks it open. He, too, is in sweatpants. Those gray ones. The ones authors write about and women lust over.

Or maybe they lust over that bare chest that's sculpted and firm and doesn't have a hint of hair.

"I hope you filmed some content in those," I say, giving him a once-over. "That's viral material right there."

A big grin filled with naughty thoughts spreads across his face, revealing straight white teeth. "You can hold the camera for me."

Is it hot in here, or is it just my hormones?

I resist the urge to fan myself. The last thing I need to do is to fawn over this man. He's not only next level, he's next stratosphere. And for some reason, he wants to take me under his wing. Maybe he's taken one too many balls to the head. Maybe he likes charity work. Maybe he's a little touched. Whatever the reason, I'm not going to make the situation uncomfortable by getting feelings.

He's objectively attractive. That's all there is to it. That, and I'm a little drunk.

I will not make a fool—a bigger fool—of myself simply because he's nice to me. Perhaps I should have thought of that before I put away an entire bottle of wine. In my defense, how was I supposed to know he'd want me to come over? Time to play it cool.

"Okay, hand it over. What's your best side?" I hold my fingers and thumbs up to make a frame and squint while I look through it. I come to one conclusion: This man does not have a bad side. "What am I going to record you doing?"

He walks toward the kitchen area. The cooktop is littered with pots and pans while a cutting board and several bowls occupy the granite counter. "I usually try to get some food prep video."

"You cook without your shirt on? Is that sanitary? Aren't you afraid of getting splattered by hot grease?" I narrow my eyes at his chest. "Also, do you wax or what?"

I truly do not know what has come over me.

Neither does TJ. "Have you been drinking?"

"Maybe I'm drunk on your physique."

He stares at me for a moment.

"Or a cheap bottle of pinot grigio," I confess.

"What are you doing going over to a stranger's apartment when you're drunk? Don't you know what could happen?"

I respond with a hiccup.

Tyler shakes his head, walks to the fridge, and pours me a glass of water from the filtration pitcher. My body shakes with another hiccup as I take the glass from him, spilling a little water over our hands. "Sorry. I've got the hiccups."

"Thanks, Captain Obvious."

I bend over at the waist and place my mouth on the far side of the rim of the glass. Then, bending a little further, I tilt the glass away from my body until I can drink from the opposite side.

"Rachel, are you okay?"

I lift my gaze, still drinking, to see Tyler bent over, looking through the veil of my hair. I stand up and say, "Voila! Hiccups are gone!" I pose like Vanna White revealing the newest letter on Wheel of Fortune.

"What was that?"

I place the glass down on the counter, slowly and methodically to ensure I don't accidentally spill it or drop it on the floor. I'm not super trusting of my motor skills right now. "That was the only useful thing my mother ever taught me. How to cure hiccups. Never fails."

It's true. I remember my mom showing me that when I was little. It's worked every time. Of course, most of the time when I do it, people have the same panicked reaction that TJ had. They think I'm about to upchuck.

He takes my glass and refills it. "Did you only come over because you're drunk?"

I nod. "Well, that and I really need to know something."

He resumes his place at the cutting board, squinting at the recipe card. He studies the directions and then moves diligently while he chops the zucchini and carrots. Of course, he would eat zucchini. I only eat it in bread form with chocolate chips added. With all of the coordination I still possess, I climb up on one of the kitchen stools and lean my elbows on the counter, facing TJ. The room spins a little.

"What do you need to know?" he asks. He consults the card again.

"Why do you care about my list? You were blowing up my phone with all these … plans." I wave my hand around.

"Why are you making plans for me? What's it to you?" Then, to soften my abruptness, I add, "I mean why are you even thinking about me at all?"

He puts down the large knife he's been chopping with. He looks at it for a moment and then moves it to the other side of the cutting board, away from my reach. He opens and closes his mouth a few times. "I just thought you could use a little help. You know, like you're too close to it, so you can't see the forest through the trees."

I squint at him, trying to figure out what he means.

"Maybe not the forest through the trees. I've never been good at those phrases. What I mean is that because of your grief, it might seem very overwhelming and like you don't know where to start. But because I'm not in your shoes, I can see that there are very easy ways to do some of the things your sister wanted to do."

He's not getting my point, although he's not wrong. It all seems like too much. "No, but why *me*? Why do you want to help *me*?"

TJ shrugs. "I dunno. You're nice. You put up with my mom and my family's antics without running screaming in the other direction. You live close by."

"So basically, proximity, and I let your mom push me around. Got it."

TJ smiles. "I dunno why. Also, I really want to know why I was on your sister's list."

"That's easy. You're hot." In the morning, I can feel mortified about my behavior. Right now, I speak the truth. *In vino veritas.*

"Okay, maybe," he agrees. It's not like being good-looking is a shock to TJ. "But don't you think it's weird you keep crossing my path? It's gotta be for a reason, right?"

"Would it be crazy to say my sister's behind this?" I ask. That's got to be the answer. Christ, she's the one who set this whole thing in motion to begin with.

"Yes, unless you believe in ghosts and possession, in which case I'm going to have to draw the line."

I spin around on the stool, which is a colossal mistake as it makes me more dizzy. I grab onto the edge of the counter to stop the world from spinning. "I wish I could say I did. But I haven't heard a word from Richie yet. I keep looking."

"Is Richie short for something? I've never heard of a girl with that name before."

"It's short for Richelle. Whenever Richie was trying to introduce herself to people, especially in a crowd, she would say, 'It's like Michelle, with an R.' She'd take her finger and draw the R out in the air. Or if it was a hot guy, on his chest." I make the shape of a capital R in the air like Zorro.

"So your names were ..."

"Yup, Rachel and Richelle Cramer. No one ever accused my mother of having good taste. Or any taste at all." I wrinkle my nose. "Her name is Renee, and her brother is Robert. Guess she wanted to keep the 'R' thing going."

"What do you have to forgive her for?" After consulting the recipe yet again, TJ tosses the vegetables in a bowl with some olive oil and then pours them onto a foil-lined sheet pan. He slides it into the oven and then returns to the counter. I watch as he unwraps chicken breasts and measures out salt and pepper. He meticulously sprinkles it on the meat.

"I've never actually seen anyone measure salt and pepper before."

"Can I tell you a secret? I can't actually cook. If I don't follow this recipe step by step, it'll turn out inedible. Trust me, I know this from experience. Also, there's a big difference between teaspoons and tablespoons, especially when it comes to salt."

I'm relieved for the change in topic. My absolute least favorite thing in the world is to talk about my mom. "Then why do you pretend to know how to cook?"

TJ looks at me, his blue eyes piercing through my drunken fog. "Isn't that what we're all doing online? Pretending to be something we're not?"

I scoff, "No. I don't pretend at all. I'm very open about what I do for a living."

He shakes his head. "No, Rachel, you're not. You're not even to the level of pretending. You're doing something much worse."

How dare he insult my job? It's not glamorous. I get that. But it's needed. Hell, I saved his parents' house four days ago. How quickly we forget.

I'm about to launch into him when TJ quietly says, "You're hiding. You're so far deep in the shadows that I'm worried you'll never find the light again."

Ouch.

CHAPTER 20: TJ

I was too blunt. Stupid Tyler. *Stupid, stupid, stupid.* I'm only trying to help her, but it came out all wrong. It's what I get for trying to be clever and deflect from the hard questions she's asking me.

"I'm sorry," I add quickly. "That came out wrong. I'm not very good at words, which is why I just take my shirt off." Instantly, I'm back in college, standing in line in the cafeteria behind a group of girls I'd met the night before at a party. The one that I thought was especially cute was in this group. They'd yet to notice me as they rehashed the events of the previous night.

My grip tightens on my tray. My hands are a little shaky from having too much to drink the night before. Coach would kill me if he knew I was hungover. I need to get some food in me ASAP to absorb the alcohol.

"Yeah, and then Jessica started talking to that soccer player," the tall blonde one says.

"Oooh, Jess, he's so hot."

I tilt my head down, the brim of my ballcap obscuring my face. Jessica. That was the cute girl's name. Maybe I'll go sit with her. Maybe we can pick up where we left off. Maybe ...

"Ugh, no, he was a PBD."

PBD? What the hell is that?

"No," the tall blonde sighs. "Say it isn't so."

"Yup," Jessica confirms. "He's Pretty but Dumb. One hundred percent pretty dumb in my book."

"Did you have to shush him so you could admire the view without having to listen to him?"

Jessica shakes her head. "Short of putting a gag on him and taking off his shirt, it wasn't going to work."

I put my tray down and walk away without eating.

I shake my head to bring me back to the present.

"So what if I'm hiding?" Rachel challenges. "What's it to you?"

I carry the cutting board of chicken breasts over to the frying pan on the stove and gingerly put them in. "It's nothing to me. Nothing at all." How do I explain to Rachel that her sister putting me on this list did something to me? That I feel like I need to earn it or deserve it? I stay facing the stove for longer than I need to, trying to come up with the right words.

Rachel finally breaks the silence. "I don't feel like explaining it all right now. I'd need another bottle of wine. Got any wine?"

I turn around to face her. "I'm more of a beer or hard liquor guy myself. Plus, I've got a game tomorrow, so no alcohol for me."

She folds her arms over her chest, her mouth turning down into the most adorable little pout. "Party pooper."

"Catch me in the off-season. Right now, my job is the priority. Most likely, I only have a few seasons left in me. I'm not going to mess it up. Plus, once you're in your thirties, you seem to lose all ability to metabolize alcohol. It makes me feel like shit."

"Oh, I'm gonna feel like shit tomorrow. No doubt about it." Her head bobs up and down in an exaggerated motion. "But it's better to feel like shit from this than from my reality."

Fair point.

Her eyebrows knit together as if she's trying to do long division in her head. "What are you going to do after soccer?"

I refill her glass with water. She's definitely going to be hungover in the morning. "I have no idea," I say honestly. Usually I avoid this question but I doubt she'll remember this conversation.

She rests her chin in her hands. "Well, what did you want to be when you grew up? Other than a soccer player."

I flip the chicken, peek in on the vegetables, and then return to my side of the counter, facing Rachel. "I wanted to be a magician."

Rachel's eyelids are drooping. Her speech is slurred as she says, "If only you were, I could be your assistant in a sexy sequined costume."

As I start to reply, it becomes apparent she's fallen asleep. Quickly I race around to her, before her head can slip out of her hands and hit the granite countertop. I slide one arm around her back and the other beneath her thighs, pulling her close to my body. I pick her up and turn, surveying my place.

Now what do I do?

Maybe I should bring her home? I can get her to my SUV, and then I'll drive over to her apartment and—shit, I don't know what apartment she lives in. It's probably not great for my image to be walking around with a woman passed out, thrown over my shoulder. Some nosy neighbor would definitely call the cops on me for that. I don't need people thinking I'm a creeper who drugs women.

I could put her on the couch. That would be respectable, yet uncomfortable. My couch sucks. It looks great, but it feels like concrete. I could put her in my bed, which would be the chivalrous thing to do. But then where would I sleep?

Tomorrow is game day. I promised Coach that if I stayed at my own apartment, I'd obey the curfew and the sleep rules. It's literally my job to be in peak physical shape. I can't be stiff and sore, and that couch would absolutely wreck my back.

Maybe I can put her in my bed for now, and by the time I'm done eating, she'll wake up and then I can walk her home.

Except by the time I finish cooking dinner, take some video of it, eat it, and then stack my dishes in the sink, Rachel is still out, snoring very lightly. As gently as I can, I shake her shoulder. "Rachel, wake up." My voice is barely above a whisper. She doesn't move. I do it again, this time a little louder and a little more forcefully.

All she does is roll over, curling herself into a fetal position, her hands in fists, bent in toward her body. She looks so small in my king-size bed.

There's so much space left in the bed. I could sleep on the other side without disturbing her at all. Normally, I'd sleep in my boxers, but tonight, I change into gym shorts and a T-shirt. I lie down and roll to my side, my back to Rachel. If I were any closer to the side of the bed, I'd be on the floor.

I scroll on ClikClak with the volume so low I can barely hear it. While I normally scroll for an hour or two, I feel sleep coming to my body almost immediately. See? I'll be totally rested. Before I know it, my eyes are closing, and I'm out.

The hand shaking my shoulder is surprisingly strong. "Wake up. TJ. Tyler, wake up!" The hissing voice is surprisingly loud, too.

I don't know how long I've been asleep, but it hasn't been long enough. I push the hand away and pretend I didn't hear anything.

"TJ. Tyler!" Someone is shaking me again.

I open one eye. "What?" It's not even light out yet. "What time is it?"

"Um, it's a little after four."

"Okay, I'll talk to you after seven. I have a game. I need my sleep." I pull the pillow over my head and go back to sleep.

When I wake up to the sound of my alarm at seven—a much more reasonable hour—I find myself alone in the apartment. Rachel's gone.

That's disappointing.

I can't think about what this means until I'm properly caffeinated.

I start coffee in the pot—the one thing I know how to make—and pick up my phone to text Rachel.

Me: Sneaking off in the middle of the night? No note, no nothing?

Rachel: It was after 4.

Me: That's the middle of the night. You still could have left a note.

Rachel: The last note I received has thrown me for quite the loop. I don't want to do that to someone else.

Me: You can leave a note, as long as you don't die on me. That's easy. Next?

Rachel: What happened last night?

I smile, knowing I'm going to have a little fun with her.

Me: Let's just say number 9 is taken care of. <winking emoji>

I give it a minute to see her response. When there's nothing, I second-guess my attempt at humor. I'm certainly not the funny Doyle. I shouldn't try to be.

Me: TOTALLY kidding. You fell asleep at the kitchen counter. I put you in bed. I took the other side. Both of us were fully dressed, and there was enough room for 3 other people in between us.

Me: I only touched you to pick you up, over clothes. I swear.

Shit, shit, shit. Rachel has massive trust issues. I know that. I was the world's biggest idiot to even joke about something so delicate. I hit the call button. This isn't something I can do through text.

"Hello?"

"Rachel, you've got to believe me. I was only trying to be funny. I'm not funny. Joey's the funny one. It takes intelligence to be funny, and we all know I don't have that. I'm sorry. I ..." I falter, not knowing what to say next.

"TJ ... Tyler, I'm not upset." Her voice is quiet on the other end of the phone.

"You didn't answer back."

"I was texting someone else, trying to make plans for tonight. Sorry."

Someone else. Those words hit like a ball to the gut. Maybe she met someone at her new job. Maybe it's someone in her building. Maybe she's on Tinder.

It's none of my business. None at all.

"What are you doing tonight?" I can't help myself.

"Not sure yet. Things are still up in the air."

"Rach." There's more than a hint of desperation in my voice. "I'm sorry I made that joke about number nine. It wasn't funny."

I hear her sigh. "Richie certainly thought it was, including that on the list. We both swore—pinky-promised each other—that we wouldn't be like that."

"Like what? I mean, pinky promises are solemn business. I've sealed all my professional contracts that way."

She breathes out a laugh. "Handshakes and notarized signatures are so last year. Pinky promises are where it's at."

I sit down on my horribly uncomfortable couch and take a sip of my coffee. "Absolutely."

There's a pause on the line before Rachel continues. "Our mom didn't know the difference between sex and love. She thought if she slept with a guy, he'd love her. She did this—a lot. She was always looking for love. Or at least the love of a man. She had two daughters who adored her, but that wasn't enough."

That would explain number ten: Forgive Mom.

I couldn't have imagined what could be so bad that you wouldn't be on speaking terms with your own mother. I think of Ma, and how she'd go to the ends of the Earth for her boys. It hurts a little knowing Rachel didn't have that.

"So Richie and I promised each other that we'd value ourselves more than Mom valued herself. That we'd never confuse sex and love, and if we didn't think we could make that distinction, we'd steer clear until we could."

I don't know what to say to that. After a moment, I ask, "Why did she put it on the list then?"

"She never really figured out the difference either, but I think she wants me to. I think she wants me to be free and liberated and to be able to experience pleasure without getting all emotional."

Immediately, a mental image of Rachel lying naked underneath me, spread across my bed, in the throes of pleasure, emerges. It's a powerful enough suggestion that it's having a real-life effect on me.

Great.

"I'm not there yet. I'm not sure I'll ever be." Rachel laughs nervously. "But enough about me. What's up with you?"

Why'd she have to phrase it like that? If I'd been taking a sip of my coffee, no doubt, I'd have spit it across my living room. "Um, nothing. Just normal game-day prep. Light workout. Pregame fuel."

"Are all the games as exciting as the last one?"

I stand up and start pacing. As soon as I get off the phone, I'm going to take a long, cold shower, but she doesn't need to know that. "I thought you read a book during that game."

"I did, but there was a big fight and two people got thrown out. Does that normally happen?"

I explain to her what happened and why and how, no, that doesn't normally happen.

"So, will you be offended if I bring a book again?"

It takes me a minute to understand what she's saying. "Are you coming to the game tonight? I thought you were making plans?"

"Yeah, I was. With your mom. Apparently your brothers can't make it, so she offered me the ticket. So, like I said, will you be offended if I have an emergency book with me?"

"What's the emergency?"

Rachel giggles again. "Um, is it offensive to say boredom?"

It's my turn to laugh. "Yes, but it's probably because you don't understand the game. I'll explain it all to you, and then you'll find it interesting."

"I don't know about that, but you can try. I need to go back to sleep for a while. See you after the game?"

"See you after the game," I say as we disconnect.

She's coming to the game. That knowledge makes me happier than it should. I barely know this girl.

Yet it still makes me happy.

Now, about that shower.

CHAPTER 21: RACHEL

I have no idea what I'm doing!" I yell at the ceiling. "I don't even like soccer!"

That's true. But I do like spending time with TJ. And, for some reason that I cannot quite comprehend, he seems to like spending time with me.

So when his mother texted practically at dawn today and asked me to attend the game with them, I leapt at the opportunity. This is so unlike me, I must still be drunk.

Speaking of which, what was that? I can count on one hand the number of times in my life I've been that drunk. *And I went over to his place.*

If my head weren't already killing me, I'd slam it into the wall a few times to try to knock some sense into myself. My entire life is spiraling into some kind of chaos that I don't even recognize.

So why not go to another sporting event with thousands of people?

Then I remember why when I'm walking into the stadium. I don't do well in crowds. Everything feels like it's closing in on me, and it's hard to breathe. I try to tap into my five senses to ground me to prevent the panic from growing when I remember the ride up to the Doyles' house. In my head, I start mentally playing "I Gotta Feeling," and by the time I find Maureen and Tom at Will Call, my heart rate is almost a normal level. Almost.

I wish I could say that, because of my budding friendship with TJ, I enjoyed this game so much more than the first. I wish I could say that, but I don't make a habit of being a liar. It's still a sport that I don't understand, don't follow, and don't care to. I mean, of course I want TJ and his team to do well. To get more points or goals or whatever.

I really should learn about soccer so I can have a conversation with him about it.

"I can't believe I willingly went to a sporting event. Again!" I say through gritted teeth as I look up at the night sky.

Pretending to watch the game, my mind wanders, thinking about the other things on the list. Obviously there's no way I can accomplish them all, but maybe I can knock off one or two more. And then, maybe if I do, I'll feel settled again. I can put the list away and just get back to my routine. Or find a new routine is more like it.

A Google search tells me there's a casino in Connecticut about an hour and a half from here. I could drive down next weekend and play some slots. I glance up at the field to see TJ running, his muscular legs pumping fast.

Or I could fly to Vegas to watch TJ play again.

I lean over to Maureen. "Do you go to away games too?"

"Sometimes. We usually save it for the playoffs and postseason games."

"So, you're not going to Las Vegas next weekend?"

She shakes her head. "No, we're babysitting the girls. Joey has a gig and Amanda wants to join him for the weekend."

The thought that I'd be able to meet up with someone I knew almost made the trip seem possible. I try to picture what it'd be like. I'd truly be solo for the entire weekend. My heart starts to pound. Maybe I could still do it. All I need is a pep talk.

I can do solo. Hell, ever since Richie died, I've been solo.

Being alone isn't bad. It's not bad at all. Especially since there is no one there to upend my routine. If I step outside my comfort zone, it's when I'm good and ready and not a moment before. Just because, historically speaking, I've never been ready, doesn't mean I can't start now.

All in all, the last week hasn't been terrible. It was better than the previous week when I sat in my new apartment all by myself. How much of that has to do with new experiences, and how much has to do with TJ?

"You're coming with us for ice cream, right, dear?"

If I've learned anything this past week, it's when Maureen Doyle asks a question that ends in "right, dear," there's only one acceptable answer, and that's the statement she's already made. Man, what I wouldn't give to have the confidence that she has.

But as I look at her with her doting husband and grown sons who obviously adore her, it becomes quite evident that I'll never possess that level of confidence. Confidence is rooted in security.

At least I know I'm reliable. I can count on me, if no one else. I'd always thought I'd be able to count on Gram and Gramps. And Richie. They showed me.

"I can follow you. Same place as last time?" I search my memory for the name. Something about ugly dogs.

"No, this week, we're going to The Flannel Cow Creamery. It's right near Tyler's place."

"Oh, then it's right near me, too." I quickly type the name into Google Maps and find that it's within a mile of my apartment. Okay, so it's not super fancy, but the neighborhood—and my neighbor—seem to have some perks. "Wait, it says they're closed."

"Yes, they're staying open for us." She explains to me the deals they've made with many of the local places, including the cost.

"So the ice cream's on us tonight. Well, it's actually on Tyler. He says it's the very least he can do to repay us for all the support we've given him over the years."

A pang of guilt hits me square in the chest. What have I done to repay Gram and Gramps? I might be angry with them now, but they did a lot for Richie and me. The least I can do is call Gram to check in and let her know I'm doing okay. I've been texting her enough so that she doesn't call the police to do a wellness check. I'm not back to telling her the ins and outs of my day yet.

Also, how adorable is this whole ice cream thing?

If the women of ClikClak only knew that beneath the firmly chiseled abs and perfect aesthetic there was a momma's boy whose insides were as gushy as the Cookie Sundae I spied on the menu, he'd break the internet.

Maureen and Tom follow me to my place so I can drop my car off and ride with them. It always takes Tyler a while to get there, so this ate up some of the time. As I slide in their back seat, Maureen says, "My, this is very close to Tyler. How about that?"

"It's purely a coincidence. I moved in here about two weeks ago when my grandparents kicked me out." As soon as the words leave my mouth, I wish I could grab them and shove them back and swallow them. They are so dishonorable to the people my grandparents are. "What I mean is that I got a promotion, but it's down in Sharon at our brand-new satellite office. Gramps said he trusted only me to run it."

"That's impressive. And lucky for Tyler too, that you're so close." She's turned around, looking at me in between the seats, so it's easy to see when she winks at me. Winking must be a family trait.

Oh no, this cannot be happening. His mom thinks we're together. "No, no, no. That's not it. We're not … We're just friends. I'm not even sure you can call us friends. We're more like …" I struggle to find the words. "Proximity acquaintances," I say. Cripes, could I be any more lame?

Of course, it's not like there's an easy term to describe "I sought him out because my dead sister told me to and fate keeps putting me in his path and he's super, super hot but he's also super kind and if I did relationships—which I don't—I'd totally fall for him because he's nurturing, but then I worry that I'd only be there because he takes care of me and that's what I've been missing my whole life."

Proximity acquaintances it is.

"Sure, dear. If you say so."

TJ doesn't help the matter when he finally arrives and includes me in on the hugs he's giving out to his parents. This is the first time we've had our bodies pressed together. The split second I realize that I want to latch on and never let go, I pull back. I will not be developing feelings just because he's nice to me.

Tonight, he's different, though. Quiet. Sullen almost. I can't help but wonder if he's upset that I'm here. Or that neither of his brothers went to the game. There's very little conversation as we eat our ice cream. There's no laughing and joking, there's none of the boisterous yelling that I've come to associate with the Doyle family.

We're finished in record time, and TJ goes to pay the employee who stayed late for us. As we walk to the door,

Maureen says, "Tyler, you'll take Rachel home, right, dear?"

He nods without saying a word. His parents get in their car and drive away. The two of us are left standing in the parking lot. I look down at the ground and kick some gravel. "It's okay. I can walk. It's not that far."

TJ sighs, walking around to open the passenger side door. "Get in." His voice is low, practically a growl.

I slide into the seat and fasten my seat belt. I focus on my hands knotted tightly together in my lap. See? This is why I don't form romantic—or any—attachments. No matter how good I try to be, I always screw it up somehow. I'm a burden that's easier dropped off on the side of the road than carried.

Still, he's been kind to me. The very least I can do is return the favor. "Are you okay? You seem upset."

He slaps the steering wheel, making me jump. "Damn right I'm upset. We're so screwed now. Brandon Nix was our best scorer. The new kid's going to be good, someday, but he's no Brandon Nix. We were *this* close to winning it all last season. Now, I'm not sure we're going to win another game."

"You're upset about the game?" It makes sense. They didn't win.

"Yeah, I'm upset about the game. Losing sucks. I'm a sore loser." He turns in the driver's seat to look at me. We're parked in front of my building, the ride from the ice cream place taking all of three minutes. "What did you think I was upset about?"

I don't say anything.

"Rachel, what happened? What did you think I was upset about?" he repeats, his tone insistent.

"Me. That I went to your game. That I came with your parents for ice cream. That you have to bring me home." *That I exist and am a burden to you.*

He slams a finger into the ignition button so hard it makes me jump, turning the vehicle off. Then he rips off his seat belt and flings open his car door. I watch him stomp around the front of the SUV until he reaches my side, where he proceeds to rip my door open. "Get out," he says, that low growl back.

"TJ. Tyler, I'm sorry. I—" I'm so flustered I've lost all motor skills.

"Rachel, now. Get out of the car now."

With trembling hands, I finally manage to unbuckle my seat belt and slide out of the vehicle. TJ doesn't back up a single step, so we're standing face-to-face with mere inches in between us. "I need you to stop."

"Stop what?" I ask. But I know. Stop coming to his games. Stop inserting myself in his life. Stop—

"I need you to stop apologizing for taking up space. I need you to stop thinking that I don't want you around. First of all, if I didn't want you around, you wouldn't have passed the Ma Doyle vibe test. Second, I'm the one texting you most of the time. The fact that you even have my number says a lot. I ..." He scrubs a hand down the back of his head and cups his neck. "I don't have a lot of friends."

"I don't have a lot of friends either," I murmur.

"I know. But it seems like we're better together."

My mouth drops open into a little O. He can't mean what I think he means. Not *together* together.

"Which is why we are good friends. It's not putting friends out to give a friend a ride home. Friends help you hose down your nieces when they've rolled in shit. Friends take care of each other when they get black-out drunk, so just keep that in mind in the off-season, you're gonna owe me one. Friends don't apologize for supporting each other. If anything, I should be apologizing to you for making you sit through that terrible game."

Now is probably not the right time to tell him that all games, no matter the score, feel terrible to me. I really don't like sports. "I don't go to see you win or lose. I go to see you. To be there for you. And because your mom had a free ticket."

He grins. "Thank you for being honest with me."

"Thank you for the ride home."

"Thank you for being my friend." He leans in and hugs me. Not a romantic one. Oh no. This is the friend-est of friend hugs. If there were a trophy for winning the friend zone, I would be hoisting it above my head.

He breaks the hug and calls a good night as he heads back to the driver's side. I wave like an idiot while he pulls away. My head is still dazed as I walk up the stairs to my apartment, where I proceed to unlock the door, walk in, and fall face-first onto the couch.

I should be happy that he wants to be friends. I would be delusional to think that a man like him would date a girl like me.

But still, being friends is better than nothing, right?

CHAPTER 22: TJ

Friends?

I must have used that word seven times. I was overcompensating for being chicken shit. But I can't put into words how being with her makes me feel. It's abundantly clear I'm not her type. I don't think she has a type. You would have to put yourself out there to have a type. But if she had a type, he would not be a barely literate, dumb jock with no life plan.

She's definitely not my type. She reads books for fun, for Pete's sake. I bet she got straight A's in school. Nicky's type, maybe. But not mine.

Yet I find myself thinking about her at the most inopportune times. Like today during the game, when I spied her sitting next to my parents. Not so much as spied as I was looking for her. No book today.

Because I was looking for her, I missed a passed ball that led to the Thunder intercepting. They didn't score on it, but they could have. I'm disappointed in myself for not being more focused. And if I'm this distracted by her friendship, there's no way in hell I could be involved with her. It would be career suicide.

So I fight with myself not to text her as soon as I get home.

And when I wake up the next morning.

And the day after that.

And the day after that.

I feel like I'm crawling out of my skin. I must check my phone twenty-five times a day to see if she's texted me. Nothing.

By Wednesday, when we're flying from Boston to Las Vegas, I can think of little else. I'm barely making content, instead relying on recycled videos to keep my views up. Doomscrolling on ClikClak is not doing anything to keep my mind occupied. Not even the magic trick videos are keeping me interested.

I power down my phone and attempt to sleep for most of the six-hour flight. I swear, I can feel the Vegas heat before we deplane. Johnson, our athletic trainer, is shouting at us to hydrate.

I turn my phone on to see a string of text messages.

Rachel: Hi.

Rachel: Hypothetically speaking, where in Las Vegas do you play, and is there a hotel close by?

Rachel: Also hypothetically speaking, is it close enough to take a cab or an Uber?

Rachel: Hypothetically of course.

Rachel: I mean, I was just thinking about it. You know, like you said, flying by myself.

Rachel: It's a stupid idea. Forget I said anything.

Rachel: Hope the game goes better.

The timestamp reveals that she texted over the better part of two hours. She probably thinks I'm upset. Or that I don't want her to come out. Nothing could be further from the truth. Excitement races through my veins, right down to my hands, and I bobble the phone as I'm trying to type.

Before my phone can hit the floor, Xavier Henry shoots out his hand and grabs it.

"Nice catch. Thanks," I say as he hands it back to me.

He tilts his head. "You okay? You look a bit off."

"Yeah, fine. My friend is looking to fly out here for the game. It's good news."

"Ophelia's flying out, too. She's never been to Vegas and wanted to see it."

"Same with my friend." Then it occurs to me that I should respond to Rachel so she goes through with making the reservations.

Me: Sorry I didn't respond. I was on the plane out here, and I turned off my phone.

The response is immediate.

Rachel: It's okay. You don't have to make excuses. I won't come.

Me: I'm not making excuses. It's what happened. I want you to come. Did you get your flight yet?

I watch for the dots, but they're not there. She's not responding.

Me: Rachel, I'm sorry I didn't have my phone on. Please don't think it's anything personal. You coming out here was my bright idea in the first place. Think of all the things you could cross off your list in one weekend.

There's still no response as I've boarded the team bus, arrived at the hotel, and made it to my room. This trip, I'm rooming with Xavier Henry. He's not a bad bloke. He's one of the quieter and more reserved teammates. That's okay with me.

Rachel: Holy shit, flights are so cheap! Gas and tolls for road trips cost as much as a flight. Why didn't I know this?

My heart soars. She's doing this. She's living for her sister. For herself. Maybe a little bit for me too.

Me: I'm proud of you. Richie would be too. I can't wait for you to see Vegas.

And me.

She fills me in on her flight information, which arrives early Friday evening, and I let her know where I'm staying. I have no idea what the going rate for this place is. We continue texting about shuttles and Ubers and hotel reservations.

"You okay?" Xavier's question startles me. We're each sitting on our beds, propped up against the headboard, legs outstretched.

"Yeah, why?"

"You're grinning like a love-sodden fool."

I drop my phone in my lap, as if it would give me away. "My friend Rachel is flying out for the game. I was just helping her figure out the hotel and transportation. She's never flown before, so she's worried about the logistics."

"Right." Xavier nods. "Like I said, my wife is coming out for the game too on Friday. Maybe Ophelia can help her? Perhaps they could bunk up. Ophelia can get a bit squirrely if left on her own for too long."

I shake my head. "I wouldn't want to put her out like that."

"I don't know you all that well, aside from what you post on social media," Xavier says. "You actually seem rather private. I don't see a lot of women in your stories, so I'd think if you have someone coming to the game, then she's special."

I never thought about that. It does seem pretty obvious. I nod. "Yes. She's a special friend."

"My wife, Ophelia, is the biggest die-hard romantic on the planet. In fact, it's the reason we got together in the first place."

I remember Ophelia's viral video heard round the world in which she went to surprise her boyfriend—not Henry, but an ex—only to find him cheating on her. ClikClak had a field day. But she met Henry, and they got married, and they appear to be living happily ever after.

"So, if there's even a hint of a movie-esque storyline," Henry continues, "she'll be all in and be happy to assist in whatever way possible. But be warned that your story might end up in one of her romance novels."

"Oh, it's not like that. Rachel's ..." I don't know what to say. There is zero chance that Rachel is looking for anything more than friendship. Math isn't my jam, but a zero chance isn't good. "Rachel's a friend," I say lamely.

"The lady doth protest too much, methinks," Henry mumbles.

"Yeah, well, she's not in a place for anything more. So even if I wanted to, which I'm not saying I do, it's not the right time for her."

"If you say so. Give me her number so I can have Ophelia reach out."

I do, and then I send Rachel a text to let her know what Xavier's offered. I wouldn't want her upset that I'm giving her information to strangers.

I get that the time is not right to pursue anything with Rachel. It's not like it's the right time for me, either. I need to be focused on the Buzzards right now. At best, my career has five years left. That's the best. The next injury could be the end. Then what? Callaghan Entay is in the process of pulling back and transitioning to more of a coaching position, working alongside the goalkeeper coach. Undoubtedly, when a position becomes open with another team, Entay will retire fully from playing to be on staff.

I'm not coaching material, nor am I suited for the front office. I should probably figure out what exactly I am suited for. "Henry," I ask, "what's your plan after soccer?"

"I've no plan other than football."

That's not helpful. "Did you go to college?"

"Nah, I was recruited to the BFL right from secondary school. Played in the Bristol Bombers organization instead of going to uni. How 'bout you?"

I shrug. "I have a psychology degree that qualifies me to do absolutely nothing. I barely graduated. I need to figure out what my next step is, but I'm lost."

"I know I can always go home to my family business."

"Something with birds?" I vaguely remember that when Xavier played in the BFL, his nickname was "Birdman." That was in the ESPN article that broke and caused a huge scandal. It's also how he was able to terminate his contract with the Baltimore Terrors and move to the Buzzards. We made out on that deal.

"Spot on. We run a birds of prey rescue and rehab. We're all falconers. I could always do that, except for one small problem."

"What? You'd have to move back to England?"

"Nah, that's not a prob. The main issue is that Ophelia is absolutely terrified of birds." He looks over at me. "Can you help her?"

I frown. "No, why?"

"Didn't you say you had a psychology degree?"

I laugh. "I remember that a fear of birds is ornithophobia, but that's about it." I surprise myself by pulling that word out of the deep recesses of my brain. "I'm not a clinical psychologist or anything useful like that. Sorry."

"No worries. Couldn't hurt to ask."

We sit there in silence for a few minutes, scrolling away on our phones. I still need to make some content. It's so much harder on the road because I'm never alone.

"Hey Henry, wanna make a video with me?"

"Hard pass. I don't dance."

"Me neither. I was thinking we could ..." Shit. What was I thinking? "Maybe talk about life plans. Like what comes after soccer. You could talk about the birds. None of us are going to stay in the USSL forever."

Holy shit. This is brilliant. I can interview everyone on the team. I can interview opposing teammates. I could even interview the referees. Their career can last a little longer, but the physical training is just as grueling.

I'm not cut out to be a broadcaster or color commentator, but I know social media. I can totally do this.

CHAPTER 23: RACHEL

This is all happening so fast. My heart is pounding so hard, I feel as if it's going to burst right through my chest wall and flop onto the floor. I put my hands over it and press, as if that's going to keep it inside my body.

"Are you okay?" Gramps is staring straight ahead, but he has the peripheral vision of a hawk. He knows I don't like to be looked at when I'm starting to panic. I called him to tell him I needed a few days off. Considering I was supposed to start at the new office yesterday, this was a big ask.

My flabbers were gasted when he not only told me to take as much time as I needed but offered to drive me to the airport as well. It turned out that the remodeling in the new building still wasn't finished, so I would have continued working remotely anyway. That makes so much more sense than this overt gesture of caring. Gramps loves me, but he's not the best at showing it. I think he would have been much more content to love us in the distant-grandfather role than as the surrogate-father role he was forced to play.

"I'm fine," I answer. It's the standard response, whether it's true or not.

"What are your plans when you land?"

"One of the other player's wife is also flying in. She's on a different flight, but she's going to wait for me. We're rooming together."

"Too bad you weren't on the same flight. I'd feel better if you weren't by yourself," Gramps says. This is about as much as he'll express his concern. He's worried about me. I've given him plenty of reasons over the years to be.

"Well, Richie said I had to fly by myself, so it wouldn't count otherwise. I've got some Xanax, movies to stream, a coloring book, and music. And I have a friend waiting for me when I get off the plane."

It's a stretch, calling Ophelia Henry a friend, but if it gives Gramps a little peace of mind, then it's worth the exaggeration. She seems lovely through text messages. Unbeknownst to me, I'd been following her on ClikClak ever since her #romanticsurprise video. She seems to like books too, so I'm sure we'll find plenty to talk about.

I'm actually looking forward to getting out to Vegas so I can meet her. Not as much as I'm looking forward to seeing TJ again. Even if it's only from the stands, it'll be enough. It's not like this trip means anything. He was suggesting it in a friendly way. Like friends do. For friends. Because he said I'm his friend.

Message received loud and clear.

Let the record state that the reason I got a haircut before this trip was not to impress TJ Doyle in any way, shape, or form. I was simply about fourteen months overdue. My hair feels—and looks—infinitely better in the chin-length bob I now sport. Like I said, I'm probably not even going to see him in person during this trip.

He'd mentioned parasailing on Lake Mead, but I think that was just to inform me that it was available for me to do on my own. He probably has a rider in his contract that he can't do anything dangerous during the season. I don't know for a fact that parasailing *is* dangerous, but it sure seems like it to me.

One year, Richie and I drove down to Myrtle Beach for our spring break. We were lying there, baking in the South Carolina sunshine, when a guy came right up to us and said, "Ladies, let me take you up. Only one dollar." He pointed to a boat zooming through the water with a large parachute attached to the back. I squinted and saw that there was a person under the parachute, at least 100 feet above the surface of the water.

We were poor college kids, so one dollar anything seemed intriguing. He had our attention, but I had a feeling that it was too good to be true. I said, "It's really only one dollar?"

He nodded. "Yup. That's it. One dollar to go up. Forty-nine to come back down."

I bet Richie was thinking about that when she put it on her list. I wish we'd spent the hundred dollars back then to be able to do it together.

The flight was not as bad as I thought it was going to be. I didn't love the taking off or the landing bit, but once we were at cruising altitude, it just felt like a car ride with less scenery. Apparently, flying is not one of the things that makes me anxious. Who could have predicted that one?

One smutty pirate-vampire romance book—*Stolen Stars* by Lia Finn—later, and we're touching down on the tarmac. The person next to me was binge-watching Grey's

Anatomy. I will still never forgive the creators of that show for killing off Denny Duquette. Even if I wanted to rewatch it, the whole Izzy-cancer-brain-tumor storyline hits too close to home. Why couldn't Richie have had a Dr. McDreamy to take her cancer out before it claimed her life? Because life is not like a TV show or a book or anything else in which we're guaranteed a happy ending.

God, I wish we were.

The first thing that greets me when I set foot in the terminal is slot machines. The second is Ophelia Henry. I recognize her from her videos. She's about my height, with her long dark hair in braids, wispy bangs dancing across her forehead.

"Are you Ophelia?"

"Who wants to know?" Her tone is wary.

"I'm Rachel. Rachel Cramer."

Immediately, the suspicion disappears from her face as she breaks into a wide grin. "Hi! You made good time. I didn't expect you for a while longer."

I don't know how to respond to that. It wasn't like I was flying the plane and made good route choices, like when you pick the faster lane of the two-lane drive-through at McDonald's. "Thank you for waiting for me. I've never flown before, and this is all a bit … overwhelming." The massive high ceilings with chrome and windows. The buzz of the people. The clanging and beeping of the slot machines.

Dear God, there are a lot of slot machines.

"If you played the slots here, would you consider it going to a casino?" I ask Ophelia as we begin to walk, following the signs to baggage claim and transportation.

She thinks for a minute. "No, the casinos are an experience themselves. You have to go to at least one. At least that's what everyone says." She whispers in my ear.

"I've never actually been here, but I've been researching it like crazy. Ask me anything. I've been studying."

"How far are they from here?"

"A little over a mile. Look there." She points at a window. "That's the Strip. The stadium is about three miles or so from here."

She does seem to know her stuff.

"Oh wow. It's all so close. I saw the mountains and the desert as we were coming in. Not gonna lie, I was a little nervous we were gonna hit a mountain. It's all so …"

"Hot and brown. That's the best way to describe Las Vegas. Hot and brown."

I consult my phone to check the temperature. It's 99 degrees. "It's mid-September, and it's almost a hundred degrees!"

"But it's a dry heat. So is the inside of your oven, but no one seems to make that comparison. Make sure you drink a lot. You'll get dehydrated quickly." She holds up a large water bottle that's half-empty. "That's what happened to me when we went to Phoenix, and the weather's pretty much the same here. Hot as Hades, and guaranteed to give you a headache if you get dehydrated."

"Thanks again for helping me out with this." We're crossing the second-floor bridge into the parking garage where our Uber is waiting. "I don't think I ever would have figured this out."

"You get used to it. I don't travel as much as some of the WAGs do, but in general, they're a friendly group. I really like Hannah LaRosa. She's with Callaghan Entay, the goalie. We've worked together a few times, and she's cool. You'll like her too. We'll hang out soon."

The whirlwind of words coming from her mouth has my brain spinning. I try to process it all. "What's a WAG?"

"Wives and girlfriends of players. I don't care for the term myself, but we are a group, and it helps to stick together. This life—being the partner to a professional soccer player—can be lonely, and the group helps with some of that."

"I'm not a WAG. We're just friends."

"Friends"—she makes air quotes with her fingers—"don't go to these lengths on a moment's notice."

Our baggage stowed in the trunk, we slide into the back seat of the Uber. "I'm not really here for the game. TJ and I are friends, and I'll naturally support him, but I have some stuff to do. Including flying by myself and going to a casino. The timing just worked well."

Ophelia raises an eyebrow. "I meant TJ orchestrating this, having me help you out, and staying in my room. Of course, I'm happy to, because you know I love a romantic storyline."

Her viral ClikClak was proof of that. She was trying for one of those grand romantic gestures. Turns out her boyfriend was a turd, and the video exposed him.

If I try to deny it again, it will not help my case. Instead, I change the subject. "So what do you do when you're traveling with the team?"

"I wouldn't call it traveling with the team. They are fairly locked down. This is one trip where they have almost a full day before they fly out, though, so we might get to see the boys a little."

"Is that why you're here?"

"Nah, I need to do some research for my next book. It's a mob romance, set in Vegas. This is a work trip for me."

"Oh, you're a writer? I thought you just liked to read books."

"That too. I write spicy romance under the name Lia Finn."

"I JUST READ YOUR BOOK!" My voice is way too loud for the confines of the car, but Ophelia doesn't seem to mind. "I don't even like smutty books, but I'd seen it so much that I thought I would give it a try. It made the flight go by so fast! My sister would have loved it."

"Would you believe someone accused me of using Xavier for research for that book and said I was only with him to get my storyline? It blew up and nearly cost me everything."

With that, we both break into laughter. The over-the-top, side-splitting, tear-inducing laughter that such a ridiculous notion can bring. Wiping the tears away, I say, "Is Xavier immortal? I've seen him outside in the sun, so that kind of discounts the vampire theory, unless you've created a new breed of sun-tolerant vampires. Something more plausible than sparkling like diamonds in the light."

We can't contain our laughter as we get out of the Uber and check into the hotel. There's something about Ophelia that immediately puts me at ease. For the first time since Richie's diagnosis, the huge crushing weight that's been threatening to suffocate me lessens.

We're at the W, which is where the Buzzards are staying as well. It's easily one of the swankiest places I've ever visited, with its gold trim and marble everything. This is a very long way from Cramer-Romero Associates Pumps. Surely they're going to kick me out for being an impostor.

That doesn't even touch the fact that I'm not a WAG.

"The guys have a curfew, but they usually have a nice meal in one of the restaurants. I'll find out which one, and we can go there too." Her fingers fly over her phone, texting away. "Okay, apparently all the restaurants they are considering are over at Mandalay Bay." She squints at the phone. "Xavier says they're deciding between Mediterranean and steak." She looks up. "Ten bucks says they're going to do Mexican. It's what they usually do."

Ophelia checks her phone and laughs. "Maybe I should gamble a little while I'm here. They're going to the Border

Grill. Oh wait, Xavier has a message for you from TJ. He says there's a casino in Mandalay Bay, right where the restaurant is, so you can hit that after. I'm here to see the casinos too, so what do you say?"

Ophelia talks so fast that it makes my head spin. She keeps going. "Let's get changed. Do you want to shower? I might shower. Like a quick rinse off. Not my hair or anything. I feel like I should dress up a little. Do you want to dress up a little? We don't have to if you don't want to. It'd be nice to look cute for our men, even if they can only see us from across the room."

My face falls. "I didn't bring anything cute. I don't own anything cute. I don't go anywhere where I need to look cute."

"You can wear one of my outfits. I totally overpacked because I couldn't decide what I wanted to wear, so I just threw a bunch of stuff in my bag." She is rummaging through her suitcase, pulling out all her clothes. Every minute or so, she stops to look at me, her eyes narrowing. "Okay, I think this one is for you."

She hands me a black sheath minidress that has a large white flounce around the top of the chest. "It's got your cute vibe, but also a little sexy too."

"What are you going to wear?" I hold the dress she's handed me, already in love with it.

"I'm feeling sassy tonight. I'm gonna wear this one." Ophelia holds up a red boatneck skater dress. "I want my husband to be chomping at the bit to get home to me after the game."

Getting ready feels like it did when Richie and I were in high school. We never did anything wild or crazy. Most of the time, doing our hair and makeup was the most fun part of the night. We've got music blasting, and when The Black Eyed Peas come on, I immediately pick up my phone to text TJ.

Me: Ophelia and I are getting ready for a night on the Vegas Strip.

I snap a picture of my leg extended, showing the short hem of my dress, a fair amount of skin, and Ophelia's strappy black heels.

TJ: You're killing me, Smalls.

"What's that grin about?" Ophelia exits the bathroom in a cloud of hairspray and perfume. She looks fantastic.

"Nothing. I just sent a picture to TJ."

A sly grin takes over her face. "Right. Your friend, TJ."

I pick up my purse. "Yup. He's just a friend. He told me so himself. That's how he sees me. That's it. That's all."

As Ophelia pulls open the door, she says, "Well, let's go make him eat those words."

I am totally okay with that.

CHAPTER 24: TJ

This girl is messing with my head. I don't think she means to, but what the hell was that picture?

It's not as if I haven't seen her legs before. She was wearing shorts the first two times I saw her. And a dress when we went to my parents. I am well aware of what her bare legs look like. So why have I looked at that picture practically continually since she sent it?

Why did she send it to me?

And what does the rest of her look like?

Is she really hitting the Strip? Is Ophelia going to be her wingman—er, -woman? Is she going to cross off number nine?

Me: Be careful. Stay together. Don't go off with any strangers.

What is she doing? I was stupid to suggest she come out here. She's totally out of her element. At least she has Ophelia.

"Um, Henry, how would you describe Ophelia's street smarts?"

Xavier is buttoning up his shirt. He stops, mid-button. "You're joking, right? You're asking about the Ophelia who flew to Baltimore to surprise her wanker ex, only to find out he was cheating on her, but she had to have all of ClikClak tell her that because she didn't realize it herself, even though it was blatantly obvious to all of us at the party. The woman who asked the internet to set her up on blind dates, but the way she worded it made them think she was a prostitute for her day job, which she's not, by the way. The woman who got drunk and proposed to me over FaceTime so I could keep my citizenship without ever researching to see if that was a valid thing, which, it turns out, it's not. That Ophelia?"

I stare at him. This is not helping.

Me: Maybe you want to have a quiet little dinner and turn in early.

It sounds lame, even to me, but desperate times call for desperate measures.

Rachel: I didn't come all this way to stay in. Ophelia and I are on a mission.

My gut churns reading this. What kind of trouble are they going to get into? I can skip dinner and head to where they're going. I've never broken curfew before, but tonight might be the night I start. Sure, there'd be a hefty fine. Dad would lose his shit over that. And maybe I'd be subject to disciplinary action that'd have me sitting out a game or two.

At this point in my career, missing games is the kiss of death. Anyone they bring in to replace me will be younger. If he has a good game or two, that could be it for me.

I can't break curfew.

I clear my throat. "Um, are you at all worried about the girls going out on the town by themselves?"

He shakes his head. "Ophelia is doing research for a book. She wants to go to a casino and see what the atmosphere is like there. I'm sure she'll be fine." We lock gazes, both knowing that could not be further from the truth.

"What do we do?"

Breaking curfew is not an option for either of us, and we both know it.

"I'll text Ophelia and tell her not to be impulsive," Henry says, pulling out his phone. "Alright, it's done. Now let's go to dinner. I'm famished."

As we get in the elevator, I ask, "Does telling Ophelia not to do something usually work?"

"Hardly ever, but one can always hope."

We've decided to eat at the Mexican place in Mandalay Bay, which adjoins the W. I can't tell if the gnawing in my stomach is from hunger or worry. It was just a week ago that Rachel fell asleep at my kitchen counter after drinking a bottle of wine. What would happen to her if she did that out here?

Henry and I lounge on a large banquette, waiting for other teammates to join us. We're the first here. I don't think this has ever happened to me before. Usually, I'm strolling in as people are ordering drinks. This gives me plenty of time to peruse the menu and think about Rachel. I'm so lost in thought that I barely notice when someone slides into the seat opposite me.

"Is this seat taken?"

My head whips up so fast I'm likely to give myself whiplash. "Rachel? What—" That's all I get out, my mouth going bone dry as I look at her. She's cut her hair. It now falls in loose waves around her face to just below her chin. It shows off her features, especially those hot fudge eyes. She's in a short black dress, with the legs she teased me with earlier appearing long and lean. Impressive on her short frame.

Her shoes can only be described as fuck me shoes.

I didn't know she owned shoes like that.

She cannot go out on the town wearing those shoes.

Rachel sees me staring at them, and she poses, popping one foot up and then the other.

"I ... I like your shoes," I finally manage to croak out. In my brain, I picture her leaving them on. And nothing else.

"Thanks. They're Ophelia's." She does the little model-y poses again. Jesus, she's adorable and sexy all at the same time.

"You should keep them. Or get a pair just like them. Or lots of pairs just like them. Your legs look ..." I don't know how to finish that sentence. Or why those words are even leaving my mouth in the first place.

She is sitting sideways on the chair. She leans back, as if on a swing, extending her legs out in front of her, crossing one on top of the other. "I mean, if you want to see sexy, you should see the rubber boots I wear when I'm filming for work." She lowers her legs and leans toward me over the table in one smooth movement. "Now those are hot," she whispers.

I lean in, matching her position. "I bet you can talk real dirty in those."

"Trust me, those boots have seen some shit."

I can't help it. I burst out laughing. The head tipped back, hands on belly kind of laugh. Ophelia sits to Rachel's right, directly across from Xavier, who's sitting next to me.

"What'd I miss?" Ophelia says.

Rachel lifts her foot again. "TJ was just admiring my footwear. Naturally, I told him they're yours."

While I wouldn't say I'm a connoisseur of women's footwear, even I understand certain labels mean a certain price tag. There's no telltale red sole from that fancy French brand. The name of Jimmy Choo isn't stamped on the bottom. In theory, there's nothing special about these heels, other than the feet they're currently on.

"Ophelia, I'll give you $500 for those shoes." The words are out of my mouth before I can stop them.

"I didn't know you had a thing for women's shoes, Doyle," Xavier says dryly. "I'm not sure how to break it to you, but they might be just a smidge too small. Not to mention, I think they look better on Rachel."

I meet Rachel's gaze. "They're not for me. They're for her."

I have no idea where any of this is coming from. It's as if I'm powerless to stop the words tumbling out of my mouth.

"Are you drunk?" Rachel raises an eyebrow.

I shake my head. "Can't drink before a game."

"Yeah, well, I think I'm gonna need a drink." She flags down the waitress and orders two Cadillac margaritas.

"Two?" She cannot hold her liquor well enough to handle two margaritas.

"One is for Ophelia. We discussed it on the way down."

"Oh, what else did you discuss?" Curiosity is definitely going to kill me where Rachel is concerned.

"Our game plan for tonight. We're going to take the tram to the Luxor to go to the casino. I'm crossing two things off in one day! My list is going to be thirty percent done, which is about twenty-nine more percents than I ever thought I'd accomplish."

Her words are like a bucket of ice water dumped over my head. She's not here for me. She's not interested in me. She's trying to fulfill her sister's dying wishes. That's it. I just happen to be one of those dying wishes.

Of course, there's no other reason. I know my worth. I just need to keep reminding myself of that. Just like she's not wearing the shoes and dress for me. She's wearing them for everyone else.

"Hey," Rachel says, placing her hand on mine. "Are you okay?"

Her eyes are full of hope and light, something I haven't seen before. The sadness has gone away, at least for now. I'm not going to do anything to bring her down.

"Yeah, just wishing I could have a margarita too. What looks good to you?" I pick up the menu to hide from her, at least for a moment. "Henry, what are you going to get?" Many of our other team members have started to arrive. Ophelia stands up. "Well, we're going to head to our table and let you boys enjoy your pregame bonding experience."

Rachel joins her, margarita sloshing over the side of the glass. I wonder what she'd do if I licked it off her hand. Probably run screaming into the void. I look back at the menu, but the words aren't making much sense.

Finally, I glance up to see Rachel peering down at me, her eyebrows knit in confusion. "Are you sure you're okay?"

"I'm fine. You have a good time tonight."

"Um, okay. I will." And with that, Rachel and Ophelia leave to go to their table across the restaurant. I can see them throughout dinner, talking and laughing. This is just what Rachel needs. A good time. She needs to be carefree. She needs to live life, not just for her sister, but for herself.

"Doyle. DOYLE!" Antonio Caster-Naples is yelling my name from the other end of the table.

"What?"

"Who's your friend over there?" He nods toward Rachel. "You haven't gone ClikClak official with anyone yet. What's the story?"

I shrug, trying to appear casual. "There's no story. There's nothing to announce. We're just friends."

"Does she know that? Didn't I see her with your family at the last home game?"

Why is he paying attention to these things?

Antonio needs to drop this. "She's noneya," I say.

"What's noneya?"

"None ya damn business," I all but growl. I glance over at her again. She's watching me. When she sees me looking, she gives a little wave. That's the margarita talking. I can tell already.

Antonio says, "Well, maybe you can introduce me to your *friend* then. She's—"

"Enough, Antonio," Landon Stubbs interjects. "Leave Doyle alone."

"Aw, but it's fun to watch him get all riled up."

I ignore him and turn to Xavier. "Henry, I know the girls are planning on a night on the town, but do you think they're okay doing that? Rachel seems a little tipsy already, and she's never been here before. I'm worr—"

"You've got your knickers in a knot over nothing. The girls will be fine. Ophelia's going to ring me as soon as they're back in their room. She won't let anything happen to Rachel. Don't worry."

I wish it were as easy as that.

CHAPTER 25: RACHEL

Vegas is … exhausting.

I'm going to need at least a week to recover from all this stimulation. It's bright and loud everywhere. I can practically feel my blood pressure rising with all those fluorescent lights. Except for meeting Ophelia and getting to see TJ at the restaurant for those few minutes, I wish I hadn't come.

I'm trying not to think about the way he was looking at my legs and shoes, and how he offered Ophelia $500 so I could keep them. What was that all about? Maybe he has a secret shoe fetish.

Ophelia and I lasted all of fifteen minutes in the Luxor Casino before we decided to blow that off for dessert at the Milk Bar.

It was much more our speed.

It also made Ophelia decide to write a romance about dueling ice cream companies with an enemies-to-lovers trope rather than a mob romance. I tell her about the Doyle family post-game ice cream tradition, thinking it would be a great subplot in her story.

"What do you think he meant about the shoes?" I finally ask her, kicking the torture devices off my feet. These were not meant for walking or standing.

"Exactly what you think it means."

"But he just wants to be my friend."

Ophelia pauses, taking a long sip from her milkshake. "Says who?"

"Says him. He said it like ten times. It was the friend zone to end all friend zones. Unequivocally. Trust me, he doesn't think of me as anything other than a friend."

"Trust me, he does. He looked at you the way you're looking at that ice cream sundae in front of you. I know romance. I know lust and longing, and boy does he have it bad for you."

That … that doesn't seem right. "Are you sure we were looking at the same thing? Tyler? TJ Doyle. Are you sure he wasn't just looking at the chips and salsa? Those were pretty damn good. I myself have experienced significant lust and longing over chips and salsa before."

Ophelia insists over and over that she's right. She offers to text Xavier and ask him, but I don't want to be the fodder for gossip. And as much as I'd like to believe what Ophelia says, I don't think I can trust her judgment. I've seen her ClikClaks.

The next day we've got time to kill before the game. I want to text TJ and tell him about our wild night that wasn't. He's got to be focused on the team. I can't be distracting him.

Since the casino life isn't for us, I suggest we find a bookstore. It's much more on brand for both of us. We take an Uber to one called The Writer's Block. It looks so cute. This time, the bright neon lights don't bother me one bit. There is stuff crammed into every single corner, with vines and plants and birds hanging from every conceivable surface. The owners must have a serious obsession with birds. There are plush birds and taxidermized birds and animatronic birds and sculptures of birds. It's so cool.

I could spend all day in here.

That is, until I realize Ophelia isn't behind me. I look all over but can't find her. Where is she? What if someone grabbed her? My heart begins to pound as my neck begins to sweat. With shaking hands, I pull out my phone to call her.

Ophelia: I'm outside whenever you're ready.

I rush to the door. It's about a million degrees, and Ophelia's standing out here, sweating. She looks pale, though, instead of flushed from the heat like I'd expect her to be.

"Are you okay?"

She shakes her head. I know that headshake. I know that expression. I've felt it a million times.

"Sit down," I order, taking charge like Gram would for me. We both sit on the step. Jesus, it's hot out here. "You know, the first time TJ ever drove me anywhere, I started to have a panic attack in his car. I didn't even have to tell him what was going on. He just knew. I've been having panic attacks since I was a kid. Everyone tells me to calm down."

"As if it were that easy." Ophelia laughs.

"Yeah, well, I have a new secret hack, thanks to Tyler."

"Tyler?"

"TJ," I correct. "He told me that friends call him Tyler."

She bumps her shoulder into mine. "Right. Friends. So what is this hack your friend told you?"

I tell her the secret of "I Gotta Feeling," and by the end, we're laughing. She looks more relaxed. "You better? Wanna go inside? It's hotter than Satan's balls out here."

The color drains from her face again as she shakes her head. "I can't go in there. Too many birds."

"Birds?"

Ophelia nods. "I hate birds. I'm irrationally afraid of them." This is the worst place in the world for her, short of an aviary.

I stand up. "Alrighty then. Who am I to judge anyone's irrational fear? I have random fears for no reason. At least you know what your trigger is. Let's get outta here and into someplace with A/C."

A few minutes later, we're in the Uber on the way back to the hotel when I spot a sign through the window. "Pull over!" I yell. "I need to get out here." I have no idea how far we are from the hotel, but I need to stop.

Ophelia looks at me. "Are you okay?"

I nod. "Yes. I ... I have to do this. I'll understand if you don't want to come with me, but I have to."

Ophelia considers for a split second. "Okay, I'm in. I like not being the crazy, impulsive friend for once."

I have to laugh. I'm not crazy. I'm not impulsive. That was Richie, not me. All this is for her and her list.

We step out of the Uber and shade our eyes, looking up at the sign. Las Vegas Shooting Center.

"I, uh, didn't pick you for a gun person."

"Oh, I'm totally not. I didn't know my sister was either, but she left it on her list for me to do." I pull the list out of my pocket and hand it over to Ophelia to read. Somehow, sharing this part is getting easier. "Are you a gun person?"

She shakes her head. "A massage gun is about it. But," Ophelia says, "it could be useful for a book, I guess."

"Wanna do this with me?" Somehow, the thought of doing the things on the list with someone rather than by myself makes them seem not nearly as daunting.

Maybe, just maybe, that was Richie's point to begin with.

"You really need to get a jersey with TJ's name on it. That way, the other WAGs know who you're with." Ophelia's wearing a shirt that says "Henry" across the back. Considering it's her name too, it's not that much of a stretch for her.

"We're just friends. And if he wants me to wear his jersey, he's going to have to give me one." I probably should have some Boston Buzzards gear at this point. It's the third game in a row I'm attending. Instead, I'm wearing a plain black tank top.

"Here, wear this. I have tons of them." Ophelia tosses me a Buzzards T-shirt. "Until you get your own."

"I can't wait to tell him about the gun range. He's going to be proud of me. No one even had to force me to do it."

I even looked into parasailing, but it doesn't seem feasible on this trip. Places in the Northeast are closed for the season, so I'll either have to travel again or wait until next summer. I can probably wait. I've made enough progress on the list for now. Richie should be happy with it.

Not to mention that I still won't be able to accomplish everything, so I really shouldn't stress, even though stressing is what I do best.

Tonight, the game is much more enjoyable sitting with Ophelia than I'm sure it would be by myself. I'm not even tempted to pull out my book. It goes by quickly, with a win for the good guys, and before I know it, Ophelia's rushing out of the stadium to go back to the hotel to get ready to go out with her husband.

I'll just settle in and read. But wait, what if they want to come back to our room? Where would that leave me? I get that Vegas doesn't sleep, but I don't want to be wandering around a strange city all by myself all night.

I wonder what TJ plans to do? What's his normal post-game routine? Ice cream is out. Or is it? I pull out my phone and find several options, the best rated being the Ghirardelli at The LINQ. According to Google, its full name is The LINQ Hotel + Experience. Everything here in Vegas seems to be an experience.

"Are you going to wait for Xavier here or back at the hotel?" I ask Ophelia.

"They ride the team bus, so I'll meet him back at the hotel," she informs me.

Makes sense since they took the bus there to begin with. Ophelia and I walked over, and we'll do the same on the return journey as well. Even with the fifteen-minute walk, we still beat the team back to the W.

"Let's go wait by their room rather than in the lobby. We don't want to draw any more attention than we have to," Ophelia suggests.

TJ and Xavier are staying a few floors above us. We don't have to wait outside their room long before the elevator dings and the guys step off. Normally, by the time TJ meets up with his family for post-game ice cream, he's in shorts and a T-shirt, his slides, and a backwards baseball cap. Tonight, he's in suit mode.

I have to fan myself, he's so damn hot.

"Friends. Sure. Friends," Ophelia mutters before running down the hall and launching herself at her husband. He scoops her up, her legs wrapping tightly around his waist, and they don't even bother coming up for air as he pushes open his door. It slams shut behind them, leaving TJ—Tyler—and me standing there, looking at each other.

He said friends call him Tyler.

"Guess I'm not going in," Tyler says, running a hand through his damp hair. "This is what sucks about away games."

"You're not going in, because we're going out." I pull out my phone and order an Uber.

"Where are we going?" he asks as he follows me toward the elevator.

"First, we're going to drop your stuff in my room, and then you're going to trust me."

He gives me a salute. "Aye aye, Cap'n."

He takes off his suitcoat—damn—and rolls up the sleeves of his black dress shirt. I finally understand the obsession that my book heroines have with forearms. Yowzas. I do a quick change out of Ophelia's Boston Buzzards T-shirt into my plain black tank top. I still look way underdressed compared to him, but I don't have many other options with me. I packed for comfort, not couture.

We don't say anything until we're in the back of the car. This is what's nice about Ubers. I can surprise him with the destination.

"So, how was your day?" he asks. "Get up to any trouble?"

"Miraculously, no, other than the bookstore incident."

"How did you get into trouble at a bookstore?"

I tell him about Ophelia's fear of birds and the decor, and the place we randomly picked.

Tyler starts laughing. "Yeah, Henry told me all about her fear. Did you know his family are—" He searches for the word. "—falconers? They rescue and rehabilitate birds of prey. And Ophelia can't handle birds at all!"

"Opposites attract, I guess," I say, realizing that Ophelia and Xavier are not the only ones feeling something for someone who is so different on paper. Yeah, that's more than just a book trope. But what if he doesn't feel the same way?

Rather than say something stupid about being attracted to each other, I continue to tell him about my other research. "I did find out that parasailing is out. When

I googled it, places come up, but then they don't seem like they actually have parasailing, just other water sports. I looked some more, and I can do it close to home. There are places off the Cape or in Rhode Island, but I have to wait until next summer. All the New England places are closed until Memorial Day."

"You're taking this list seriously, then? Like actually trying to do it all?" he asks.

I shrug. "Maybe? I don't know. It feels good when I get to cross things off. Like some of me is being put back together. Slowly." Parts I didn't even know were broken, but so obviously are.

The Uber pulls to a stop, and we get out, standing in front of the Ghirardelli Ice Cream & Chocolate Shop. "Let's get our ice cream."

His face breaks into a wide grin, those blue eyes sparkling. He cocks his head slightly, as if trying to figure out a puzzle.

"What?" I ask, unsure if this was the right thing to do. Maybe he's tired and wants to rest.

"You ... this ..." He gestures at the store. "It's amazing. That you thought of this."

I shrug. "It's what you do after games, right? I love that you and your family have this tradition."

Tyler leans in and whispers in my ear, "And I love that you planned this for me. *Love.*"

With his hot breath on my face, my knees go weak and my insides turn into mush, like the bottom of an ice cream sundae that's been melted with hot fudge. Yes, he's definitely the hot fudge to my ice cream.

Even though it's almost ten p.m., the area is still bustling. This place is open until one a.m. on Saturdays. After ordering, Tyler and I take our sundaes to go so we can check out the neighborhood. There's a comedy club next door, and we're just in time to slide into the ten o'clock show.

Tyler leans over. "I'm doing this for research for my brother. One of these days, he'll be headlining in Jimmy Kimmel's club. I just know it."

"You're pretty proud of him, aren't you?"

He nods, his face still close to mine. "Yeah. What he does takes so much brains and courage. You have to be very smart to be that funny. Most people think humor is easy, but it's not. Both my brothers are super smart."

The opening act takes the stage, and Tyler sits back, relaxing into his chair. This is not the first time he's made comments about his intelligence—or lack thereof, especially compared to his brothers. I watch him throughout the act. He's laughing, his face totally relaxed for once. There's no tension around his mouth. His eyes aren't sad and lost. If I thought he was attractive on the soccer field, or wearing a suit, or in those gray sweatpants, it has nothing on laughing Tyler Doyle. This is a side of him I don't see very often. This isn't the soccer player. It's not the ClikClak sensation. It's him, in his most genuine form.

My heart clenches. It would be easy to fall in love with him. So easy. So stupid, but so easy.

After the show, we're walking out when Tyler stops abruptly. So abruptly that I run into him, my front slamming into his back. His hands clasp around mine, holding me to him. I peek around his arm to see what has his attention. It's a poster for a magician who performs at this club every day.

"Do you want to see a magic show? Maybe we can get tickets. What time is your flight tomorrow? I'm flying back on the red-eye. Monday morning is going to be hell."

I look it up, and there's not a show that will work with our schedule. Dammit.

His trance is broken, and Tyler starts to walk again, keeping a tight grip on one of my hands. We're holding hands. Walking around Vegas, just casually holding hands, like it's no big deal. I don't know that I've held hands with a boy since I was in junior high. Dating has never been my thing.

Now, I'm walking around Las Vegas holding hands with a professional soccer player.

How did I get here?

Richie. My sister manifested this for me. Maybe she didn't have a crush on TJ Doyle. Maybe she picked him for *me*. Maybe that's why meeting him was number eight on the list, and then number nine is to have a one-night stand. She knew I wasn't impulsive, so she appealed to my organized side by giving me a to-do list.

She didn't want me to be alone. She knew, with our history, there'd be no way I'd ever open myself up to anyone. She knew I'd never be able to trust anyone not to leave me, like she was doing. But still, she didn't want me to be alone.

Dammit, tonight I'm not going to be.

CHAPTER 26: TJ

I like touching Rachel. She hasn't pushed me away yet. I hope she never does.

"Do you want to keep walking or should we grab a cab?" I ask. We've been wandering around Las Vegas Boulevard. We're right in front of the Fountains of Bellagio. "How far is it?" I should lean in and kiss her here. This would be a romantic place to do it.

She lets my hand drop to consult her phone. "Almost two miles from here. Let's grab a cab so we can get back quicker. I know you're a super-fit pro-athlete and all, but I'm not, and I'm tired."

Right. She's ready to be done with me. "Sure." I flag down a cab. We slide in, and she keeps shifting in her seat until her thigh is pressing into mine. We're so close that I either need to put my arm around her or my hand on her thigh. I go for option A, stretching my arm across the back of the seat.

"Are you having fun out here?" I ask, practically murmuring into her hair. I really like her hair. Did I tell her that yet? I should have told her that already. I should say something sly and smooth and clever. Instead, I say, "I like your hair."

I am an idiot. But then, by some miracle, I swear she leans in a little closer. There's no mistaking it. She's leaning her head on my chest. Maybe she's tired. I want to remember this feeling of Rachel in my arms forever. With my free hand, I lift my phone and snap a picture.

"You're not putting that on your ClikClak or Insta, are you?" she asks.

"You don't want me to?"

"I'm probably not right for your image."

I sit up a little straighter, pulling away to look at her. "What do you mean by that?"

"Oh, come on. Look at you. Look at me. You're in Vegas. You should be club hopping with someone in a painted-on minidress and stilettos, not me in my Walmart tank top and jorts."

"Jorts? What the hell are jorts? Are they some kind of fancy sneaker?" I look at her feet. She's wearing flip-flops. No wonder she doesn't want to walk another two miles. Her feet have got to be killing her.

"Do I look like a fancy sneaker girl to you? Jorts are jean shorts. And you prove my point. You don't even know what jorts are. You have a brand. I'm not it. Don't tank your aesthetics by putting a picture of me up, especially not when I look like this."

I don't know what to say. Of course, she would think that I care about stuff like that. It's all my social media is. The perfect image. I've worked hard to keep it that way.

I know, it's a dick thing to say, but it is how my social media looks. What I have to decide is if I want to keep it that way. I need to come up with a plan.

I choose my words carefully, because the last thing I want to do is hurt Rachel's feelings. "I understand what you're saying. I—" I break off because whatever I say will come out wrong. "I ... I just wanted a picture of us. To remember the night. To remember what a good time I had."

Like I'll ever forget it.

She took me out for ice cream after my game. And paid.

I will never be able to eat hot fudge again without thinking about her.

Once back at the hotel, Rachel marches across the lobby, straight toward the elevator. I put my hand on her shoulder to make her pause. "Wanna get a drink?" I ask. "There's a bar on the sixty-fourth floor. We can look out over all of Vegas."

She looks unsure.

"I'm not sure if I can get into my room yet," I say, hoping the desperation to continue my night with her isn't evident.

We step into the elevator. "I'm not the glitzy rooftop bar type." Her gaze drops to her feet.

"Aw, come on. You only live once."

She freezes for a moment. Then she says, "How 'bout we have a drink in my room?" She looks at me hopefully.

Since I'm only doing this to prolong my time with her, I nod. "Sounds good." I pull out my phone and order a bottle of prosecco from room service to be delivered to her room. "Drinks are on the way."

There's no hint of Ophelia when we get back to the room. This is good. The longer she spends with her husband, the longer I get to stay with Rachel. The room is virtually identical to ours, with a view of the stadium we played in. Was that really just a few hours ago? The after-game high is starting to wear off. Not to mention the time difference. Three days is not enough to adjust my body to the Pacific Time Zone. I feel like it's 3 a.m.

I might just ask Rachel if I can crash on the couch in her room.

"Um, so Ophelia just texted and asked me if you can spend the night here." Rachel is practically pacing around the room. She's picking up and folding clothes, straightening the pen and pad of paper on the desk. If I didn't know better, I'd think she was nervous.

"Yeah, I can take the couch. It's pretty late. I was eyeing it anyway."

She laughs, a high-pitched, squeaky kind of laugh. Definitely a nervous laugh. "Don't be ridiculous. You can sleep in the bed. My bed. The other is Ophelia's bed, and she already slept in it." She pauses to hang up the dress she wore last night. "I mean, it's not like we haven't shared a bed before."

There's a knock on the door. Rachel rushes to answer it, but I'm close behind with the tip.

"You got us an entire bottle of champagne?"

I want to tell her that it's not champagne, but I don't want to correct her. I never want to do anything that makes her feel small. I'm familiar enough with that feeling.

"I thought we could celebrate crossing two things off your list." I pop open the bottle and pour the fizzing drink into the flutes provided.

"Three things. I've done three things on this trip."

I try to remember what's on the list, other than flying and going to a casino. She said parasailing was on hold. "Did you appear on stage in a sexy sequined costume and I missed it?" My mind is flashing back to her legs in those shoes.

She shakes her head.

"I'm guessing there wasn't a moose on the loose in downtown Vegas."

Another shake of the head.

"Any emergency baby deliveries?"

She laughs. "Um, no."

A pit forms in my gut. The prosecco tastes like sawdust. I swallow the whole glass in one gulp and immediately pour myself another, forcing myself to choke it down. There's only one other thing on that list that she could have done out here.

The thought of some guy—other than me—putting his hands on her makes me want to punch someone. Go full-on Brandon Nix on them.

"Wanna see?" She's scrolling on her phone.

No. Yes. No.

I need to see the guy she had a one-night stand with. I have to see who she chose. What's her type? I can't picture her with anyone that's not me. I have no idea what to expect when she hands me her phone.

I definitely don't expect to see a ClikClak from Ophelia's account, with the two of them in protective eyewear, noise-canceling headphones, and holding rifles.

"Ophelia and I went to the gun range down the street. I did it! I fired a gun."

"You fired a gun?" Relief rushes through my entire body. Even the proof in front of my eyes is not enough to slow the racing beat of my heart.

"It's one more thing off the list."

I'm finally able to meet her gaze again. Now it's her turn to take a long drink. "Congratulations," I manage, trying not to stare at her slender throat as she swallows. Knowing that she wasn't with someone else should be calming me down, but it's not. I'm still spiraling.

Quietly, she says, "So, you know that whole 'what happens in Vegas stays in Vegas' thing? Do you believe that's true?"

Where is she going with this? If she's going to confide in me, I need her to know she can trust me. "With the right people, it is." I start to move toward her, to assure her, but she's doing that pacing and fussing thing again. "You can trust me," I say, my voice soft.

Rachel nods a few times, almost as if she's trying to give herself a pep talk.

I move closer to her, taking both her hands in mine. "Rach, you can trust me. Just tell me what it is."

She inhales a shaky breath before pulling her hands from mine. "It's about number nine."

Here it comes. I promised I would be someone she can trust. I'll do that for her, no matter how much I'm going to hate hearing the words coming out of her mouth. I nod and hope my face looks open and inviting. Trustworthy.

Rachel turns toward the window, her arms tightly hugging her body. Every second that ticks by is agony. "So, what happens in Vegas stays in Vegas."

"Yeah." Where is she going with this?

"And we're friends, right?"

I nod again. I want to kick myself for ever telling her that.

"Can you be my friend tonight and help a friend out?"

"Anything you need." Thoughts whiz and whir through my brain with the catastrophic possibilities of what she is about to tell me. Are brain tumors hereditary? Is she dying like her sister?

Rachel sucks in a deep breath and exhales slowly. "I think Richie was onto something. She knew how broken I was. Am. She knows trust isn't something I do easily. It's why she put number nine on the list. She doesn't think I can do a relationship, which I probably can't. But she didn't want me to miss out on the—*other stuff*—like she did. She wanted me to have my cake and eat it, too."

I nod, unsure of what else to do. I have no idea what she's trying to say.

"I know we're friends. You made that clear. I don't have any expectations other than friends. I really don't. But tonight, I want my cake."

"We just had ice cream, but I can see if room service—"

Rachel takes a hesitant step toward me. "TJ." Her voice turns soft. "Tyler, I want you to be my cake. Just for tonight. Be my one-night stand. I promise, I'll never ask you for anything again. But I trust you. Be my cake."

I close the distance between us in two steps. Cupping her jaw with both my hands, I hold her face, staring into those chocolate eyes for just a split second before I put my lips on hers.

Her eyes grow wide for a moment, and then her lids flutter shut. She exhales into me, her hands holding onto my wrists. It's as if she's afraid I'm going to let go of her. As our lips and tongues and breath mingle, she relaxes, pressing her body into mine. Her hands reach into my hair, pulling it into her fists.

"Rachel," I pant, breaking our kiss for a moment, "are you sure?"

She nods, gazing deep into my eyes. "I've never done this with another person. I know you'll be kind."

Oh shit. She's a virgin. I should have guessed that but leave it to me to miss the cues. "Then this means a lot."

This is a big responsibility. I'm honored she even considered me to fulfill this role in her life.

She shakes her head. "I promise it doesn't. I don't want the pressure of thinking this is love. Or that it means anything. I know it doesn't."

"Rachel, of course you mean something to me."

She takes a step back. "I know. We're friends. I'm only asking you for more tonight. Tomorrow, we forget it ever happened."

I shake my head. "That's not how it works."

She raises an eyebrow. "So you can stand here and tell me every person you've ever slept with? Details. Names. Faces. Places. Positions."

My mind immediately goes blank. "Uhhhh ..."

"You'll be able to forget me, too. I promise. I ... I just need this." She looks at me, her eyes pleading. "Please?"

Because I will never possess the kind of courage it takes to do what she's doing—to ask what she's asking—I let her believe the lie.

I let her believe that I'll be able to forget about her after tonight.

CHAPTER 27: RACHEL

I lied to Tyler. I told him we could forget all about it after it happened. I'll never be able to forget him. But he doesn't have to know.

He did me a favor. A kindness.

A wonderful, surprisingly pleasurable kindness.

"Is it always like that?" My legs feel like rubber. I don't think I could get up and walk, even if I needed to.

Tyler lies next to me, sweaty and panting himself. "No."

No? What does he mean by no? Is no a good thing or a bad thing? I don't expect to have rocked his world, because I had virtually no idea what I was doing.

Not gonna lie, everything I needed to know, I learned from romance novels. Suddenly, I'm grateful to my sister for making me read all those spicy books out loud to her. Hell, I'm grateful to my sister for a number of reasons right now, but mostly because of the orgasm I had.

It's different when it's with another person.

It's so much better.

I'm determined not to let his words crush me. I prop up on one elbow, clutching the top of the sheet around my chest, and lean over to give him a quick kiss. "Well, I'm sorry for you, but thank you from me. I have nothing to compare it to, so I think it was fantastic. I really didn't expect to enjoy myself, if you know what I mean."

Tyler smiles. "There was no way you were going to get through your one-night stand without enjoying yourself." Then he rolls out of bed and heads to the bathroom, his fantastic naked buttocks on display. Seriously, I could bounce a quarter off of those.

It'd probably be out of line to ask.

Though almost everything I've done since I met him has been out of line.

Alone in bed for a moment, I have to remind myself it was just sex. It was just sex. *It was just sex*. I promised him it would be just that. He did enough for me.

I can't go and do something stupid like fall in love with him.

That's what my mother would do. She'd mistake kindness for love. Then she'd hang all her hopes and dreams on someone who just wanted a good time. No, I can leave it as just a good time.

I pull the hotel robe over my shoulders and tie the sash before wandering over to the bathroom door. Knocking lightly, I say, "Do you want to get some breakfast?"

He opens the door. He's fully dressed. I hadn't even noticed him picking up his clothes from the floor where he'd discarded them last night. "Yeah, sure. I want to go back to my room and get my stuff packed up first, if that's okay."

"Yeah, probably a good idea. I should shower and pack, too. I think checkout is eleven."

"Okay. Meet you in the lobby then?"

I nod. Tyler leans in and kisses me. It's slow at first, but it quickly deepens. It's definitely not a quick good-bye peck. I can feel his mouth smiling against mine. "That was just a friend kiss. See you in a few."

With that, he's gone. I place my hands on my lips to see if they feel any different. They're a little swollen, perhaps. Quickly, I run to the mirror. Do I look different?

My face is flushed. My hair is a mess. I have a hickey on my chest, just below my collarbone. He gave me a hickey!

I'm in the bathroom putting myself back together when Ophelia comes back. "Hope it wasn't too much of an inconvenience having TJ crash here."

It's a good thing I've got my toothbrush stuck in my mouth so she can't scrutinize my expression. "It's fine. We got ice cream and went to a comedy show. Did you know his brother's a comedian? Has a Netflix special and everything."

Distract, distract, distract.

"I think we're gonna get some brunch as soon as we're all packed. Did you and Xavier eat yet?"

"No, can we join you?"

Several series of text messages follow, and before we know it, we're a party of twelve having the brunch buffet at The Wynn. Normally, that many people would be too much for me. Today, I'm counting on the crowd to help me sit there without things being weird between Tyler and me.

I just need a few minutes to remember how to act around him. To be able to be in the same room and not think about his lips on my breasts and his hands *there*. For as long as I live, no matter how hard I try, I don't think I'll ever be able to forget what he felt like inside me.

And no matter how many times I tell myself that it was only a one-night stand, my brain is hijacking the conversation by dreaming about seeing him again, hanging out with him, and sleeping with him again. Most definitely that.

I 100 percent understand my mother. Promising herself she won't get attached and then letting herself down immediately. The only difference is that I don't have two little kids. She has spent her whole life chasing love that she didn't deserve.

Guess this apple didn't fall far from the tree.

Once in the lobby, Tyler immediately starts introducing me to his teammates. One name after another. Maliq. Merriweather. Andy. Crew. I smile and shake hands, knowing I'll never remember who's who. It's easier when they have their names and numbers on their backs, but I guess they can't wear their jerseys everywhere.

Would be helpful though.

The guys have arranged for several cars to pick us up. Ophelia and I check our bags with the concierge and follow the Buzzards out. The two of us end up crammed in the back seat together. Tyler's not even in this car with me.

Okay, that's fine. He's not blowing me off. He knows I'm with Ophelia, and I'm fine with that. Friends wouldn't care about such a trivial detail. Nor would they care when they don't get to sit together at brunch. There are a lot of people. We're all friends here.

This is not a rejection. At least that's what I keep telling myself. If I say it enough, I might start to believe it.

"So, you're friends with Ophelia?" the guy sitting to my right says. I think his name is Crew. Ophelia's on my left, so I can see why he'd think that. "Um, yeah. I mean, we roomed together."

I don't know what else to say to him. I don't want to get into why I'm on this trip to begin with. Most people wouldn't understand. They'd think it's lame and stupid. Desperate even. Maybe that's what Tyler thinks of me this morning.

I should have known better than to ask him for a pity screw.

Also, now I know why one-night stands are a bad idea. No matter how much you tell yourself you're not going to catch feelings, it starts to happen. Not for everyone. Probably not for a lot of people. Not for Tyler. But for someone like me. Someone who has always wanted unconditional love and acceptance.

Someone who has never deserved it.

I didn't anticipate what the physical aspect of it would do. How I'd turn to mush in his hands. How I'd part my legs and take him in and never want to let him go. My brain chemistry isn't the greatest to begin with, and now my hormones are definitely messing things up even more.

But I won't break my promise to him.

Plus, if it were anything more, it wouldn't be a one-night stand, and I wouldn't be able to cross it off the list. I'm not going through all of this for nothing.

Speaking of which, that sort of makes me feel bad for Richie. I mean, I feel terrible for her a lot of the time, with her being dead and all. But it's really a shame that she never got to have the pleasure I had last night. Her two minutes of fumbling with Jason Flemming in the back of his car was a dismal experience. I will grant her her honorary virginity back.

It's also a shame she never got to come to Vegas. It truly is a sight to behold. Especially this buffet. There is so much food, I hardly know where to begin. I'm standing there, holding my plate, when Tyler steps up beside me. I know it's him before I even hear his voice. "Don't forget to leave room for dessert. This is a place where you can have your cake and eat it, too."

I glance up at him. If we were in a romance novel, the look he's giving me would best be described as a smolder. I never knew what that was until now. Now the image is seared into my brain. Jesus, my knees threaten to buckle right then and there, and my girl parts are panting and fanning themselves.

I also now officially know what a panty-dropper is. Merriam-Webster should have a picture of TJ Doyle as he looks right now.

"Friends don't talk about cake," I remind him. "Friends forget about the cake and move on to brownies. Or cookies. Or chocolate pudding."

"Chocolate pudding? On a buffet?" He wrinkles his nose.

I look around at the massive selection of food. There's an Asian station, a Mexican station, a seafood station, carving stations, as well as traditional breakfast offerings. "Well, my grandparents were big fans of Golden Corral and Old Country Buffet when we were little. Those buffets always had chocolate pudding on them. I'm not so sure this is in the same league."

"Trust me, you're still in Vegas. There are many more decadent things to find on this buffet than chocolate pudding."

My eyelids flutter closed for a second. This is going to be harder than I thought. Not just making sure my pants still zip after I'm done here, but making sure my pants stay on around him. Not flirting with Tyler. Not touching him. Not wanting what we had last night. Again.

I promised him, though. Just because no one's ever been able to keep a promise to me doesn't mean I won't keep mine to him. I'm going to be better. I'll keep my word.

I head back to the table with my first selection of food—eggs Benedict, a pancake, and a loaded Tater Tot. Gramps, a true connoisseur of the buffet, has drilled his mantra of "take all you want, but eat all you take" into my head. However, being at an all-you-can-eat buffet with professional athletes is quite mind-blowing. They put Gramps to shame. Even that stodgy old man would be impressed. I take some pictures so he doesn't think I'm making things up.

An hour later, I'm so full I can barely move. I'm not the only one. Most of us around the table are groaning and rubbing our bellies. I don't think I'm ever going to eat again.

Tyler stands up. Crew says, "Jeez Doyle, you're not going back for more, are you?"

"One more thing." Tyler disappears for a moment before returning with what has to be his sixth plate. On it sits a lone piece of chocolate cake with ganache and sprinkles. I can't stop staring at it and then him.

"How do you have room for that?" one of his teammates asks.

Without breaking eye contact with me, Tyler scoops up a piece with his fork, shoves it into his mouth, and then slowly drags the fork back out. He licks his lips and smiles. "I just wanted to have my cake and eat it too."

Reflexively, I cross my legs under the table, squeezing my thighs together. Holy shit, what does he think he's doing to me?

It's going to be hard enough continually replaying every kiss, every touch, every secret moment we had. How am I ever going to go back to being friends when he's doing stuff like that?

CHAPTER 28: TJ

The lie I told her keeps swishing around my brain. Okay, it wasn't a *lie* exactly. It was more of an intentional misleading. When she asked if it was always like that, I told her no. I saw it flash across her face that she thought I meant I hadn't enjoyed myself.

I let her believe that.

I let her believe that every touch of her smooth, soft skin was not going to stay seared on my fingertips forever. That's my cross to bear. I knew going in she couldn't give me more. I don't deserve more.

Yet I couldn't help but tease her at brunch, and for the few hours afterward when we walked around the Strip, taking in the sights. I couldn't stop touching her. A brush of the arms here. My hand on the small of her back there. All too soon, I have to report back to meet up with the team, while Ophelia and Rachel are on their own to get to the airport. We're flying back on different airlines out of different terminals from the girls, which sucks. I would have loved to spend that overnight flight with Rachel leaning against me. Instead, she's waiting in Terminal One, while I'm a mile away in Terminal Three.

I'm playing with fire, and we all know how that turns out. I'm going to have to be more careful. I just need to put some space between us. The duration of our flights won't be long enough, but it'll be a good start. I'm glad Rachel and Ophelia ended up on the same flight. Rachel shouldn't be alone after last night.

Last night.

It was a mistake. A huge mistake. I'd one hundred percent do it again in an instant.

It would have been better to never know what she tastes like, what she feels like, than to know I can never have her again. Even if she wanted more, which I know she doesn't, what do I have to offer her? A career that could be over at any moment? No other appreciable skills beyond looking pretty for the camera? I don't even know how to take care of myself.

Rachel needs—no, deserves—someone who can take care of her, like my dad takes care of my mom, and how my mom takes care of us.

The only thing I could offer her is loyalty, but that seems weak, considering my only source of income would be from taking my clothes off for other women to ogle my body. Somehow, that doesn't seem so loyal.

So friends it is. It's going to be hell. It's going to be torture. It's going to be my reality. I'm the one stupid enough to catch feelings for her. It won't be the first time in my life that I have to pay for my stupidity. It won't be the last either.

See what I mean about Rachel deserving better?

This trip has completely and totally messed with my head. My brain hurts from thinking so hard, trying to find an answer that will be right for everyone. How I'm going to support myself after my soccer career. How I'm going to make my parents proud. How I'm ever going to be enough for Rachel.

Sitting at the gate, waiting for our plane, I stare at the phone in my hand, as if it'll provide me with some magic answers. ClikClak, with its wealth of knowledge, does not have any solutions. Crew Benequista drops into the chair next to me.

"Waiting blows," he says. "I hate this part."

I glance over at him. This is his first away game with the Buzzards. "This's got to be nicer travel than what you had in the reserves."

"Oh, yeah. This is a lot better. But I wish we didn't have to waste so much time traveling. Like, we're here in Vegas for four days, but we only got to party one night. This part sucks."

"Yeah, well, you get used to it. The final two rounds of the playoffs are here in Vegas, so if we can get our shit together, maybe you'll get some of your Vegas partying in then."

"Were the playoffs awesome last year?"

Jesus, he's like an exuberant puppy dog with boundless energy. "How old are you?"

"I'm twenty."

Christ, I knew he was young, but I had no idea how young. "You're not old enough to party. You can't even go to the casinos. And the playoffs sucked last year because we lost."

In every national championship game, one team goes home a winner, but one goes home a loser. We were on the big L side.

"But you got there, man. We're gonna avenge it this year. This is our year. I just know it."

Oh, the unbridled optimism of youth. "Yeah, well, you're gonna have to step it up then. Brandon Nix was our leading scorer. You've got big cleats to fill. So it's on you to pick up the slack if you even wanna make it out of the wild-card round."

His eyes narrow as he nods. "I know. I'm working on it. I've been following some of your training videos to do in my downtime."

My training videos? "Dude, those are thirst traps for the ladies. They're not meant to guide you."

Crew shrugs. "Maybe. Maybe not. I've picked up a few different exercises. Or different ways to combine things for a more efficient workout. I like the way you explain what you're doing. Helps me know what I should be feeling. You ever think of being a personal trainer?"

I have to laugh at that one. "Nah, I just know what I've been taught over the years. There's no big secret."

"I hope you're right, and I hope I figure it out soon, so we can have a shot at it this year. I hear Entay's retiring, so this year might be his last shot."

I've heard the rumors about Callaghan retiring as well. CC has been getting more time in goal since the Global Games, so it's probably not as much of a rumor as it is an inevitability. It's yet another reminder that I need to figure out what I'm going to do with myself when my soccer days are over.

If I can figure out what I want to be when I grow up, then maybe, just maybe, I'd be in a position to be able to date Rachel. I have to get my life together before I could even consider asking her to take a chance on me.

In the meantime, I've got to keep feeding the algorithm that is my current cash cow. Hopping up, I swipe open the app. "Hey guys, let's make a video." There's a collective groan. "All I'm gonna do is ask you who on the team is the ..." I search my brain for something—anything—that will get views and laughs. "For who has the best pregame playlist."

By the time I'm done interviewing my teammates, the consensus is that Merriweather Hayes has the best pregame playlist. Maliq Miller got an honorable mention, and Andy Bracer was voted to have the lamest playlist. We board the plane, and I spend a large chunk of the flight editing the video. I should be trying to sleep like most of my teammates are doing, but there's something fulfilling about taking raw footage and turning it into a polished video.

Not bad multitasking while cruising at 40,000 feet above the country.

We arrive, and while I'd like to wait for Rachel, the bus isn't going to wait for me. I'll call her as soon as I get home. She should be on the ground by then. I wonder what her arrangements are for getting home.

I should have asked her. I should have made sure she was okay. That she was taken care of. As soon as I get on the bus, I'll text her.

Except the minute I'm on the bus, fatigue sets in, weighing my eyelids down like sandbags. One second later, we're pulling into the parking lot where our cars have been for the better part of the week. Even though everyone is talking and jostling me, I can barely keep my eyes open long enough to stand up. I struggle to my feet and shuffle down the aisle.

I have never felt so tired in all my life.

"Doyle!"

I can't even figure out who's yelling my name. I feel drunk or drugged or something.

Coach Janssen shakes my shoulder. "Doyle? You alright?"

I nod, my eyes threatening to close again. "A little tired."

"You sleep on the flight?" he asks. "Don't tell me you didn't."

The time changes are hard enough on our bodies. We're still practicing and training. We need sleep. I committed a cardinal sin by not sleeping on my flight. "I was stupid, I know. I got involved in a project."

Coach calls over one of the training staff to drive me home. I'd argue, but I'm too tired. I don't remember getting home. I don't remember walking into my place. I remember nothing until I awake with a start in the fading evening light.

My watch tells me it's almost six p.m. I feel like I went on a bender last night. All I did was stay up for way too long after a night of barely any sleep because of Rachel.

Rachel.

I fumble for my phone, but it's dead. Shit. My bags are sitting neatly next to my door. I have no recollection of carrying them in. Probably because I didn't, according to the note on my counter. Apparently, Berat brought me home. My car is still at the facility. He didn't want me panicking when I couldn't find it.

I feel like a moron. How could I have been so stupid as to stay up for that entire flight? Just so I could do what? Make a stupid video? Because I wanted to try something new? Because I wanted to make content that didn't involve me stripping down?

My phone has enough juice to power on. There are no missed calls or texts from Rachel. My mom, yes. She always wants to know if I got in okay. But nothing from Rachel.

I can't believe that after everything, she wouldn't at least text me.

The first text goes to Ma, who responds with a string of texts, using all shouty caps, dressing me down for worrying her like that. She finally stops her rant with a threat to pick me up from all my games and travel to make sure I get home safely.

Thirty-two years old, and my mom is still treating me like I'm twelve.

She means well. She loves me, and this is how she shows it. I'm lucky to have her. Some people don't have caring mothers in their lives. People like Rachel. I can't even imagine what that does to a person.

I can't hold out anymore. I'm texting her.

Me: *You get in okay? I got in trouble for not texting my mom when I landed. I didn't sleep on the flight back, so I passed out on the bus. One of the trainers had to drive me home.*

I wait. Nothing.

Me: *Please tell me you're okay.*

Me: *Rach?*

Okay, now I'm starting to feel like my mom, panicking that she's not okay. Pacing around my apartment does nothing to make me feel more calm. Neither does incessantly checking my phone to see that she hasn't yet responded.

I can go over to her place and see if she's there. Except I don't know what apartment she's in. What kind of friend am I?

I could go over and be like that guy from that movie who holds a boom box above his head and plays music until she comes out. Chicks seem to dig that.

Minutes tick by. No response. Then it's an hour. Then it's two hours. I'm going out of my mind. I haven't eaten since the snacks on the plane. My body doesn't know if it's day or night. I certainly haven't worked out today. None of that matters.

All I can do is worry that she's not okay. I send a text to Xavier to see if Ophelia made it back home. She did.

Shit. Shit. Shit.

Out of desperation, I look up Oh Crap on ClikClak. There haven't been any posts today. I hit the bio and follow the links to their website. There's an emergency after-hours number. I startle when the voice is Rachel's, only to realize it's a recording.

"Thank you for calling Cramer-Romero Associates Pumps. You have reached the after-hours emergency line. This is for true emergencies only. If you are having a true emergency, please leave your name and number, and someone will get back to you within the hour. If it is not an emergency—in other words, if you don't have sewage backing up into your house—please call again during normal business hours."

"Hi, this is Tyler—TJ—Doyle. I'm, uh, a friend of Rachel's. I'm her neighbor, too. Um, well, we were just out in Vegas together. Not together-together, but she was there to see me play a game. Anyway, I haven't been able to reach her since I got back, and now I'm worried she didn't make it home. So, um, have you heard from her? Can someone let me know if she's okay? Please?"

As soon as I disconnect, I feel like an absolute moron. Who calls the family business and leaves a message like that?

CHAPTER 29: RACHEL

R achel, I need you to check the emergency line."
Gramps never calls me, so when he does, I know something's wrong. "What's wrong?" I jump up off my couch, where I've been in an alternating state of reading and sleeping for the better part of the evening.

Jet lag sucks.

My phone has been on "Do Not Disturb," and the only reason Gramps's call made it through is because I have three numbers that bypass that setting. Only two will ever ring my phone again.

"A call came in, and we need you to handle it."

"How am I supposed to handle it? You want me to call the guys and assemble a crew? Do you want me to video it? Why is it such an emergency? Are you sure—"

"Jesus, Rachel, just listen to the damn message." Gramps disconnects.

He didn't have to be so snippy.

I call our number and then press the prompts that lead me to the mailbox. I've got a yellow legal pad and pen ready to write down details, as well as my laptop opened up. I'm ready to work.

The minute I hear Tyler's panicked voice, the pen drops from my hand. I replay the message. And then I replay it again. I want to save it forever.

Or I could, you know, just call him back.

Indeed, there is a string of missed calls and text messages from Tyler. Whoops.

I dial his number.

"Rachel! Are you okay?" His voice is full of panic.

"Yeah, I'm fine. I hadn't turned my notifications and ringer back on."

"I'm so sorry I didn't check in sooner. I stayed up the entire flight back working on editing videos, and then I crashed. Like, I was so out of it. I woke up, and I couldn't get a hold of you, and I didn't know if you were safe—"

"TJ. Tyler, stop. Take a breath. I'm fine. I get it. That flight was brutal." I want to mention that we didn't get much sleep the night before either, but I promised him it would stay in Vegas. I won't even mention it. He doesn't need to know I've been obsessing about our time together. I made a promise to him, and I'm going to keep it. "What do you mean you didn't sleep?"

"I'm an idiot. Everyone's already told me that."

"No, you're not. I wish you would stop saying that. You say it a lot." For a man with so much physical perfection, he's awfully hard on himself.

"I speak the truth. Dumb jock here. Never pretended to be anything else."

I wish we were having this conversation in person so I could hug him. I could ask him to come over, but I don't want him to think I'm clingy and trying to manipulate him.

"Why do you say that?" I have to know what's made him like this. His family is perfect, the kind I dreamed of being a part of when I was a kid. Why is his self-esteem in the crapper?

"Because it's the truth. Look at my family. Joey's the clever, funny one. Nicky's boy genius. He's a Harvard freaking lawyer, for Pete's sake. And then there's me. I barely got through school. I can barely read. I mean, I can read, but it's hard. Like a lot of effort, and then by the time I get through, I can't remember what I read. I say stupid things all the time. I do stupid things all the time. God had to make me pretty and athletic because He didn't give me any other decent traits. I literally can't do anything other than play soccer, and when that's all done, what will I have?"

Until this moment, it never occurred to me that people with perfect lives have issues too.

"I don't want to be stupid. I ... I just don't have a good brain. So I make bad decisions. Lots of bad decisions."

Like sleeping with me. He doesn't come right out and say it, but he doesn't have to. I can infer his meaning. I clench my eyes together and will the tightness in my chest to dissipate. I'm curled into my ever-favorite fetal position on my couch.

"Rachel? Are you still there?"

I didn't realize how long I'd been quiet for. I sit up a little. "Yeah, I'm here. You seem like you needed to vent, so I was letting you have the conch."

"The what?"

"The conch. You know, like from *Lord of the Flies*?" As soon as the words are out of my mouth, I want to shove them back in. He just said he can barely read, and there I go referencing a book. I don't want him to feel any smaller than he already feels, but I undoubtedly did.

"Oh yeah. That." His tone is flat.

Shit.

"You know," he continues, "thinking back, that was probably the last book I read. I liked the movie better, but that's because it was easier for my brain to process. And that says a lot, considering it was in black and white."

Relief flows through me. If he'd been talking about the early '90s movie version, it might be a dealbreaker. The 1960s version is critically acclaimed both as a film and a book adaptation. "Normally, I'd fight anyone who says the movie is better than the book, but that's one answer I'll accept."

He laughs. "I'm glad to have your approval."

I approve of everything you do, especially everything we did in Vegas! "Duly noted." Something occurs to me. "You know, I saw this ClikClak once, and the person was talking about how they were late-diagnosed dyslexic, and that explained so much about all the trouble they had in school growing up. I don't know anything about it, but maybe it's something to look into?"

He's quiet for a minute. Then another minute. Then another one. "TJ? Tyler?" I ask quietly. "Are you okay?"

"Lemme call you back." He disconnects abruptly.

Shit. I overstepped. I shouldn't have said anything, especially when I don't know anything about the topic. I should learn a lesson from this. I'm better off alone than trying to be with people. They're all just going to leave me anyway, so why put myself through this in the meantime?

About fifteen minutes later, he texts.

TJ: Can you come over? Or I can come over to you. Can I come over? What apartment are you?
Me: 3108

About three minutes later, there's an abrupt knocking on my door. I stand on my tiptoes to look through the peephole. I've seen too many TV shows where the unsuspecting young female pulls the door open, only to find a serial killer or mobster on the other side of the now wide-open door.

"It is you," I say, opening the door.

Tyler does not smile in return. His hair is a mess, standing straight up as if he's been pulling it to attention.

He steps in, not looking directly at me. He looks up and down, over and around. Anywhere but at me. I place my hand on his arm. "TJ." I correct myself. "Tyler. What's going on?"

Finally, he meets my gaze. "I need to call my mom, and I want you here for it. I need you with me. Okay?"

"Okay." I nod. I have no idea what's going on, but if he needs me, I'm here for him. It's what friends do.

He dials his mother, his phone on speaker. He's yet to sit down, instead pacing around my apartment.

"Oh, Tyler, to what do I owe this pleasure? Do you need something? I'll be down tomorrow to grab your laundry. You know I always get it on the Tuesday after an away game."

"Ma, when I was little, did you have me tested for dyslexia?"

There's silence on the line. Tyler looks at me before repeating, "Did you have me tested for dyslexia?"

"Well—"

"Jesus, Ma. Rachel told me about dyslexia. I just looked it up. Reading a paragraph and forgetting what I've read. Having trouble decoding. Remembering words and sounds. Letters jumping around on the page or in the word. All of it. It sounds like me."

"Yes, we had you tested."

I suck in a gasp, hoping she doesn't hear.

"Ma, how could you not tell me? Didn't you see me struggling?"

232

"Of course, we knew it was hard, but we figured you'd be okay, and you were. They said that your IQ was normal."

With those words, Tyler melts onto the couch, his knees giving way, and stares at the phone. Utter devastation washes over his face.

"Actually," his mother continues, totally unaware of the bomb she's dropped on her son, "if I remember correctly, your IQ was a little higher than the average. About the same as Nicky. Higher than Joey, but don't tell him that. So we figured you'd be okay. You just had to work a little harder. It was good preparation for the rest of your life. If everything comes easy, you never learn to push through."

"I'm not stupid?" His face is breaking in pain. I sit down next to him. I'm tempted to slide my arm around his shoulders and hug him to me, like they do in movies. But this isn't a movie. This is real life, and his entire sense of being has just been shattered open, and I don't know what to do for him.

"No, of course not, honey," his mom coos. "Why would you say such a thing?"

"Um, maybe because Joey and Nicky are constantly telling me I am."

"You know your brothers are just picking on you. That's how boys are. They think it's funny."

His face is so hard right now. "Well, it's not. I gotta go."

"Tyler, don't hang up. We need to talk." The desperation in his mother's voice is evident.

"No, Ma, I gotta process this. It's a lot. I ... I'll talk to you later."

He disconnects, and we sit there for a moment. I'm not sure what to say or do. I try to think of how Gram would help me when I'd start to spiral. Quietly, I admit, "This is a lot to deal with."

He looks over at me, his eyes red-rimmed. "Did my mother just use the 'boys will be boys' excuse for my brothers?"

I nod.

"And did she just admit that she and Dad knew I had … dyslexia," he stumbles over the word, "but kept it from me to make me tougher?"

I could offer a hundred excuses. I'm sure they're out there if I tried to find them. But the truth is, I have no idea what his parents were thinking. It's not my place to say. So I say the only perspective I'm qualified to share. "It's obvious that your parents love you and your brothers so much. I don't know them that well, but I would bet that everything they've done, they did to protect you, to help you, and to nurture you. It might not have been the right thing, but the intention was right. That's got to count for something."

"So I'm dyslexic?" he asks. I don't think he's looking to me for an answer. I have none to give. He runs his hands through his hair again. Then, he unleashes.

He's ranting and raving, pacing back and forth. There are enough curse words coming out of his mouth to make a sailor blush. He's carrying on, and I half expect him to either start throwing things or drop to the floor, kicking his feet like a toddler. He finishes with, "God, a simple diagnosis and … now what? How do I deal with this? How can a few words about my brain change my whole life?"

His words, though innocent in intention, are a punch to my gut. He's not thinking about me, which is understandable. This isn't about me or my sister. Yet, when you're struggling to put one foot in front of the other, it's hard not to view the world around you in relation to yourself.

With the flip of a switch, he's been thrown into the grieving process. What no one tells you is that moving through the five stages isn't linear. I've spent most of the year in the depression phase. Through meeting Tyler and his friendship, I'd finally moved on to acceptance. Yet here I am, with the mere utterance of thoughtless words, back in the anger phase.

I'm angry for Tyler and at Tyler all at the same time. He doesn't know how good he has it. Yes, his parents messed up big with this one, but they care. They care so much. That is such a gift. Not all parents care. They messed up, but they tried their best. And yes, he's been told his brain is different, and his life will change from it. But dyslexia isn't terminal. It's not going to put him in the grave in eight short months.

He'll continue to be alive and kicking, and my sister will still be dead.

CHAPTER 30: TJ

Rachel has gone rigid, sitting on her couch next to me. I sink back, suddenly depleted of the strength needed to overcome gravity. Her couch is infinitely more comfortable than mine. "Where'd you get your couch?" I ask. It's easier than talking about what just went down. I'm pretty sure I acted like my nieces during their terrible twos phase.

I'm not sure if I'm still livid or embarrassed for acting like a spoiled toddler.

"It's a Bob-o-pedic from Bob's Furniture," she answers, her voice robotic.

"It's comfy." I scrub my hands down my face. "Did that just really happen?"

Rachel doesn't say anything. She's staring off into space.

"Rach? You okay?" I sit up. She doesn't look so good.

Finally, she whispers, "I'm processing."

"Right." I don't move. "Processing what? How my parents lied to me my whole life? How they kept a ... a mental defect from me?" I know my words aren't accurate.

But hell, words have never been my strong suit. Now at least I know why.

I also neglect to ask her if she's processing my childish behavior.

Rachel is still and calm. Like, freakishly still and calm. "Tyler, I think maybe you need to deal with this in private. You don't need someone you barely know getting all up in your business. Maybe it'd be better if you left."

She's kicking me out? Now? "Rach." I swivel to face her, taking her hands in mine. "Rachel, I just found out that my entire life is a lie. That my family betrayed me. That—"

Rachel stands up, pulling her hands from mine. She hugs them tightly around her chest and turns to look out the window. I have no idea why she's acting like this.

"Rachel—"

"Tyler, please. I'm trying so hard right now, but I don't know how much more I can take." The words strain coming out of her mouth. "But I can't say what I'm thinking, either. You'll hate me for it."

"I think you should let me be the judge of that, because I can't think of anything you could say that would make me hate you." She's probably going to rant about my parents. I won't hold it against her. They deserve to be ranted about.

She turns around, her face ashen. I raise my eyebrows to encourage her to start.

She sucks in a deep breath and then says, "My rational brain is having a war with my irrational brain. I don't know that either side will be the victor." Her eyes are huge right now. She rolls her lips into a flat line for a minute. "This is about you. What you've experienced your whole life, and what—and how—you found out about it. It's about you and your relationship with your family. I understand that it's upsetting. I know that, but I can't be upset for you. I'm too upset at you, which is stupid. I know this isn't about me. It's not. So I'm trying not to say anything until I can regain that perspective."

She's upset at me? "What? How? Why? None of that makes any sense."

Rachel's voice is so quiet I can barely hear it. "I know it doesn't, but I'm angry that you're this upset when it's just dyslexia."

"Just dyslexia?" If my eyes bulged any more, they'd pop out of my head. Just dyslexia? Where does she get off?

"It's not glioblastoma. It's not terminal brain cancer. You're not going to have seizures. You're not going to puke your guts out and lose your hair from the chemo. You're not going to lose motor function and the ability to see. You're not going to die. You're going to keep living. Your mom is going to keep taking care of you. You're going to keep playing soccer. You're going to keep cruising through life, never knowing how lucky you are."

In an evening full of shocks and surprises, this was not anything I'd even have remotely expected.

"I'm sorry that I feel that way, but that's where I am right now. So, have a nice life, I guess." She walks toward the door and pulls it open. "Thanks for everything. I do appreciate it."

"You're kicking me out?"

She falters. "Don't you want to leave?"

Her words aren't making any sense. "I … I don't understand. Why would I leave?"

Her gaze darts around the room. She's looking anywhere but at me.

"Rachel? Do you want me to go?"

She shakes her head. "But why do you want to stay?"

"Um, cause I'm having a super shitty day, and I want to talk to a friend about it." I think about what she said. "And my friend is going through shit too, and I want to be there for her. Two things can be true at the same time. We can work on them together. It's what friends do."

"You're not mad at me? I'm a terrible person for even thinking ... for making this about me and my experience. Don't you want to leave now?"

There's a lot to unpack in that statement, and I'm in no place to do it.

My brain hurts; it's so full of conflicting thoughts and emotions right now. I gingerly sit back down on the couch. It really is comfortable. "Can we have a quick recap, just so I'm not confused as to what's going on here?" I think I understand, but there's a piece missing that's making it not make sense for me.

Rachel remains by the door, but she allows it to close gently. I take this as a yes. "I'm upset that my parents withheld the fact that I'm dyslexic, allowing me to struggle my entire life. They let me think that I was stupid and worthless because I couldn't keep up academically with my brothers. Knowing them, they thought they were doing what was best for me, but they may have done more harm than good. That's where I'm at, agreed?"

Rachel nods.

I continue, "And while you see that perspective, this whole situation, especially me talking about my brain, is triggering for you because your sister died of brain cancer and, from what you've told me, your parents are not in the picture. So while you can understand that I'm mad at my parents, it's still infinitely better than any interactions you have with your parents. Am I correct?"

Another nod. She's staring at the floor as if it holds all the secrets of the world.

"And you understand that your reaction to me right now is a little skewed because you've just lost your sister, and you want to be supportive, but you still have your feelings, and you're trying to work through them." I don't wait for a response before I continue. "So, if that's what's going on, why do you want me to leave? That's what I don't understand."

Finally, she looks up at me, tears shimmering in her eyes. "I don't *want* you to leave. I expect you to leave."

These words are like a knife to my heart. She expects me to walk out on her.

In a voice so faint I can barely hear it, she whispers, "Everyone leaves me."

I'm off the couch and crossing the small room before I can stop myself. I pull her into me, pressing her tightly to my chest. My arms engulf her, and I kiss her forehead. "I'm not going anywhere."

"That's what they all say."

I hold her tight, feeling her body slump into mine. My chin is on the top of her head. She seems so small. I wish I could use my body to protect her from all the hurt she's endured in her past. "I mean, physically, I do have to leave at some point. I still have a job to do, and unfortunately, I can't do it remotely."

I feel her body shaking against mine.

"Are you laughing or crying?"

Rachel sniffles. "A little of both."

I pull back slightly so I can look at her. Her eyes are red and puffy, and her face is slick with tears. "We can fight, not that that even was a fight. You had feelings, which you're entitled to. You also showed a tremendous amount of self-awareness in your feelings, which I think is interesting. People usually have no idea when they're being self-centered. Trust me, I know what I'm talking about. I'm one of those people."

"I've always had to be more aware. When I was growing up, I thought it was something I was saying or doing that was making Mom leave. Or that I was unlikeable—unlovable—and that's why she always chose her boyfriends over us. If I just did better, or was better, or was more quiet, or took up less space, then she'd love me too. I mean, if my own mother doesn't love me enough to stay, then why would anyone else?"

I can see why she was upset with me and my reaction toward my parents. To her, it's like complaining that your wagyu steak dinner is slightly overcooked when the person next to you is eating SpaghettiOs.

Number ten on her list is to forgive her mother. When I first read that, I couldn't imagine ever being so mad at my mother that I would not be able to forgive her. Today, I understand a bit more.

"Do you ever think you will be able to forgive your mom?" I ask.

Rachel shakes her head. "Maybe, at one point, I could have forgiven her for leaving us when we were little. She was young herself, and she didn't know what she wanted from life. People make mistakes. But I can't forgive her for not being there for Richie. She only came to see her one time after she got sick. Toward the very end, when Richie couldn't see anymore and could barely speak. She was only semi-conscious. That's when Mom breezed in. But then, at the services, there she was, playing the role of the distraught mother."

I wouldn't be able to forgive that either. "Do you think Richie wrote the list before your mom came to see her?"

Rachel pulls out of my arms. She cocks her head, considering. "She would have had to. There's no way she was still writing by the time Mom came."

"So Richie thought she was going to die without seeing your mom, and yet she still wanted you to forgive her. I wonder why."

Rachel starts walking aimlessly around her apartment. She finally ends up in the kitchen, where she pours herself a glass of water. "You want anything to drink?"

"Water'd be great. I still feel dehydrated from Vegas and the flight."

Rachel sets the water pitcher down and looks at me. "Was that really only yesterday?"

It feels like a million years ago.

"In about three days, your body will get back on schedule. Speaking of which, I am going to have to leave soon, but it's not because I'm deserting you. I have to eat and get to bed at a decent hour. I need to sleep in my own bed tonight."

Rachel says, "I understand. I ... I've never been good at long-term relationships of any kind. I didn't have a lot of friends growing up. I had Richie, who was all I needed. She wasn't just my sister. She was my very best friend. But she still left me, too." Her voice is so small.

I move to her again, taking her in my arms. She fits into me so perfectly. "Rachel, I'm guessing if Richie'd had a choice, she wouldn't have left."

"I know. I know it wasn't her choice. And Gram and Gramps kicking me out wasn't to hurt me. It was to help me. Kind of like your parents. Good intentions, shitty results."

I look around. Her apartment is still newly lived in. There isn't artwork on the walls, and there are a few boxes here and there. I wouldn't call her totally settled yet. "Seems to me like you're taking steps to build a life. You picked out one hell of a couch. You made a new friend. You're accomplishing Richie's list."

"I've made two new friends. Ophelia and I really hit it off. I may have to pretend to be your girlfriend so Ophelia and I can do WAG events together. She's a lot of fun."

The voice inside me is yelling, *"You don't have to pretend!"* It's all I can do not to kiss her again or sweep her up in my arms and carry her to the bedroom. That would most certainly complicate the situation. I want

Rachel to be with me for the right reasons, not just because she was swept up in complex emotions.

I want her to want me like I want her. Simple as that.

CHAPTER 31: RACHEL

I'm going to need a week to recover from everything that's happened, not to mention at least a dozen years of therapy. To be fair, I could use the therapy, even if the last week hadn't happened. Tyler is texting and calling multiple times per day, as his schedule permits, to let me know he's not blowing me off. I am using every tool in my toolbox to take him at his word.

I'm failing miserably.

I want to believe him, but I know Mom believed all her loser boyfriends. Not that Tyler is my boyfriend. We've lived up to our agreement to keep Vegas in Vegas, and we're back to being strictly friends.

Just because no one's ever kept their promises to me doesn't mean I'm going to break the ones I've made, no matter how much I want to.

Saturday morning, I receive a text from Ophelia, asking if I'm going to the game.

Me: Hadn't planned on it.

Ophelia: Damn. I was hoping we could hang out. It's a lot more fun with friends.

She considers me a friend. I don't want her to be by herself. I know what that feels like. Quickly, I text her back.

Me: Where are you sitting? I'll see if I can get one in the same section.

Ophelia: TJ can get you one. Like he did for the Vegas game.

My hand hesitates before typing the next text. These tickets are reserved for very special people only. The wives and girlfriends. I'm neither. I don't like lying. How can I expect people to be honest with me if I lie to them?

A voice in the back of my head screams at me that I'm already lying to TJ by pretending to be his friend when I want so much more. I figure if I suppress these feelings long enough, I'll get over my crush. Every woman with a pulse, and probably a fair number of men too, has a crush on TJ Doyle. And they don't even know him. The real him. The one who is nurturing by nature. The one who is so worried about what everyone else will think that he spends hours reshooting and editing his videos so no one can criticize him.

I understand that a whole lot more since everything with his parents went down. Still, I decide to text him nonetheless. I'll let him decide about the deception.

Me: Good luck today! What time do you leave?

TJ: I was just going to text you. Leaving around noon.

Me: I was texting with Ophelia. She wants me to come to the game. Would you be able to get me a ticket so I can sit with her?

Me: I know I don't technically meet the criteria..

TJ: Done.

Me: Are you sure? I don't want you to get in trouble.

TJ: It's fine. But if the ticket police investigate, you're going to have to kiss me to prove our relationship.

TJ: With tongue.

I suck in a sharp breath, pressing my knees together, thinking about that mouth and that tongue.

Me: <sigh> I guess I could take one for the team.

TJ: It'll be waiting for you at Will Call with your pass for the lounge. Have Ophelia pick you up or take an Uber. I'll bring you home.

He's just being nice. Maybe he's looking for an excuse not to see his parents after the game, if they even show up. We haven't talked much about them this week.

I spend the rest of the morning catching up on work. Then I shower and get ready for the game. No glasses today. I even use the curling iron on my hair. I don't think twice about mascara and lip gloss.

While it's been a seasonably nice day for the end of September, the evening promises to be cooler. I still don't have any Boston Buzzards merch, so I plan to buy a hoodie once I get to the stadium. It'll cost more, but that's the price I have to pay for not thinking about this earlier. Speaking of cost, Tyler never said how much the ticket was.

Me: How much do I owe you for the ticket? I'll Venmo you.

Then it occurs to me. Shit.

Me: I never paid you for Vegas either. I'll send you the money for both.

TJ: Shut up.

Me: No, really. How much do I owe?

TJ: I get them for free. It's a perk for the WAGs.

Me: But—

His text interrupts my objection.

TJ: No buts. It's one of the perks of my job, and if you want to pretend you're my girlfriend to come to the games, I'm ok with that.

TJ: There is one but ...

I wait for his condition.

TJ: Tongue and maybe I get to feel you up a little. You have a nice rack.

I blush at his forward text. I look down at my chest to make sure we're talking about the same thing.

Me: That's not the kind of text you send to a friend.

Me: And thank you. I always thought they were on the small side.

TJ: All of you is on the small side, so they are perfect for you. And for tonight, you're my girlfriend, remember? <winky smiley face emoji>

I will not get all swoony over this. I should be offended. I should be filled with righteous indignation. I should not be thinking about kissing him again.

Or letting him get to second base.

I know, wrong sport.

Me: Perv.

Me: If I have to take one for the team, it's a sacrifice I'm willing to make.

TJ: Your dedication to the Buzzards organization is appreciated. Not all heroes wear capes.

When Ophelia's text comes in that she's here, I'm still smiling. I smile as I walk out my door, down the hall, and descend the steps out of my apartment building. The smile falters when I realize that it's not just Ophelia in the car. The driver is ... holy shit, it's Hannah LaRosa. She's super ClikClak famous. I love her dog park series.

"Hey!" Ophelia greets. "So glad you decided to come. This is going to be so much fun! Let me do introductions. Rachel, this is Hannah LaRosa and Carlos Cruz-Collado. Hannah is with Callaghan Entay, the goalie, and Carlos is with Landon Stubbs. Hannah and Carlos were roommates before they started shacking up with their respective players. Landon's a midfielder, just like TJ. He's right and TJ is left. Rachel is dating TJ Doyle, though she continues to keep up a cock-and-bull story that they're just friends. Do you fly out to Vegas for 'just a friend'? I think not. Rachel," she says to me directly, "I just realized I don't know your last name."

"It's Cramer." One of the reasons I like being with Ophelia is that she does all the talking. I never have to carry the conversation.

"So, Hannah runs the social media account for the New England Patriots. Carlos is a makeup artist. They are both huge on ClikClak, but they don't like me to mention that." She smiles sheepishly. "Did you say you worked for your family business? What is it?"

I suck in a deep breath. I've just met these people. Even though Tyler and I aren't *really* together, would it damage his image to be associated with me and my ClikClak account?

"Ophelia, give the poor girl a break and let her get a word in edgewise," Carlos chides. He turns around to look at me. "God, you're cute. Adorable."

My face fills with heat. "Um, I don't wear makeup," I say apologetically.

"Don't apologize to me, girl."

I wish I could be like Ophelia and be unabashedly open with total strangers, saying something like, "*My mom was really into it. She wouldn't go anywhere without putting her face on. She'd spend hours at a time on it. I swear, she looked like a completely different person. You know, like practically catfishing. Maybe that's why her boyfriends never lasted long. They woke up with someone different than they went to bed with. Anyway, she pretty much sucks, and I don't want to be anything like her, so I've never gotten into the makeup thing.*"

Instead, I sit quietly while Ophelia continues to ramble, and Hannah and Carlos occasionally chime in. They're a funny group, and I'm having a good time.

Richie would love them.

I smile, knowing I'm here because of her. Though losing her was the worst experience in my life, I'm emerging on the other side, better and stronger. Maybe even happier. All because of her list.

We've arrived at the stadium, and we head inside to the lounge reserved for the WAGs. Carlos is the only man in here, but he doesn't seem to mind. There are snacks and drinks. There's even a staff person dedicated to running and getting our alcoholic beverages so we don't have to stand in line.

This is so cool.

There are only about six other women in here. I'm not sure if most of the team is single, or if coming to games isn't super popular.

It's almost time for the game to start, and I've yet to get myself a sweatshirt or hoodie to wear. I let the crew know that I'm stepping out and that I'll meet them at our seats. Ophelia offers to come with me.

"So, it's basically like high school all over again?" I ask. Even though there weren't that many other women in the room, the social structure was evident. I was smart not to disclose my place of employment.

Ophelia shrugs. "I guess. I think? I'm new to all of this. We all are. It's the first season for any of us. We're definitely the new kids." She thinks for a minute. "Probably not the cool ones, either, in case you couldn't tell."

"I've never been invited to sit at the cool kids' table," I admit. That should shock exactly no one. "I'm not sure I'd want to, either."

"Me neither, which is why we vibe."

"I don't know anything about soccer. Do the players' positions determine their rank? Like that Victoria woman— is her husband the ... what's the soccer equivalent of quarterback?"

"She's like that because her husband, Pressley Samson, is one of the two captains. She thinks it makes her special."

"Who's the other one?" There wasn't another snooty WAG in the lounge. Maybe the other captain isn't married.

"Callaghan Entay. Hannah's boyfriend. He's the goalie, which is probably the most equivalent to the quarterback."

"But Hannah's so nice!" I say. It's true. She is smart and funny, and if she was passing judgment on me, she kept it to herself.

"Like I said, we're all new here. But we're determined to have a good time, so I'm glad you came with us tonight."

In all honesty, if I'd known there would be more people, I probably wouldn't have agreed to come. On the other hand, Tyler's response was worth having to people when I didn't plan to. His words dance through my head again. He was flirting with me. No doubt about it. The mere thought of it feels like soda fizz in my stomach.

I'm torn between the red-and-navy camouflage-patterned sweatshirt that matches their home jerseys or a simpler navy hoodie. I'm not the flashy patterned type, so I land on the plain navy hoodie with "Boston Buzzards" in red and white across the chest. I pull it over my head, and we make our way to our seats.

I probably should look at getting a shirt or jersey with TJ's name on it, if only to keep up the pretenses of being his girlfriend to get cheaper tickets. It sits uncomfortably in my gut, the lying and deception. What if TJ gets in trouble for abusing the system? Also, I don't want to lie to people I could be friends with.

I turn to Ophelia. "TJ and I are really just friends. I probably shouldn't be in the lounge or these seats."

"You can say you're friends all you want. He doesn't look at you like a friend. He wouldn't be buying you these tickets if you were just a friend."

Buying? "Tyler told me he got me the tickets for free!"

Ophelia shrugs. "It's complicated. They're not free. They're part of his contract, so they're considered taxable income. Even then, the Buzzards still have to pay about twenty-five percent of face value, so while they are discounted, they're not free. I don't know that a lot of the players understand about the taxable income." She pauses and glances my way. "Once an accountant, always an accountant."

I laugh. "I do a fair amount of bookkeeping myself, so I get you." Ophelia and I do get along. I've never made a friend this quickly before.

I make a mental list of things to talk about with Tyler after the game. Number one: he's not buying my tickets. Number two: does he have a good accountant to help him with the financial stuff? Number three: I'm not going to lie about being his girlfriend. Number four: where can I get a jersey with his name on it?

It'll be good that I have things to talk to him about. Maybe it'll keep his mind off his parents and not going out for ice cream.

The game is slightly more interesting than the last one. The cocktails didn't hurt. Neither did laughing with Ophelia, Hannah, and Carlos. Seeing their men on the field, rooting for them to do well made the game pass by quickly. I didn't even think about a book this time.

As the stoppage time minutes wind down in the second half, that fizzy feeling is back in my stomach. Tyler is going to find me, and he's going to make a show. I just know it.

Yes, I need to put a stop to this farce. I will. After I steal one more kiss from him.

CHAPTER 32: TJ

eating the Milwaukee Steins, moving us one step closer to the playoffs, is a good feeling. Knowing Rachel is in the stands to watch me is a great feeling. Knowing I get to kiss her, and she can't pretend we're only friends, is the best feeling.

The minute the final whistle blows and the teams exchange handshakes, I'm headed over to the WAG seats, which are located in the section behind where my parents usually sit. I don't want to think about them right now. My focus is on Rachel.

I climb up the railing and swing my legs over to reach the stands. I take the steps two at a time, ignoring the burning in my fatigued legs. She's wearing a Buzzards hoodie, the kind they sell here at the stadium. The tip of her nose is red from the cool autumn air. I cannot control the grin that spreads across my face as I walk up to her.

"Hello, girlfriend," I pant, suddenly out of breath from the exertion. I put my hands on my hips and try to take a deep breath. Or three.

Rachel glances right and left. "Hello, boyfriend. Good game." She leans in, whispering in my ear, "I still don't know anything about soccer to say more than that, but I don't want to blow my cover."

Her breath, hot on the side of my face, nearly undoes me. A mental image of us lying in bed together, me drawing out the schematics of soccer plays on her bare abdomen, flashes through my brain. Yes, I'll have to take the time to explain it to her. Slowly.

Rachel starts to pull away. This is my chance. I scoop her jaw with both my hands, cradling her face. Damn, those hot fudge eyes get me every time. Gently, I guide her mouth to mine, watching her eyes flutter shut. She tastes like sweet hard cider. Her lips part, and I slide my tongue in. She's now gripping the back of my hair with both hands, pulling me deeper into her.

Electricity zings through my body. This may be a show for her, but tell that to every hormone in every cell that is shouting at me to keep this going. I can barely hear the catcalls and whistling, the cheers and jeers. What I can hear is Rachel moaning softly into my mouth. I could kiss her all night long.

"Hey, dumbass, you wanna come up for air? That girl can barely breathe with you swallowing her face like that." Joey's voice is like a vat of ice water dumped over my head.

I feel Rachel go rigid. I give her one last little kiss to reassure her before pulling back. I'm still gazing into her eyes and holding her face when I say to my asshole brother, "I don't hear her complaining."

"That's because you were swallowing her tongue."

I finally let go of Rachel, only to drop my arm around her shoulder and pull her into my side. "Can I help you?" I ask my brother.

"We'll see you at Tom and Jerry's. The one in Raynham." He brushes by me, clipping my other shoulder, and continues up and out of the stadium.

I turn back to Rachel, who's staring at me with confusion. "Are ... are you still meeting up with your family?" She pulls back slightly, so I let my arm fall to my side. Probably a good move since I really need a shower.

"Yeah, it's what we do. It's a little harder this time of year because a lot of the places are closed for the season. Tom and Jerry's is open year-round. They just opened a new location that's a little bit closer to here. You're coming with, right? Give me a few minutes to shower."

"But ... but I don't understand," she stammers and repeats herself. "You're still meeting up with your family?" Her face looks like that meme of someone trying to figure out advanced calculus.

"Yeah, it's tradition. We don't mess with that. Do you know what kind of fate could befall the team if we mess with it?"

"But ... you're upset with them. Rightfully so. I ... I can't believe you're still speaking to them."

"Yeah, I'm mad, and at some point, we're going to have to talk. They're going to tell me they did what they thought was best. I'm going to blame them for my life going the way it's going. Nicky'll stand there, looking at his phone because he's too good for us, and it's beneath him to get involved in such plebeian affairs. Joey'll still call me stupid, even when shown evidence that I'm actually smarter. He'll take it the hardest. I'm smarter, and better looking, and my penis is bigger, so he can say whatever he wants. I still win."

Facts. He can put *that* in his stand-up routine.

"And ... what'll happen tonight?"

"We'll get ice cream. We'll talk about tonight's game and the game next week. Ma will hug me and tell me she'll

254

be down for my laundry on Monday, because she picks it up on the Monday after home games, but not until the Tuesday after away games. She tells me this every week. Every. Single. Week."

"That's just like the other times."

I nod. "Yup. Now let me go get showered and changed. You can wait in the lounge where you went before the game. I won't be long." I lean in and give her a quick kiss on the forehead, like it's the most natural thing in the world.

I jog back down the stairs, hop the rail, and sprint to the tunnel that takes me to our locker room. Normally, I take my time in the shower, but tonight I don't want to keep Rachel waiting.

Rachel.

Her reaction to finding out we're still seeing my family was interesting. I can't get the expression on her face out of my mind. She was honestly and truly bewildered. I'll bet she has no idea what it means to be able to trust.

Sure, I'm still upset with my parents. I don't agree with how they handled the situation at all. However, I can honestly say that whatever decisions they made for the three of us when we were growing up, they did out of love. I know without a shadow of a doubt that they will always be here for my brothers and me.

Hair still dripping, I make my way up to the WAG lounge. It's got an actual name, but no one calls it anything but *the WAG lounge*. Rachel's in there with Ophelia, Hannah, and Carlos. Oh good, she didn't have to wait alone. They're all laughing and smiling, and they look like they're having a good time.

My heart threatens to jump out of my chest when she turns that smile toward me. I'm tempted to do something foolish like bow and extend my hand, saying something corny like, "Are you ready, my lady? Your chariot awaits."

Instead, I shove my hands in my pockets and give a quick head jerk toward the exit. "You ready?"

Rachel stands up, and she's quickly enveloped in a tight hug by Ophelia and then Carlos. Hannah hangs back and gives her a little wave. Rachel walks up to me and nods. "I'm ready." She glances back over her shoulder. "Thanks again! I ... I had fun!"

I don't think Rachel has fun very often, so I hope the rest of her squad realizes how huge it is for her to say that.

We walk out to my Trackhawk in silence. As we approach, I press the key fob in my pocket, the lights flashing as the vehicle unlocks. I open the passenger side for her to get in, closing her in before walking around to the driver's side. Once I'm in the car, I start to plug the name of the ice cream shop into my GPS, but I freeze.

Shit.

My hand stays frozen in mid-air as the letters dance in my brain. Shit again.

"What's wrong?" Rachel asks, concern filling her voice.

"I can't remember the name of the place. We call it Tom and Jerry's, but that's not it. It's something *like* that." I run my hand through my hair. I feel like I'm back in high school, trying to take the World History final, while names and dates swim through my head. I bang the steering wheel. "Fuck!"

Rachel puts a very gentle hand on my arm. "I'd tell you to calm down, but I know that helps about as much as tits on a bull. So let's see what other ways we can figure this out. You could text your family," she suggests.

"Yeah, so they can laugh at me for not being able to remember the letters. I'm the one who called it Tom and Jerry's in the first place. You know, like the cat and mouse cartoon? That's how my brain processed it, and I can't get it out of my head."

"Okay, so we won't text them. We'll figure out another way."

"It's in Raynham. There can't be too many ice cream places there." I pull up Google and type in, "ice cream Raynham, MA Tom," knowing for certain that Tom is in the name. There it is. Tom and Jimmy's. Relief floods my body.

"Thanks for your help," I say as I shift the car into drive.

"You're the one who figured it out. And listen, Tom and Jimmy's is pretty damn close to Tom and Jerry's. Plus, I don't think it's a dyslexic thing. Richie had a friend growing up whose name was Molly McKinney. My grandfather continually referred to her as Molly McButter. If I called him up right now and said that name, he'd automatically say McButter. Sometimes brains just do that."

"I don't believe you. Call him right now." I totally believe her. I am curious to hear her interaction with her grandfather. I need to know more about her family. "And put it on speaker."

Rachel glares at me for all of three seconds before retrieving her phone from her back pocket. "Hey, Gramps, it's Rachel."

"I know it's you. What's wrong?" His voice, dancing through the speaker of her phone, sounds gruff. This is a man you don't want to cross.

"Nothing's wrong. I, uh, I'm here with a, uh, friend, and I have a question for you."

"Who's the friend?"

"TJ."

There's a quick bark of laughter. "Oh, the young man who left the message on the emergency line."

My face fills with heat, thinking of how desperate I felt in that moment, needing to know Rachel was okay. I'd one-hundred percent do it again.

"Yeah, him. Okay, question for you. Do you remember Richie's friend Molly—"

"McButter," he finishes before she can even get the question out.

She smirks at me. "That's it. That was the entire question."

"Fine. Call your grandmother. You've got to get over this."

Quickly, Rachel disconnects. She doesn't move, simply staring at the phone in her lap.

"You haven't been talking to your grandmother?" I ask after a moment.

"I'm mad at her," she says quietly.

We're almost to the ice cream shop, so I pull over to give us a little more time. "What are you mad at her for?"

Rachel remains staring at the phone in her lap. Her hands are fidgeting with the case, pulling the corner off and then popping it back on. "Okay, not mad as much as hurt by her. She kicked me out. She made me leave my home. She said I'd always have a home with her. She told me that for my entire childhood, every time my mom dragged us out to live with her. Every time my mom dropped us off because she was sick of being a parent. Every single time, she told me I'd always have a home with her. But then she made me leave when I needed home the most."

I'm quiet for a minute, trying to think about what to say. "If you called your grandmother right now and said you were stranded on the side of the road, what would she do?"

Without missing a beat, Rachel says, "Either hop in the car herself, or send Gramps or Uncle Robert to pick me up."

"If you had surgery and needed care, what would she do?"

The corners of Rachel's mouth turn down. "She'd rent a hospital bed and convert her house into a skilled nursing facility."

I bet she knows that from experience. It was a stupid—no, it wasn't the right question to ask. Or maybe it was.

"If you called her and said you were getting married, what would she do?"

"She'd start baking cookies for the bridal shower and start fussing about where she was going to find a dress and complain about how she can't wear nice shoes anymore because her ankles are bad."

I press my luck and ask one more question. "If you were having a panic attack, what would she do?"

"She'd ask if I want a hug. She'd sit with me, talking in a low voice, trying to distract me with stories about the cats, giving me anything else to focus on. She'd drop everything to be with me."

"All of this, even though you don't live there anymore?"

Rachel finally turns to look at me. "I've been a bitch to her, haven't I?"

"I wouldn't go that far, but you could probably call her tomorrow. Couldn't hurt, right?" As I'm saying this, I know I will need to call my mom tomorrow too. I reach over the center console and pull Rachel into a hug. For a moment, she rests her head on my shoulder. If it weren't for how horribly uncomfortable this is, I would stay like this forever.

"Thanks. I needed that," Rachel says, breaking away from the hug. One of these days, she won't pull away so quickly. When she's ready, I will be too.

I put the car into gear, knowing I'm going to catch hell for being so late. It doesn't matter. All that matters right now is Rachel.

CHAPTER 33: RACHEL

The ice cream shop, which I'll forever think of as Tom and Jerry's too, is not as awkward as I thought it would be. Perhaps a skosh more tense than the last time, but more relaxed than the first time when Tyler accused me of being a stalker and his brothers sat on him.

It seems like a normal night. There's talk of the game, most of which I tune out, instead thinking about the kiss after the game. If I didn't know better, I'd think Tyler took advantage of the situation just to kiss me, like he wants more. But that's nuts. Why would he want more with me? It'd be death to his image. Not to mention, it's me.

No, it must be in my head that he's hinting at more. I drank those ciders a while ago, but maybe I'm still a little tipsy.

Tyler orders a chocolate chip sundae, which looks almost as delectable as the man eating it. I opt for a single scoop of birthday cake ice cream.

"That's it? A single scoop?" TJ asks me.

"Don't hate on my birthday cake ice cream. Not everyone needs a monstrosity of a dessert." Defiantly, I stab at my ice cream with my spoon.

TJ leans in, our shoulders touching. "Is that your favorite flavor?"

I shrug. "It's what I was in the mood for. It's pretty good."

TJ takes that as an invitation to reach over and spoon out a scoop. I watch him bring it to his mouth. The same mouth that was on mine after the game. The same mouth I'm not supposed to be thinking about. Then, just as he did in Vegas, he turns the spoon over in his mouth, dragging it out through his teeth and lips. "So you're still looking to have your cake and eat it too? Insatiable little appetite there." Then he winks.

Lord help me.

I press my thighs together as warmth floods my body. Why is he teasing me like this? What does he want from me? Would it be conspicuous if I started fanning myself?

We're with his family, for Pete's sake.

"So Rachel." Maureen leans in, tenting her hands beneath her chin. "Is soccer growing on you at all? This is what—the third game in a row you've been to?"

"Um, I think it's the fourth. I don't know that it's growing on me, but I don't dread it like I did the first game, so I'd say that's an improvement. I had a lot of fun tonight."

"The game or the sucking face after the game?" Joey certainly likes to stir the pot.

"I didn't want to get in trouble for sitting in the wife and girlfriend section, so we thought we had to make it believable." I don't know why I'm telling his parents, of all people, this.

You see? This is why I do better staying in my apartment by myself. It's nearly—but not totally—

impossible to open yourself up to humiliation when you're at home.

Even as I think that, two thoughts race through my head. I referred to my apartment as my home, and I'm happy I went out tonight. Sure, I'll have to recharge my social battery for a solid five days after this, but it was much better than staying in. Even if Tyler hadn't kissed me, tonight at the game was still better than staying in all alone.

You know on all those medical TV shows, when the character flatlines, and all the doctors are working on the dead person? There's the sound of the flatline on the monitor, and people are yelling, "Clear!" and shocking the person over and over. And just when you think that person is dead and gone, there's a miraculous beep and the person sucks in a huge gasp and sits up, and everything's wonderful?

I think I've been coding for most of my life. I was "circling the drain" as they like to say on all those TV shows, and once Richie died, I flatlined too. Every item on her bucket list was like a shock from the paddles. Clear. Fly on a plane by myself. Charge the paddles to 100. <shock> Clear. Go to a casino. Charge the paddles to 200. <shock> Clear. Meet TJ Doyle. Charge the paddles to 300. Clear. Have a one-night stand. <shock>

That's all I needed. I'm alive, gasping for breath, ready to live again.

Is it clichéd to say I was brought back to life by a magic penis? It's the stuff of legends in my romance books. The best part of this realization? Knowing that I'm ready to live again, and I don't even have to forgive my mother.

And for the record, it wasn't the magic penis itself, but the connection to the owner of the magic penis. It's not like it's just an organ (God, I hate that term) free floating throughout the universe. No, it's the man attached to the penis. Though, for the record, and keep in mind I have nothing to compare it with, it was pretty magical.

And then, by extension, the connection to Ophelia and her friends. Maybe they're going to be my friends, too. I can see the four of us hanging out, even when it's not at a game. I don't know the last time I wanted to go out and be social. I don't know the last time I laughed this much.

The rest of the time at the ice cream parlor passes by in a blur. The Doyles are talking, mostly about soccer, I think, but my brain will not stay focused. The weight of my entire life has started to lift from my shoulders. If I weren't in public—and with other people—I'd yell to the ceiling, "Richie, I'm free!"

I hope heaven has granted her this same feeling.

My elation lasts until we're in Tyler's SUV, driving home. He glances over at me. "I know I'm a great kisser and all, but I don't think my powers are enough to make you this ... happy?"

He has no idea.

"I had a really great time tonight."

"I'm glad," he says.

"No, you don't understand. I went out. With people. People I didn't even know. I went out in a crowd. I didn't worry about whether people were going to like me, or if people were going to laugh at my family business." I stop, thinking back. "No, wait, I did worry about that. I think I'll always worry about that. Comes with the nature of the business. But what I do for work didn't matter. It was fun. And flirting with you was fun. And kissing you was super fun. Before I met you, I never had any fun. At least not since my sister got sick."

"That's over a year at this point, right?"

I nod. It seems like forever ago and yesterday all at the same time. "And I didn't cry today. I didn't even want to. Not even when I wanted to talk to Richie. I feel like a huge weight has started to lift off of me."

Admitting it to Tyler boosts my confidence. It swells inside my chest like an overinflated balloon. I said it, and nothing bad happened. For the first time in my life, I start to think that maybe I'm good enough. Maybe, just maybe, Tyler wants more than just friendship.

He certainly acts like he wants more.

I know what Richie would say. She'd tell me I only live once, and that I'd better climb him like a tree before she does. I have the advantage, being corporeal and all, while she's, at best, a spirit, but nonetheless, I take her advice.

Safe in the dark vehicle, as we're zipping up 495, I do something very un-Rachel-like. I channel my inner Richie. "I don't want to be friends. I want more. I want my cake." There it is. I drop it like a bomb—and then immediately want to vomit. He's made his feelings about my upchucking in his car very clear, so I know it would be a dealbreaker.

Tyler stares straight ahead, his fingers tightening on the wheel. The SUV swerves, almost imperceptibly, which is his only tell that this has thrown him. Oh shit. What have I done? He doesn't want more. I promised him, and now I'm breaking my promise. I'm no better than my mother.

Shit.

My good mood is instantly gone as I quickly descend into the shame spiral. Hello darkness, my old friend.

I have to fix this. Quickly, I say, "I'll get over it. Don't worry. Forget I ever said anything. I'd be horrible for your image. Your views and traction would tank because of me and my job. I couldn't do that to you. We can just be friends, but you can't kiss me anymore then. Not even for show. I'll pay for regular tickets. I can't handle the flirting and the touching and the kissing. It makes me want more, and I'm okay if you don't want more. I'll get over you. Just give me time."

Why, why, why did I think blurting something like that would be a good idea? I'm not impulsive. This is a terrible time to develop the trait that so irritated me about my sister. Jesus, what if she's possessing me? Or, more likely, what if I have a brain tumor too?

I know neither is true, and it's simply me, making a disaster of my life after I finally felt happiness for all of thirty seconds.

You don't get yourself into these kinds of messes when you are home, by yourself, with a good book. You can cringe with second-hand embarrassment from the character's idiotic actions, but you're never the one acting like an idiot.

He pulls into my parking lot and shuts the SUV off. I wait for a moment for him to say something—anything—but he sits there, still and staring straight ahead.

"I'm sorry I said anything. I didn't mean to fall for you. If it's any consolation, I think my feelings would have developed even if we didn't spend the night together. I flew across the country for you."

"You flew across the country for *you*," he corrects. "It was something you needed."

"And now you're something I need." My words hang in the darkness. He doesn't have to respond. I get the message loud and clear.

My hand is on the handle, I'm a millisecond away from jumping out of the vehicle and never looking back when he says, "It's not you, it's me."

His words confirm my deepest, darkest fear. It's what one says when it is most definitely you. My initial instincts to never leave my house again were the right ones. Putting myself out there only leads to rejection. Again. When will I learn that no one will stay with me? There's something inherently lacking in me that's completely unlovable. I wish someday someone would tell me what it is.

My eyes burn with tears, and the lump in my throat is so thick I feel as if I can barely breathe.

He puts his hand on my arm, as if he knows I'm going to run away and never look back. "Rach, I mean that. I ... I'm not ready to give you what you need. I'm too messed up still. I want to, but I don't want to hurt you because I'm a train wreck."

"You're the train wreck? Your life is perfect," I spit at him. No wonder he doesn't want me. He has impossible standards that I must fall quite short of. Silly me for dreaming.

He rakes his fingers through his hair, slamming his head back against the headrest. "Rachel, there's no such thing as perfect. I live every day with the thought that the next practice or game could be my last, and then what? I have no marketable skills. It's not like I have what it takes to work in the front office. I'm not polished or smooth enough to be on air for one of the networks, plus, do you know how steep the competition is for that? All I can do is take my shirt off and pretend to know how to cook. But when it's not my job to be physically fit, I doubt people will still tune in. Then what? What do I do? There's an expiration date on both my looks and my skill, and we all know it's sooner rather than later. You see what Joey looks like, and he's only five years older than I am. When I don't have those things, what am I good for? How am I going to provide a life for you?"

My mouth opens and then closes. I try to make sense of his words. "I never asked you to provide a life for me." The tears that have been stinging the backs of my eyes make their way forward and spill down my face.

"It's tempting to want more. Because I do. But I'm not ready yet. And, frankly, neither are you. Because when this happens, I will never ever want to let you go. So, when this happens, I want the best version of myself to be there for you. And don't take this the wrong way, but I want the best version of you for me. So let's slow this down, work on ourselves, and get our shit together before we do anything stupid."

I want to tell him his words make sense. I want to reassure him he's not stupid. I want to beg him to reconsider so we can grow together. Instead, I hop out of the SUV and run inside, never once looking back.

Once safely behind the door of my apartment, I slide to the floor, the tears flowing freely. I yell at the ceiling, "This is all your fault!" Once again, my sister doesn't answer.

I'm right back to where I started.

CHAPTER 34: TJ

Monday morning finds me heading into the Buzzards' facilities at the crack of dawn. Well, 7:30 a.m., but close enough. It was the only time the team psychologist, Watson Ross, could squeeze me in.

I've never been one for therapy, but so many of my teammates swear by it that I figure this guy is either the smartest man in the world or a miracle worker. I don't care which, as long as he can help me.

Yesterday felt like the longest day. All I wanted to do was talk to Rachel or go see her. She was not okay when she got out of the car. I was trying to be mature and reasonable. It would have been so much easier to fall into bed with her. It's all I wanted to do.

But I know how delicate she is, and I didn't want to hurt her by messing up our relationship, which I'd eventually do. So instead, I hurt her by telling her the truth. I wasn't rejecting her. It's the reverse. I'm not good enough for her.

"What brings you in today?" Watson asks.

Do I start with Rachel? Or do I start with the thing with my parents keeping my learning disability from me? Or about ClikClak and how I get sucked in and then can't do anything else. Maybe I should tell him that I don't know what I'm going to do when I'm no longer playing for the Buzzards.

Shit. I'm going to need a lot more than an hour session.

"Hey, there's no wrong answer here. You look a little nervous. Don't be. Tell me what's on your mind."

"Everything." It's the truth. "I feel like I'm spinning around in circles, and I don't know which way is up anymore. I want to get off the ride, but I don't know how. I'm afraid if I try, I'll fall down and never get up again." I have a mental image of me stepping off a fair ride only to get sucked up underneath it, whipping around like a rag doll as it continues to spin.

"So what do you do about that?" he asks, leaning back in his chair, his fingers carefully tented under his chin.

"Nothing. And then I hate myself for doing the same thing day in and day out." At least I'm still buckled into the ride.

"Tell me what your days are like."

I fill him in on the doomscrolling and the aesthetic videos, including pretending to cook, when I can barely follow a recipe. "No matter how hard I try, I seem to mess up the stupid directions." Then it dawns on me why. "I'm dyslexic. I just found out. Do you think that could be why the recipes are hard for me?"

"Undoubtedly. Has reading always been challenging?"

I nod. "Everyone thought I was being lazy or that I wasn't trying. I was, so I thought I was just dumb. It certainly seemed that way. Whatever I did, it wasn't good enough."

"You said you recently found out that you have dyslexia. Tell me about that."

I recount the conversation with Rachel, and then with my parents. "They didn't think it would be a big deal because I had a high IQ. I've spent my entire life thinking the only option I had was to cash in on my athletic talent and my looks, both of which are short-lasting and temporary."

"And now?"

"That's the big question, isn't it? I need to go back to high school and work with the guidance counselor and take one of those career-readiness tests. Although I'd probably still bomb it because it's not like reading is easier, just because I know about the dyslexia now." It feels good to open up about this stuff, like I've primed the pump and now the water's ready to flow. "And that's the thing. I need to figure out what comes next because I need to be better."

"Why do you need to be better?"

"I ... I'm interested in someone. Someone I want to have a future with. I don't think I should be taking my clothes off for other women if I belong to her. So then what do I have?"

"Before soccer, what did you want to do? What did you want to be when you grew up?"

"A magician." It's the God's honest truth.

"Ooookay," Watson says, drawing the word out. "That's a starting place."

"Not really. I beat the odds by becoming a professional soccer player. I don't think becoming the next David Copperfield is in the cards for me."

Watson laughs a little. "Would it help you to know that you're not the only player in the twilight of his career to have this same kind of identity crisis?"

I look up from staring at my hands, which are much less interesting than the bombshell the psychologist just dropped on me. "What?"

"This is not uncommon," he says. "Frankly, I'm more concerned when a player does not go through this process. You've been playing this sport for as long as you can remember. It's probably all you've ever wanted to do. It's been your focus, your purpose, your identity. It makes sense to be stressed out about what comes next. Not very many athletes prepare for life after sport during their career. It's something that the industry needs to address."

Relief floods through my body. "I kind of feel like I've been spiraling with this. Maybe even a little depressed." It feels good to say that out loud instead of letting it silently fester.

"And you may continue to struggle with those feelings. They're natural when facing a transition. I'm going to refer you to a life coach, so you can work on figuring out your goals and whatever obstacles might be in the way. Together, you'll develop a plan for your post-soccer life." He hands me a business card as I stand to leave. "I've had several patients work with Brooke, and they seem highly satisfied."

Walking out of the office, my body feels lighter, but the card weighs heavily in my hand. What if I can't come up with a plan? What if I can't figure out who I am outside of soccer? What if I never find my calling?

I make it to the practice facility and drop my bag in front of my locker. Because of my appointment, I'm early. This has never happened before. Just as I'm about to start berating myself for being habitually late, I remember the podcast I listened to about dyslexia. Time management—specifically time blindness in my case—can be part of it. So maybe I'm not rude. Maybe it's not that I don't care about my team or others. Maybe it's just that I haven't given my brain the support it needed to be on time.

Wow, the breakthroughs are hitting all over the place.

I pick up my phone to text Rachel, but then I put it down. I need to have myself a little more together—have more of a plan—before I ask her to be in the audience of the shit show that is my life. I will figure it out and arrive on her doorstep, a new man. And then I'll tell her that I don't want to be friends and that I don't want our one night in Vegas to be the last time I ever hold her or make love to her. I'll tell her that I can see myself falling for her. Or maybe that I've already fallen.

She's on the same page—at least she said so after the game. She's falling for me as much as I'm falling for her. Maybe if we can *both* work on ourselves a little bit, we can have a future together.

Despite my early arrival, I'm not the first one there. The new guy, Crew, is sitting on the chair in front of his locker, head in his hands. He's way too early in his career to be this dejected. Of course, my telling him that he was no Brandon Nix probably didn't help. I need to be more supportive and encouraging to the players at the start of their careers.

"What's up, man? You okay?" I ask. "Thinking about the game?" Crew has yet to score since joining the Buzzards. He's gotten close, but close isn't going to get us to the playoffs or the championship.

Crew looks up. "No, my girlfriend dumped me."

"Oh." I don't know what else to say. Prior to meeting Rachel, I'd probably have said something epic like, "Yeah, bitches. Can't live without 'em, don't want to live with 'em." That feels wrong on so many levels.

"You screw up?"

He nods. "Yeah, I hooked up with someone in Vegas. She was waiting for me to cheat. Expecting me to fail. I like to live up to expectations."

"Maybe if she was expecting you to fail, she's not the type of person you should be with. Try to surround yourself with people invested in your successes, not your failures. There are tons of haters out there. You don't need them in your inner circle."

My impromptu pep talk dances around my head throughout the rest of the day. I can't stop thinking about it. At the end of practice, I make another locker room ClikClak, this time asking the team who their biggest supporters are. For most, it's their parents. A few, like Callaghan Entay, list coaches they've had along the way. Pressley Samson says his wife.

I stash the footage in my drafts as inspiration hits again.

I turn the camera on myself. "What's the harshest criticism you've ever heard about yourself that's totally untrue? I'll go first. I'm lazy and stupid. Turns out, I'm just dyslexic, and I learn differently."

The guys practically line up to answer this one. Xavier Henry's answer is obvious. "That I'm a drunk who nearly left a poor woman to die in a ditch, when in fact, I was trying to help her out."

Callaghan Entay says, "That I never quite lived up to my potential. It was very early on in my career, and I hadn't hit my peak yet. I think I've proved that wrong, but those words have lived rent free in my brain for a very long time."

Crew Benequista sits thoughtfully for a minute. "That I can't be loyal. I can be loyal when someone believes in me."

On and on it goes. This is awesome. By the time I'm done, I have tons of small interviews that I'll be able to edit into multiple videos. None of it requires me taking my shirt off, though several of my teammates were in various states of undress.

It takes me hours to edit the videos. I don't bother making any cooking videos, instead choosing to heat up a frozen meal my mom stashed for me. My freezer is packed with the black containers.

> Me: Ate one of the frozen meals tonight. Came in handy. Thanks.
> Ma: I'm glad to hear that. That's what they're there for. I can make more. Let me know what you want.
> Me: Ma, I don't need you to cook for me. I'm appreciative of it, but I don't need it.
> Ma: Old habits die hard.
> Me: I'm an adult, you know. I am 32.
> Ma: I know, though I don't know how that's possible, considering I'm only 35.
> Me: 35? What happened to 27?

For years, that's how old my mother claimed to be.

> Ma: I don't want people to think I'm a liar.
> Ma: I'm sorry that we didn't tell you about the dyslexia.
> Me: Why didn't you?

I have to know. My parents are big on the truth. This is out of character for them, which is why it's so hard to digest.

> Ma: Lots of reasons. Honestly, it was hard for us to accept. But also, we didn't want you using it as a crutch. You know, an excuse not to try. You were the kid to look for the easy way out, and we didn't want to open the exit door for you.

That makes a lot of sense. I tend to follow the path of least resistance. I still look for the easy way out. Like with my video content. Except now, I'm trying. I'm working at it.

> Me: I can kind of see that, but you know it did a number on my self-esteem.
> Ma: <laughing emoji>

Laughing emoji? What the fuck? She thinks this is something to laugh at? I hit the call button. I don't even wait for a greeting once the call connects. "I'm not being funny. I'm being serious. My self-esteem has been terrible my whole life."

"Oh, Tyler, I beg to differ. You're a professional soccer player in the USSL. You got there because you believed in yourself. You make an additional six figures a year from your social media. You got there because you believed in yourself. You can't do either of those things without a healthy self-esteem."

"So I can kick a ball, and I'm conventionally attractive. I'd rather be smart."

"But you are smart."

"I've never felt like it." I think about it. Could it all be my perception? I think about the way my mother still hovers. Still treats me like I couldn't make it on my own, with the cooking and the laundry. "And you didn't either. You didn't—don't—think I'm smart enough to make it on my own. That's why you're always hovering. Doing my laundry. Cleaning my place. Stocking my fridge. Treating me like a child."

She lets out an exasperated sigh. "Tyler, I do those things to help you out! You have an incredibly demanding job. Your job is 24-7-365 for a limited time. While you're in this world, I thought I'd help you out by not wasting your time with some of the more menial, time-consuming tasks that suck to do because they never go away. Do you know how many times I wished when you boys were little and I was running here and there and everywhere that someone would break in and clean the house? Or do the laundry? Do you know how tedious and tiresome it is to have to meal-plan *every single night* because the people in the house won't eat if you don't do it? Your father and I made the decision that this was the best way we could support your career. Dad would help with your accounting, and I would help with the housekeeping. Not because we didn't think you could, but we wanted you to only have to focus on your career. We wanted you to be able to put everything into playing soccer and not worry about the other bullshit." Her voice has risen several decibles by the end of the rant. I have to hold the phone away from my ear, otherwise I'd risk damage to my hearing.

"Well, you don't have to yell about it," I say.

"I wasn't yelling. I was expressing my thoughts with feeling and volume."

A smile betrays me. "Dammit, Ma. So it's not because you think I'm too stupid to be able to work my washer and dryer?"

"No, it's because you'd probably let your clothes grow mold in the washer because you're too busy to get them to the dryer. There'd be clothes all over your place, because you'd never fold them and put them away. Your place is too nice to become one big laundry hamper. Plus, when I come over, I want a place to sit, and I don't want to have to dig out the couch from under Mount Laundry." She pauses for a second. "Though maybe the laundry would make it more comfortable. That couch is really hard."

"Yeah, it's awful. Rachel's couch is super comfortable. She got it at Bob's. It's a Bob-o-pedic. I might have to get me one."

"Oh, how is Rachel?"

Shit. I shouldn't have brought her up. I can't lie to Ma about the situation. "Um, well, we're on a little break."

"A break? What did you do that she needs a break from you?" It feels like the question I asked Crew. *You screw up?*

Suddenly, I'm six years old again and just got caught with my hand in the cookie jar before dinner. "Um, I asked for the break. I wanted to get stuff figured out. I talked to the team psychologist, and he suggested I see a life coach. I have an appointment with Brooke later on this week.

Once I've had some sessions and know what I want to do with my life, then I'll be good enough for Rachel."

"Tyler Jeremiah, that's probably the stupidest thing I've ever heard you say."

She did not just call me stupid. "Ma! You said I wasn't stupid."

"You are not inherently stupid, but that's one of the most boneheaded maneuvers you've ever pulled. You can't ask that girl to wait for you until you get your life figured out. Spoiler alert: there's no figuring it out. Most grown-ass adults are still trying to figure out what they want to be when they grow up."

Huh. I thought I was the only one who didn't have it figured out.

"And another thing—I saw that poor girl sitting all by herself at the game, reading a book. Sadness wafted out of every pore. That's not the same woman who was with you on Saturday. And frankly, you're not the same man either. So, and I say this lovingly as your mother, pull your head out of your ass before it's too late and you lose her for good."

CHAPTER 35: RACHEL

J ust tell me one thing." Gramps is doing little to conceal his annoyance. "Are you doing this to punish us for making you move out?"

I tuck the pile of papers into a file folder before looking up at my grandfather. "No, I'm doing this because if I don't get out now, I'll never leave. I've stayed alive here, but it's no place for me to thrive." Giving my two weeks' notice at Cramer-Romero has gone over like a fart in church.

He's mad. He's disappointed. He's grumpy. Well, he's always grumpy. But he still loves me. He's not going to stay mad forever. I hope.

"I swear, I went to the bookstore, and they had a help-wanted sign. I thought maybe I could do part-time, but they need full-time. I'll still have time to do the social media for you, so your business won't suffer. If I can't get out to a site, Dale's going to shoot the video for me. I already talked to him about it."

"Do bookstores pay that well?" he huffs.

"Not at all, but you can't put a price on happiness. I'll figure out a side hustle. I could probably do some remote bookkeeping for you, if you need it. I just don't want to be running the Sharon office. I don't want Cramer-Romero to be my only thing. I need something for me."

"Well, your mother has been asking me for a job for a while. If you're not going to be in the office every day, I could offer her something."

"What?" It's a good thing I'm sitting down already. You could knock me over with a feather. "You've ... you've heard from Mom?"

"She's been around a lot since Richie died. Hit her hard."

The image of our birth giver crying and wailing at Richie's funeral comes flooding back, and so does the anger. "If she's been around so much, why haven't I seen her? Did she forget she still has a daughter?"

"She's been asking to see you. Sharon and I thought it was best if she didn't bother you. We told her you'd be in contact when you were ready."

My inner child is standing there with a big ole grin on her face, all excited because her mom is coming back. My adult self is backhanding that fool for having any hope that Mom will change.

Gramps continues, "Renee seems to have turned over a new leaf, but we've thought that before too. We've been worried about you, and we didn't want to add one more thing."

"Smart move," I grumble. My grandparents know me well. I wouldn't have been able to handle my mother's unpredictability right now, especially not on top of my grief.

"You know I'm not the one to defend Renee. I leave that to your grandmother. I've been disappointed by Renee more times than I can count. But I think I see a difference in her since Richie died. It was a wake-up call."

"It came too little, too late," I grumble.

"That's what she's realizing. She missed out on everything. I think she thought she'd always be able to make it up to you when the time was right," Gramps says with a shrug. "I can't figure out where we went wrong," he adds, staring out the window.

He's now lost in his thoughts, so I don't interrupt him. Over the years, I've heard him and Gram fighting about my mom. It's easy for me to forget that she's not just my mother; she's their child. It hurts me to see my grandparents hurting. They stepped up when our mother failed us. They gave Richie and me a home. They gave us everything. And now I'm walking away, like they don't mean anything.

"Gramps, I don't need to quit. I can keep working for you. I ... I'll tell the bookstore that I can't take the job. I can be here for you the way you were here for me." I stand up from my new desk and go to hug my curmudgeonly grandfather.

He bats me away. He's not the hugging type.

"Have you lost your damn mind? You don't belong here anymore, and I was wrong for trying to force it on you. You were only supposed to help out over the summers when you were in high school. This wasn't supposed to be your career."

"Yeah, but I had to pick up the slack for Mom. She was supposed to be in the family business. I had to take her place."

"You can't live your life for Renee any more than you can live out your sister's bucket list. You have to live for yourself. Do what you want to do. Get what you want from life, not what you think other people want you to have."

The intrusive thought that so often guides my life once again bobs to the surface. "I'm afraid no one will love me if I don't do what they want me to do." This is the first time I've ever admitted it out loud.

Gramps slams his hand on the desk. "Are you kidding me with that bullshit?"

I jump. "N ... n ... no," I manage to squeak out.

"Is that really what you think?" He waves his hands in front of his face. "No, don't bother answering that. I ... dammit, where is Sharon when you need her?" he blusters and then storms out.

Alrighty then.

About three minutes later, my phone rings.

"Hi, Gram."

"Gramps told me you're upset."

I sigh. "I'm not the one who stormed out of here. He didn't even get that upset when I turned in my resignation."

"You know Albert isn't good with the feeling stuff. He's all prickles on the outside, but on the inside, he's a big softie. You know that. He's upset by what you said."

Historically, I would have hung my head and apologized profusely, doing anything to make it so no one was mad at me. Today, I feel different. Emboldened maybe. "Gram, I'm allowed to have feelings. I'm allowed to say that I have a deep-seated fear that if I don't do exactly what someone wants me to do, they won't love me anymore. I've earned it. I have a deadbeat dad, if he even knows I exist, and a mom who's not much better. When the people who make you don't even love you, then who else will?"

"Gramps and I tried to make up for it." Gram's voice sounds so sad.

"I know you did. But I have these abandonment issues. And then Richie left me, and then you kicked me out. You can see why maybe they're not getting better."

But they are getting better. Okay, not by much, but I'm at least able to admit that they exist. Gotta start somewhere.

"We ... mistakes were made, with you and your sister. We didn't know what to do for you."

It breaks my heart to hear my grandmother talk like this. "You took us in. You kept us out of foster care, or even worse, from potentially getting abused by one of Mom's boyfriends."

"Yeah, but we were scared. We'd messed up so much with Renee. She had your grandfather wrapped around her little finger when she was younger. He spoiled her, and she could manipulate him like nobody's business. We didn't want to make the same mistakes with you and Richie. So we just stood by and watched you make mistakes."

"I think Richie and I turned out pretty damn good, and that's all because of you and Gramps."

"Rachel," she says quietly, "you're kind of a mess."

I jump to my feet, my voice rising to a level I've never taken with my grandmother before. "I am not!" That's it. That's my whole argument. I guess this is why I never considered law school. I would have sucked ass.

"Rachel, you are still working the same job you had when you were fourteen years old."

"No, I'm not. I just quit. And, back then, I was just answering phones and filing paperwork. I do so much more now. I'm the South Regional Director. At least I was until I resigned to take a different job. A job I want. A job that will make me happy." Take that, Gram. I still don't think arguing in a court of law is my chosen calling. That's one profession I can rule out. Nine billion left to go.

"Yes, but it's not your passion. It's not what you want to do."

"Yeah! It's why I turned in my notice to take a much poorer-paying job at a bookstore. At least that gets me excited to go to work everyday. Plus, I think there will be much less shit."

I can practically see Gram nodding. "Language, young lady. But I admit, it is a step in the right direction. Al said you've stayed there all this time because you were afraid that if you quit, we wouldn't love you anymore because you let us down."

She's got me there. Gram continues, "Did he tell you that while we've been happy you've been a part of Cramer-Romero all these years, we always expected you to go off and find your own path? Were we upset with Richie when she wanted to go to PA school?"

"No, but I thought that was just because I was still holding down the fort. Someone had to pick up Mom's slack. It obviously wasn't going to be Richie, so it had to be me," I say.

"Or else we wouldn't love you?"

Okay, maybe that seems a little ridiculous when she puts it like that. "I see what you're saying, but try telling my brain that. It had a rough start in life." I think people, especially older folks, truly underestimate the effects trauma can have on kids and people in general. But especially kids. "I think taking a new job is a good start for me."

I want to tell her about Tyler, but then I remember that he shot me down. Maybe I'll tell her about the next guy I'm interested in.

Who am I kidding? I don't see myself getting over TJ Doyle any time soon.

"It is a good start," Gram says. "I don't want to rush you or push you, but Renee has been asking to talk to you."

"Yeah, I'm growing as a person and all, but I'm not there yet. I'm not sure I ever will be." Before Gram can say anything else, I add, "And it's not even about when we were little. It's about Richie. She didn't come when she was sick. She should have been here for her daughter."

"She didn't know how to be there."

"I can't forgive her for letting Richie down."

"Even though Richie explicitly asked you to?" Gram questions.

She's got me there.

"Trying to do Richie's list has brought me nothing but heartbreak. It's stupid, and I could kill her for leaving it for me." I think about Tyler and how he can't have feelings for me the way I have for him. Why not? Don't I deserve to be loved, like everyone else?

Yes, I do.

Yes, I do.

All the lies my brain has told me over the years part like clouds, and the truth shines through. I deserve to be loved. I am worthy of love. Not just because I don't speak up, or because I do what's expected of me, but because I am. I exist, and I deserve to be loved.

I'm *ready* to be loved.

CHAPTER 36: TJ

The idea hits me in the shower. I've heard that's where many great ideas strike. I was doing a mental inventory of things I'm good at: playing soccer, doing social media. Then I made a list of everything I'm not good at: everything else. It doesn't help tremendously with career planning. Normally, I'd think about reading a self-help book about finding fulfillment in life and then berate myself because reading is hard. That seems like a bad cycle to venture into.

Watson Ross suggested I look into audiobooks and podcasts as source material since people with dyslexia often find those easier to glean information from. And then—BOOM—it hits me.

Podcasts.

I could start a podcast. I could talk about soccer things, but also about life after soccer, when the time comes. Maybe I could try out different jobs and talk about my experiences. I bet a lot of people would be willing to let a professional athlete shadow them for a day. It could help drive business to those places. I immediately think of

Rachel's account for Oh Crap! I could use my name for good, especially helping small businesses.

Would anyone even tune in? Yes, I think they would. Even if I was bad at a job. Especially if I were bad at the job. I've been the butt of jokes for so long that this wouldn't even be a stretch for me. My videos of my teammates have hit all-time high views for me on ClikClak. I record a note in my phone to talk to Leora, our public relations person. She might have some ideas for me. Joey might be able to help, too. Maybe we could do the podcast together.

Putting notes in my phone is new for me, too. The simple act of recording the note helps me remember that I have a task to do. Look at me, getting my shit together.

This is killing an entire flock of birds with one stone.

As soon as I talk to Joey and Leora, I'm calling Rachel. I'll have a plan. A direction. An adventure to go on that she can ride shotgun for. Or maybe she drives sometimes, too. It'll be a journey we can take together. Our own bucket lists.

I step out of the shower, energized by my brilliance. This is going to be great. Then I hear it. There's a thumping sound. It takes me a moment to realize it's the door. Someone's knocking.

Dripping wet, I fasten the towel around my waist. No one ever knocks on my door. Ma has a key and lets herself in. This can't be good. I yank open the door, expecting to see police or something like that.

I do not expect to see Rachel standing there, her feet planted, trying to make her petite frame seem big. She doesn't say anything. Her eyes do a slow blink, and her jaw goes slack. I glance down. Oh yeah, I probably have that effect.

"It's not like you haven't seen it before," I offer.

"Yeah, but it's wet and ... hot." She licks her lips. She'd better stop looking at me with so much lust in her eyes. This towel isn't forgiving, and my reciprocated feelings are about to become very physically evident. I turn around. "Give me a second."

In my bedroom, I grab the first thing I see, which are my gray sweatpants. Why is she here? What does she have to say? Will she listen to me? Will she give me another chance? I slide them on without even bothering to put on underwear.

"Yeah, I don't know that's much better. Can you at least put a shirt on? It's hard to think with all that"—she makes a circle motion with her hand—"on display."

"Fine." I stomp back to my room and grab a T-shirt. She wants me fully dressed. That doesn't bode well for ... anything. I pull the shirt over my head. She wants something from me. No matter what it is, I'll give it to her, even if it means letting her go.

Rachel is perched on the edge of the couch. "I deserve love," she announces before I'm even close to her.

I cross the room and kneel in front of her. "Of course you do." I want to take her hands in mine, but they are knotted tightly in her lap. Her body language is screaming, "Don't touch me!" I have to respect that.

"I am worthy of love." Her voice breaks.

"Of course you are."

"Will you just let me finish?" She stands up and brushes past me. She starts pacing the length of my living room and then takes a deep breath. Her voice still shaking, she says, "I deserve love. I am worthy of love. I am lovable. I'm ready for love."

I wait for her to continue.

She turns and looks at me. "I deserve love. I am worthy of love. I am lovable. I'm ready for love."

Almost imperceptibly, I nod.

Rachel throws her hands in the air. "I'm ready for love! Ready for love with you. To love you and to be loved by you. And maybe we're not there yet. Maybe we don't know each other well enough yet, but the keyword there is *yet*. So maybe you're not ready for love. Can you be ready for yet?"

I wait for a minute to make sure she's done. The silence fills the apartment. Okay, I think she's done.

"Can I talk now?"

She nods, those big, hot fudge eyes taking up her whole face.

Now I'm pacing. Then I turn back to face her. I have to see her expression when I say this to her. "Before I met you, I was lost. I didn't know who I was or where I was heading. I was stuck in an endless cycle of doomscrolling and self-pity. Turns out, at least if the team psychologist is to be believed, I'm having an identity crisis, which is totally normal for athletes toward the end of their careers. My whole life has been soccer, and it's going to end within the next few years. I don't know what comes next. I'm in a little bit of an anxiety-depression-panic cycle because of it."

"I can relate," she says flatly.

I smile. "I bet you can. You just unknowingly jumped into the middle of my downward spiral. And all I could think of was that I wasn't enough. It turns out that it's not really because I'm not enough, it's just that I don't know who I am yet. Outside of soccer, obviously."

"Obviously," she echoes.

"And how can I be with you if I don't know who I am?"

"I don't know who I am either, but I'm starting to branch out," Rachel says quietly.

"ME TOO!" My voice is entirely too loud for the situation. I don't care. I feel like a kid on Christmas Eve. I'm expressing my thoughts with feeling and volume. "But

I'm working on it. I ... I have a life coach, and now I have a plan. Can I tell you my plan? I think it's a great plan. It came to me in the shower, the plan. This plan is the answer to everything."

"You can tell me if you don't use the word plan. You sound like a book that didn't go through enough editing." I see a hint of a smile. "It's a serious pet peeve of mine."

"Okay, my ... idea is a podcast. Maybe even with Joey, because he can be funny occasionally. I want to interview other athletes and talk about sports, naturally, but then about life after sports. Career planning and career readiness. I was also thinking about a segment where I try out different jobs." As I'm saying it, I realize the problem. "Shit, that wouldn't be good for a podcast. That's more visual."

"But you could probably spin that off into a YouTube series. It would definitely be good to cross-post on ClikClak as well."

I look at her. "You don't think it's stupid?"

She shakes her head. "I think it's brilliant. I think you and your brother will be good together, and it will help both your careers."

"And I was thinking that it would help the businesses that I feature when I try out jobs."

"Yes. They could sponsor an episode, which would help with production costs, as well as get the publicity and traction. Cramer-Romero has sponsored all sorts of things over the years. Never a podcast, but it's not out of the realm of possibility."

When she doesn't comment about my idea, I prompt, "So?"

"So what?" she asks.

"So I have a pla—an idea for what I'm going to be when I grow up. When my time with the Boston Buzzards is done,

I'll have the roots for this in place so I can step seamlessly into a new career."

"That's great, Tyler. I'm happy for you." Is Rachel looking at me expectantly? She holds my gaze for a moment before standing up. "I'm happy you have your plan. I think it's great. You're going to be just fine." She turns and walks toward the door.

I grab her wrist, spin her around, and pull her back to me. Her body collides with mine with a soft thud. "Where do you think you're going?"

She keeps her head down, her arms hanging limply at her sides. I reach down and, with the most delicate touch I can manage, gently lift her chin with my fingertips. "Where do you think you're going?" I repeat.

Her eyes brim with tears. "I told you I was ready for love, and you told me about your podcast."

Holding her chin steady, I lean down and give her lips a soft kiss. I can't stop there. I kiss her again, parting her lips with mine. She opens wider, inviting my tongue in, meeting it with her own. My hands move to the sides of her face and then back into her hair, the silky short strands sliding through my fingers.

I will never tire of kissing this woman.

"I was telling you my plan so you'd know I'm ready. I'm not some screwup who's going to drift aimlessly. I'm getting my shit together, and you're going to get your shit together, and our shit will be together and we'll be together, shitless."

Rachel pulls back slightly. "I'm not sure if that was romantic or terrible."

I laugh. "How about terribly romantic?"

It's her turn to laugh. "I happen to know for a fact that no one is ever truly shitless, but I think I know what you mean."

"I'm ready for yet and whatever comes after yet. I'm ready for it all, as long as we can do it together."

Her body presses into mine. I slide my hands down her shoulders and back until I'm cupping her petite ribcage in my hands. It's not enough. I bend forward so my hands can reach down further, underneath her buttocks. In one swift move, I scoop her up. Reflexively her legs wrap around my waist.

I carry her to the bedroom and make a plan never to let her go again.

EPILOGUE: RACHEL

Two Years Later

A re you sure about this?" Tyler asks. I'm not sure which one of us is more nervous.

"It's going to be great," I say through clenched teeth, tugging down the edge of my shorts. "I mean, it would be great if my ass weren't hanging out."

"But it's a great ass," Tyler says, leaning back to admire the view.

I turn around and straighten his tie. "It's a party for children. There are seven- and eight-year-olds here. They do not need to see butt cheeks," I say, pulling the shorts down again. "And they're itchy and scratchy all at the same time. They're hurting in my nether region. And under my armpits!" My voice rises.

"You don't need to yell."

"I'm not yelling. I'm expressing my displeasure for sequins with feeling and volume."

Tyler slaps my hind end. "I'm personally enjoying the show."

I brush his hand away. "There are children here," I hiss. I turn back to the mirror, Tyler standing right behind me. "I look ridiculous."

"Ridiculously awesome," Tyler says, his arms circling my waist. He leans his chin on my shoulder. "You're going to be great. And even if everything goes horribly wrong, I want you to wear this tonight—after. I have plans, and most of them involve stripping you out of this very slowly."

Before I can admonish him again that there are children present, he plants a kiss on the top of my head and walks over to his setup. I turn back to my reflection in the mirror. There I am, Rachel Cramer, clad in a skin-tight, red sequined, booty-short romper. The long sleeves make it difficult to move my arms, and I'm worried that the scoop neck is scooping a little too low for the audience. I'm not gifted in the boob department, but thanks to the push-up bra I'm wearing underneath the outfit, my cups are threatening to runneth over.

It was a compromise from the rest of the outfits Tyler picked out for me, most of which included corsets and much more cleavage and were far more suited to the bedroom than a child's birthday party. I did give in a little for him, and I am wearing fishnets and red high-heeled boots. He said it would make him less nervous. As previously suspected, Tyler has a thing for shoes. I have an entire shelf in the closet of shoes that never leave our bedroom.

I look up at the ceiling. "I just know you're laughing your ass off at me. I wondered about a lot of the things on the list, but I know this was just to troll me." I do a little twirl so my sister up in heaven can get the full view. "But this is it. Last one. Then what am I supposed to do with my time?"

Tyler comes back over to me, moving stiffly in the black dress shoes. He's wearing a black button-down shirt and dress pants, along with a red satin vest and bow tie. It's not his best look, but on brand for a magician.

That's right, Tyler has finally taught himself enough magic tricks to string together for a show. I'm his lovely assistant. Turns out, the reason Tyler could never learn how to successfully do magic tricks was that he was always trying to read books on it. It was too nuanced for him to be able to get it successfully. Once he started watching video tutorials, it was a whole different ball of wax.

I swear, if I got to keep every quarter he pulled out from behind my ear, I'd be ... well, I could afford a venti drink with extra shots at Starbucks, if that tells you anything.

Our first official gig is at Tyler's niece's birthday party. The deck has been converted into a stage, complete with curtains that open and close. We even have microphones and everything, though my super-tight, super-short outfit doesn't leave much room to conceal it.

The backyard at Joey and Amanda's house has been transformed into a glitzy, glittery wonderland. There are disco balls everywhere, reflecting the strobe lights. Most of the attendees are dressed as "pop stars." We're the opening act, followed by karaoke on the stage. Apparently, Cami and her friends have been choreographing routines to go along with their singing since the invitations went out.

Tyler's set is about fifteen tricks that he's been practicing for the better part of a year. He's replaced doomscrolling with magic trick scrolling. It's fine, except for when he wakes me up because he's finally unlocked a new trick.

He'd really wanted to start learning tricks with doves. With his practices, games, and travel, it'd be too hard to take care of a pair of doves. Tyler says when he retires from playing soccer, he's branching out. I'm not so sure about that. Ophelia is terrified of birds and said she will never, in no uncertain terms, hang out at our house if we have birds indoors. Xavier, of course, is encouraging Tyler to get them, and he's even offered his expertise in caring for birds.

I've yet to tell Tyler that I promised Ophelia we wouldn't get them in exchange for being able to be in the delivery room when she had her baby, Penelope. I mean, when else would I get the chance to cross *that* item off the list? In all honesty, it was kind of gross. Miraculous, but gross. Not only did Ophelia let me be in the room, but I'm one of Penelope's godmothers. It's what best friends do for each other.

I haven't had to deal with this issue just yet, as Tyler's career continues with the Buzzards. Barring a catastrophic injury, he's on contract for at least one more season. I can figure out the bird thing then. Maybe I'll convince him to use rabbits in his act instead.

As planned, I went parasailing off the Rhode Island coast as soon as the season opened. It was not nearly as scary as it looked from the ground. Kind of relaxing, really, and super easy to cross off the list. I should have started with that one.

A random road trip one Sunday in May to the outlets in Lee helped fulfill number five. There I was, minding my own business, driving west on I-90 when I spotted the moose on the side of the road. Granted, I nearly crashed my car looking at the damn thing, but I also felt like Richie was there in the car with me. I could practically hear her laughing.

Forgiving Mom? That was the toughest. It wouldn't have been possible without Tyler showing me what love can do for a person. That, and the help of a good therapist. Forgiving her past transgressions didn't mean she got an automatic pass into my life. I was pleasant to her when I had to show her the ropes at Cramer-Romero. The guilt of missing out on our lives is her bag of rocks to carry. I no longer need to add to it. I'm lucky to have Gram and Gramps and my sister, for as long as I had her, and now the entire Doyle clan, not to mention the Boston Buzzards crew. I went from feeling like I wasn't worth being loved to having a life full of love and acceptance.

All because of Richie's list.

I still miss my sister. I always will. There will always be a part of me missing, but the rest of me has continued to grow around that hole. It's not as much gaping and treacherous anymore as it is a tripping hazard. I wish Tyler could have known her, but I feel like maybe he does because I talk about her so much. I used to think that her dying was the end of my life too. Funny, it's only because of her death that I learned to live.

So now it's time to cross the last item off the list. I'm about to perform on stage in a sexy, sequined costume. We have practiced the routine so many times, I could do it in my sleep. I just want to get through it so I can change out of this outfit. It really is itchy. I'm going to have to slather myself in hydrocortisone cream before I put it on later for Tyler. That'll be super sexy.

I look at Tyler and smile. Beads of perspiration form on his hairline. His gaze darts back and forth. Oh shit, he's starting to panic.

I take both his hands in mine and start singing "I Gotta Feeling." He adds his woo-hoos and ad-libs, smiling at me through it. "This is one of the many reasons why I love you," he says, leaning in and kissing me gently. "You've always got my back. Now, are you ready to do this?"

It's my turn to nod, and then, following Joey's introduction, we take the stage. The set starts with a bunch of scarf tricks, and then some card tricks. He's got a magic coloring book, which is met with impressed oohs and ahs. The kids are eating this up, Cami especially, who's stopped doing back walkovers for once and is sitting in the front row, transfixed.

My grandparents even made the trek down to see the show. I'd talked to Gram about it so much that I couldn't exclude her from my debut. Joey and Amanda understood about fulfilling Richie's list, and why I needed them here for this moment. They were surprisingly gracious about my inviting my septuagenarian grandparents to their eight-year-old's birthday party. On the other hand, all the Doyles have welcomed me into the family, and by extension, Gram and Gramps.

Tyler calls up Cami and a few volunteers and begins pulling quarters out of their ears right and left. The girls are squealing and giggling. Once all the ears have been rid of quarters, the girls return to their seats on the lawn. Tyler walks over to me. "And what about you, young lady? Do your ears need to be checked, too?"

This is not part of the routine, but he's doing it to mess with me. He knows how much I'm over this trick. It was the first one he learned, and he's done it a lot.

"I'm good, thanks."

"Oh, come on, I think I see something."

"I'm quite sure there's no quarter behind my ear," I say flatly. The girls in the audience laugh. They don't know this isn't part of the routine.

"No, let me check," he says, stepping closer.

He's not going to let this go. "Fine," I say, facing the audience. I pull my hair away from my ears to make his approach easier.

"Oh, what's this? What did I find?" Tyler says, looking out at the audience and winking, as he pulls his hand away from my head. The audience erupts, yelling and clapping.

I turn to glance at Tyler to see what he's doing that's worthy of such a reaction. The glint of the metal catches my eye first. It's gold when it should be silver. There, in Tyler's outstretched hand, is a sparkly diamond ring.

My mouth falls open, and I cover it quickly with my hands.

Tyler drops to one knee. "I know how much you love it when I talk about my plans, but no plan will ever be complete without you right beside me. I love you, Rachel. I love watching you curled up on the couch, reading while your face morphs into the expressions described in the book. I love how you still don't understand the rules of soccer but show up to support me nonetheless. I love how you loved your sister so much that you did all these things that didn't matter to you, just to make her happy. I love how you feel in my arms. I love waking up with you beside me and falling asleep with you every night. I love loving you. Rachel, will you marry me?"

I start jumping up and down, hands still over my mouth. I cannot remember how to form words. Finally, my brain reminds me that Tyler's waiting for an answer. "Yes. Yes. YES!" I shout.

Tyler stands up and slides the ring on my finger. He sweeps me into his arms, his mouth meeting mine. Applause and a few catcalls ricochet through the audience. Then I remember where we are and what we're doing. This is Cami's birthday party, and we just stole all the attention.

I break the kiss and look for the birthday girl. She looks thrilled, rushing up onto the deck to hug us. "That trick was my idea. I told Uncle Tyler to propose to you like this. This trick was my idea."

"You're sure it didn't ruin your birthday?" I ask her.

"No, but you have to promise me that I can be in your wedding. I want to be a bridesmaid."

I laugh. "How about junior bridesmaid? Only if you promise not to do any gymnastics down the aisle."

She holds out her hand for me to shake. "Deal."

I turn back to Tyler, who's being hugged by his parents and brothers and sisters-in-law. Next come my grandparents, Gram's eyes shining with tears. Ophelia and Xavier move forward to congratulate us, baby Penelope squirming in a carrier strapped to Xavier's chest. Tyler told me he asked Ophelia to record the magic show to use on his social media.

He really did make a great plan.

"Oh my God, this is the most romantic thing ever, and we got it all!" Ophelia waves her phone around. "This is going to go so viral."

Tyler pulls me in to kiss him again when Cami interrupts. "I know it was my idea and all, but can you guys leave the stage? My friends and I want to do our karaoke now."

I look up to the sky and say quietly, "That was one hell of a finale. Did you know it was going to end up like this? Was this why you did it?"

Tyler slides his arm over my shoulder and pulls me into him. "Did you like my magic trick?" he asks. I look at the stone sparkling on my hand. It's gorgeous.

"I love your magic tricks. And I love watching you play soccer. And I love listening to you record your podcasts. And I love how you fight with your brothers. And I love how you let your mom take care of you because she needs to feel needed. But mostly, I love how you love me, and I'll never stop loving you."

"Good, because I'm never going to stop loving you either."

And I say okay because I am worthy of love. I deserve to be loved. I am ready for love. Richie was right.

You only live once.

THE END

ACKNOWLEDGMENTS

To Dianna Koch for beta reading and for taking the job so seriously that you had pages and pages of notes.

To Amanda Hansel for giving me the idea that Rachel's grandparents should own a septic company

To Kim Demarest for answering questions about owning a septic pump and grinder business

To Susan Traynor: thank you for making this cover come to life before the book even existed.

To all of my ARC readers who so thoughtfully and diligently read and wrote reviews. I don't know that I can ever truly express how much your words mean to me.

To my editors, Tami Lund and Regina Dowling: Thank you, thank you, thank you for taking this book to the next level.

Michele, I know 2025 is a year you want to forget, but please remember that yet another one of your pets made it into my book. And if you want to think that Richelle is named after you because I can't possibly have another Michele in my books, I'll let you think that.

Dad, the idea for Tyler's struggle with reading was inspired by you. You were one of the smartest men I'll ever know, and you accomplished so much without ever understanding how hard it was. I miss your wisdom every single day. We all miss you, but especially Jaboc and Spohia.

ABOUT THE AUTHOR

Kathryn R. Biel writes low-to-no spice contemporary romance, rom-com, sports romance, and women's fiction full of humor, heart, and happily-ever-afters. Her books balance the drama and challenges of real life with witty banter, strong heroines, and swoony cinnamon-roll heroes. Whether she's writing laugh-out-loud romantic comedies, emotional women's fiction, or heartfelt sports romances, Kathryn delivers stories where resilience, love, and laughter take center stage.

Kathryn is the author of more than 20 books, including the award-winning *Live for This*, *Made for Me*, and *The UnBRCAble Women Series* (*Ready for Whatever, Seize the Day*, and *Underneath It All*).

If you've enjoyed this book, please help the author out by leaving a review on your favorite retailer and Goodreads. A few minutes of your time makes a huge difference!

Stand Alone Books:

Good Intentions
Hold Her Down
I'm Still Here
Jump, Jive, and Wail
Killing Me Softly
Live for This
Once in a Lifetime
Paradise by the Dashboard Light

Boston Buzzards:
XOXO
You Belong ith Me
Zero to Hero
Alive and Kicking

A New Beginnings Series:
Completions and Connections: A New Beginnings Novella
Made for Me
New Attitude
Queen of Hearts

The UnBRCAble Women Series:
Ready for Whatever
Seize the Day
Underneath It All

Center Stage Love Stories:
Act One: *Take a Chance on Me*
Act Two: *Vision of Love*
Act Three: *Whatever It Takes*